THE USUAL
FAMILY
MAYHEM

ALSO BY HELENKAY DIMON

THE USUAL FAMILY MAYHEM

A NOVEL

HELENKAY DIMON

AVON

An Imprint of HarperCollins*Publishers*

THE USUAL FAMILY MAYHEM. Copyright © 2025 by HelenKay Dimon. All rights reserved. Printed in the United States of America. No part of this book may be used or reproduced in any manner whatsoever without written permission except in the case of brief quotations embodied in critical articles and reviews. For information, address HarperCollins Publishers, 195 Broadway, New York, NY 10007.

HarperCollins books may be purchased for educational, business, or sales promotional use. For information, please email the Special Markets Department at SPsales@harpercollins.com.

Avon, Avon & logo, and Avon Books & logo are registered trademarks of HarperCollins Publishers in the United States of America and other countries.

FIRST EDITION

Interior text design by Diahann Sturge-Campbell

Homemade pies illustration © kamenuka/Adobe.Stock.com

Library of Congress Cataloging-in-Publication Data has been applied for.

ISBN 978-0-06-324058-2 (trade paperback)
ISBN 978-0-06-342759-4 (hardcover library edition)

24 25 26 27 28 LBC 5 4 3 2 1

This one is for my grandmothers, Helen and Kathleen. The part about serving poison pies to bad men is fictional (probably), but some of Mags's and Celia's personality traits and quirks should look familiar to all who loved them.

THE USUAL FAMILY MAYHEM

CHAPTER ONE

I needed a good idea. Not an *interesting* one or one with potential. Nope. This had to be a real stunner. The kind that would cause the men sitting around the conference room table in their plain white, nine-hundred-dollar Tom Ford sneakers to break out in a chorus of *oohh*s and *aahhh*s.

Hell, I'd settle for tepid approval and a few half-hearted nods at this point.

Living in Washington, DC, and being single meant wading through a dreary dating pool of guys in striped ties. I didn't have a problem with stripes, in general, but these stripes tended to be worn by a specific clout-chasing Capitol Hill type. This clout-chasing Capitol Hill type asked the same two questions at the start of every date: *Where do you work?* and *Where did you go to college?*

Being twenty-six and no longer actually in college, I didn't understand why the latter mattered but College of Charleston. Go Cougars! The answer to the former was Nexus Opportunity Ideas. I'd worked there for four months and three days and still had no idea what I did for a living other than sit at my desk and play games on my phone.

NOI was a business incubator that *found and developed business opportunities for savvy investors.* The description came right from the company website. I know because I memorized it and repeated it with confidence whenever anyone asked me about my job. The explanation was only slightly more comprehensible than the company name, which sounded like pure gibberish.

My best friend, Whitney, worked in human resources at NOI. She'd texted, emailed, and called me about an open position the second before the official listing went live to give me the chance to "get in fast." Yeah, no pressure.

Whitney made enough money to buy a sweet one-bedroom two blocks from Logan Circle. Sure, it barely measured six hundred square feet, but it had a private terrace and a walk-in closet. I rented a studio apartment on the fourth floor of an in-need-of-renovating building with a leaky faucet, wallet-depleting rent, and a broken elevator.

Whitney easily won that round of adult bingo.

If only to rescue my ego and bank account from obliteration, I needed to survive the six-month probationary period at NOI. Two months to go.

The position sounded great in the employment listing. Talk about false advertising. *Dynamic work environment! Innovative teams! Breakfast and lunch provided!* The promise of a daily free bagel won me over. But to get the job I had to . . . let's say embellish.

Lie. I had to lie.

The job requirements were vague, or I pretended they were. Business or finance degree? Not really or at all. The ability to *quickly and effectively develop new investment opportunities and strategize about their implementation and financing*? No idea what that even meant. But Whitney vouched for me, and I owed her big-time.

One problem remained. I hadn't pitched a single actionable idea since starting at NOI. I kept my head down, made calls, attended meetings, and researched other people's projects. Basically, a computer program could do my job and no one would need to feed it a free bagel, so my days were numbered. I had to start doing something or get better at faking being busy.

"Kasey?"

Kasey Nottingham. That was me. Unfortunately. I stopped staring out the window at The Wharf, the strip of restaurants, businesses, and residences on DC's southwest waterfront where NOI was located. That location being the best part of the job. Food everywhere and if I squinted I could see the tail end of the National Cherry Blossom Festival from the smaller conference room. A perk the company recited with pride at the initial interview back in November, months before the cherry blossoms appeared.

This town took its flower festivals very seriously.

Brock Deavers had called for my attention and now he had it. He managed to be the most annoying *I went to Yale* blowhard I'd ever met and that was a high bar to clear. He was my immediate boss. I'd been foisted on him without his input and clearly over his objection, and now worked on his team. Lucky me.

That team consisted of other guys who went to Yale or Yale-like schools. They played around in canoes or kayaks—not sure about the difference—on the weekends as they traded stories about their college rowing days. Never mind that they were in their thirties. In Brock's case forties but pretending to be thirties.

At CofC we called these guys assholes.

Every member of the five-person team was an assistant director because this company handed out titles like free bagels, but Brock was a full-fledged director. *The* guy in charge. Dressed to perfection in his expensive-but-trying-to-look-casual black pants and zip-up hoodie.

He hated me. He never said the actual words out loud, but he telegraphed his disdain at every opportunity. He sighed whenever I opened my mouth. He trampled over the few comments I rarely offered. He'd also delivered a lecture yesterday about my *workload* that should have lasted five minutes max but droned on for forty.

His smirk now shouted *gotcha!* "You wanted to talk about a business idea today?"

Ah, okay. We'd entered the passive-aggressive portion of the meeting. This was a challenge. Brock's way of testing. Worse, of showing everyone I didn't belong in this super-dynamic and not-at-all self-important company.

He wasn't totally wrong but still. Screw him.

The charged silence dragged on just long enough for people to start shifting around in their leather chairs. If they thought they were uncomfortable they should have tried being me.

"Pies." The word popped out of my mouth to a round of frowns. Some guys in the room leaned forward in what looked like the body language equivalent of *what the hell did she say?*

The most pronounced scowl belonged to Michael Bainbridge, the owner of NOI. The same Michael who had some sort of epiphany or spiritual awakening and now insisted on being called Micah. Because it was totally normal to change your name if you thought a different one sounded cooler. His parents must be so proud.

Fifty and trim, Micah ran more miles each day than I had in my entire life. He'd also taken a class on effective listening and spent the majority of every conversation repeating back whatever anyone said in the form of a question.

"Pies?" Micah asked, right on cue. His eyes narrowed behind his black-framed, very serious glasses that matched his newly minted name. "Are you hungry?"

Yes. Always. Wasn't everyone? But this was the time for babbling, not eating. Full-on, cover-your-ass, try-to-make-sense babbling. "Food is big business."

Micah nodded. His version of encouragement. That and the repeating thing. "Big business?"

Brock sat up, clearly intending to interrupt. His shifting made my brain spin faster, spewing words about the one business model I knew a little about. Very little. Like, almost nothing. "Imagine homemade desserts, with pies being the star, made by two older Southern women using time-honored family recipes that elicit a feeling of nostalgia and luxury."

Brock snorted as he shook his head. "Food is a crowded field. There's no way—"

Micah held up a hand. "Let her finish."

Yeah, dumbass. Let me finish.

"This is about more than pies and desserts. It's about the story behind the desserts." I was in it now and didn't have a road map to lead me out again. "The backstory is inspiring. Two women of a certain age were married to completely useless men and ultimately forced to fend for themselves."

I let that last sentence splash around in the room's testosterone for a second.

"They rebuilt their lives by making and selling pies. Creating a business and a community around the pies that later expanded to include other desserts."

"So?" Brock excelled at missing the point and didn't disappoint here.

"Frankly, they're damn good pies. Right now, they're sold on a small scale all over the South via word of mouth and a website. They're special. Curated. Artisanal." I'd moved into the part of the pitch where I threw phrases together that may or may not have applied to pies, cupcakes, and other assorted dessert items because this room loved fancy buzzwords. "Now imagine taking this small grandma-run business nationwide. Making it the go-to dessert option for special occasions. Putting it in high-end grocery and specialty stores as well as on direct delivery. Creating demand like that lady did with cupcakes a decade or so ago."

Big fan. Loved the whole dessert family. And those cupcake vending machines? Genius.

Now I wanted a cupcake, so time to wrap this up. "If we focus on the pies for a second, once you convince people they need the pies, they'll pay anything for those pies. Plus, you have built-in marketing gold in the form of two very feisty, self-made women who people will see as their grandmas."

There. Done. Not brilliant but not a complete fumble either. No one said a word.

Maybe I didn't stick the landing. The pitch wasn't real anyway. I counted on it getting shot down. The hope was to buy a few more months on the job while I figured out how to do it.

"The scale is too small," Brock said.

Micah frowned. "Too small?"

"Yes?" Brock looked a bit less confident about his attempt at sabotage than he had a minute ago.

"Everyone has a grandma." Micah made the statement as if he was delivering a grand revelation and not merely commenting on a biological fact. "Combined with the reality that people with money are willing to pay for items they're convinced are luxuries, something special their neighbors don't have, even though anyone could buy or make that item for far less, you have a recipe for success."

Like how the sneakers I got on sale for fifteen dollars looked a lot like Brock's expensive ones. Just as an example.

Micah continued. "Our job is to convince an investor who already has a foothold in the specialty food market that they can make these pies, produce them at a substantial return, and create sustainable demand."

Wait . . . did he say . . . Was Micah actually considering this?

He shrugged. "Then our client can sell the entire company, grandmas and all, for a huge profit to some big grocery chain."

Selling grandmas sounded like a problem, but I played along because Brock looked ready to explode into a giant fireball of ego and hair gel. I didn't want to miss that.

"We can start making calls and testing interest levels. First thing we'll need to do is secure our rights and get these grandmas under contract." Micah pointed the end of his pen at me. "You have two weeks."

Huh . . . Well, that went sideways fast. The extent of my overpromising hit with the force of a freight train.

My grandmother was going to kill me.

CHAPTER TWO

The intoxicating mix of brown butter, sugar, and bubbling blueberries hit me the second I crossed the threshold into Gram's kitchen two days later. I would have gotten there sooner but it took that long to pack, plan, and work up the nerve to dive into this business mess. But here I was in Winston-Salem, North Carolina, the magnolia-strewn area where I grew up.

The old house calmed me. Provided a sense of much needed peace. From the outside, an impressive Federal-style three-story painted a crisp white with navy-blue shutters. A historic home set back from the road on a lot filled with a vegetable garden, winding stone paths, a few small outbuildings, including a mostly unused shed and greenhouse, and flower beds in a burst of color. The place was grand and welcoming. Almost regal.

Inside was a different story. Patterned wallpaper and flowered sofas launched an all-out assault on the senses the second you walked through the door. Gram had a thing for frilly touches. Lace table runners. Pillows with fringe. Pops of color. Not a lick of white paint anywhere.

Magnolia Grace—Mags to anyone who knew her and didn't want to get scolded for using her "given" and much hated name—Nottingham was seventy-five and moved with the energy of a person half her age. Born and raised in North Carolina, she had a standing hairdresser appointment—not a stylist, a hairdresser—every Thursday morning at ten, which was as sacred as Sunday church service.

She donned one of her conservative no-pattern dresses, along with the perfect matching handbag, whenever she ventured out in public or had lunch with the ladies at her favorite restaurant in Reynolda Village. At home, she morphed into a different person. A color and pattern devotee who exclusively wore plaid bedroom slippers around the kitchen.

She was a deeply Southern woman who loved hats and sweet tea and the granddaughter she'd raised from age six. I hoped that last part survived my visit.

"Kasey!"

"Gram." You didn't brace for a hug from Gram. You let it happen. Drank in the familiar scent of jasmine and vanilla from Gram's perfume and sank into the half-cranky, always-loving warmth only Grandma Mags's arms could provide.

The smell and the touch kicked off memories. I was transported back to the years when I ran through the big house or stretched out on the velvety green lawn, looking up to see the puffy clouds roll by. Creating stories. Eating pies and cupcakes. Crying when Johnnie Pace dumped me two days before prom. The jackass.

"Let me look at you." Gram pulled back, never letting go of my arms. A second later the corners of her mouth fell into a tight line. Her pursed lips carried more than a hint of *what did you do now?* "What's wrong? Tell me straight."

Pummeled by grandma radar once again. "I'm just here for a visit."

"Hmmm."

Her humming was never good. The sound beat me into submission every time.

People let the bob of white hair and sweet smile fool them. Amateurs. Intelligence and strength lurked behind Gram's blue eyes. The woman didn't miss a thing.

Stay calm. "Is it that weird for me to visit?"

Gram could smell fear. She was the queen of not talking and letting people trip up in the silence. I'd fallen for the wildly successful trick so many times I'd lost count. Not today . . . hopefully.

A few minutes ticked by as Gram assessed and I choked back the words that would condemn me to a heap of lecturing. What was the right way to say *I used your pie story as an example at work and now some big company will want to muscle its way in here and try to buy the business and you?*

Not weird at all.

"Did you lose your job?" Gram asked.

"What? No. Why would you ask that?" Okay, sure. Fair question. Even I could admit I possessed a bit of a professional follow-through problem.

It all started with what could only be called *the law school fiasco.* Dropping out before the end of my first year meant owing student loans for a career I didn't have. In my defense, leaving law school had been the right answer because I needed to and *oh my God, how boring.* Leaving *before* the tuition refund cutoff for second semester would have been a better plan.

"You've only been working at your newest company for a few months. How do you have vacation time saved up?"

The woman hadn't worked outside of the house in decades, yet she somehow knew about office politics. "Companies are more employee-friendly these days. Did I tell you about the free bagels?"

"Kasey!"

Celia's high-pitched voice cut through the room. I pulled away from Gram and hugged Aunt Celia. Not my biological aunt. Frankly, my birth father proved that blood ties were over-rated. Unlike my feelings for him, which were hostile at best, I loved Celia. She lived with Gram and, well, that was a *whole thing*.

"Auntie." Celia's squeezing hug enveloped me. "It's good to see you."

Celia Windsor was about eight years younger than Gram, though that was a guess. Celia offered different birth years, depending on who asked the question. She also hid her driver's license with the stealth of an undercover operative, so good luck trying to verify a date.

Celia ended the hug with a wince. "Did something happen at work?"

Apparently I had a reputation to overcome. Time to get the conversation off my résumé and on to something safer. "How have you been?"

"It's okay, sweetie." Celia rubbed her hands up and down my arms. "Come back home. We have plenty of room and more work than we can handle."

Gram snorted. "She can't cook."

Hey . . . "That's rude. Right but rude."

"Her cooking skills don't matter." Celia shrugged. "We bake."

Gram managed a double snort. "Not her strength either."

"Listen up, you beautiful ladies." I spied what looked like homemade scones at the end of the massive kitchen island and grabbed one as a diversionary tactic. I ripped it in half and took a bite, barely swallowing before continuing. "I missed you and . . . sweet baby Jesus, what is in this thing?"

Celia beamed. "Peaches."

"It's our newest addition. The menu expansion opened us up to a whole new clientele." Gram's hand slid over Celia's forearm for just a second. "Celia perfected this recipe."

Pride. Love. I heard and saw both, as I had since I moved in almost a year after Celia did. Even at age six I understood they were a team. But back to the outside crunch and pillowy, buttery inside goodness of the scone. I dropped the pastry before I stuffed the whole thing in my mouth and dove in for a second.

"At least now I know where my carb addiction comes from." As if that had ever been a question.

"Oh, please." Gram snorted for the third time in the same conversation, which was nowhere near her record. "Carbs never hurt anyone."

"The entire healthcare industry would argue otherwise." That made me think about my doctor and his *you could stand to lose a few pounds* lectures. All that meant was I needed to find a new doctor, preferably one who didn't blame every problem on weight. Mine, by the way, was perfectly fine and within the range for my height . . . or close enough.

Doctors meant health insurance, which meant I had no choice but to hold on to this job. Which meant the time had come to spill the truth about what I'd done.

Gram and Celia liked new clients. It just so happened I could help with that.

"I thought we could . . ." Looking at their two shiny, loving, totally skeptical faces made me stumble over my words. Probably from the rush of adrenaline and panic. I fell back on my greatest skill—avoidance. A business discussion could wait one more day. "DC sucks and the dating pool is enough to make me yearn for a dog, so I needed some family time."

"Aw, honey." Celia unleashed another loving hug. "Dogs are always better than men."

"Why didn't you tell us you needed home cooking and lots of spoiling?" Gram asked.

Because that wasn't the real reason for the visit, but the idea grew on me as I stood in the homey kitchen with those yellow-and-blue-flowered curtains. A few days of carbo-loading? Excellent.

Gram walked over to the cabinet and took out three fancy antique teacups with matching saucers. "You stay as long as you need."

She said that *now*. Chances were her good mood would vanish once I coughed up the truth. Until then? More scone eating.

CHAPTER THREE

Jackson Quaid ruined everything.

Probably not fair and a bit too general but I'd known him for a long time and had some experience in this area. He was Celia's nephew. A real nephew. Not a "nephew" in one of those Southern everyone-is-considered-family kind of ways. Actual kin.

Jackson's mom, Savannah, was Celia's baby sister. Two of the five kids in the Windsor clan with Celia being the oldest and Savannah being the youngest. That was the good side of the family. Then there was Harlan, Jackson's father. A glad-handing, rarely genuine lobbyist type who had been immersed in politics for so long that he'd forgotten how to tell the truth.

Harlan came from a long line of blowhard, pontificating Quaid men. He was the kind of guy who made a compliment sound condescending. He used to talk about what a good housewife Savannah was . . . then would say she didn't have the skills to be anything else.

Maintaining a certain public image guided every move Harlan made. Except when it came to women. Dealing with women made him extra messy. He'd waited five whole weeks after Savannah died following a lengthy battle with breast can-cer before moving his pretty "real estate friend" into the family home. He, and only he, was shocked when people gossiped about his appalling timing.

It might be faint praise, but Jackson was the best of the Quaid men by a mile. He was also an only child. His parents clearly realized their tragic mistake after having him and stopped making kids. At least that was my working theory.

People described Jackson as focused and smart. I'd add humorless and prone to mumbling under his breath. He was a successful lawyer because he'd actually finished law school without dying of boredom or failing out. The show-off.

He stepped out of the French double doors off the dining room and onto the back flagstone patio. He wore a buttoned-up dark suit, giving off his usual put-together vibe. Objectively handsome—not that I noticed—but only as long as he didn't talk.

I'd been at Gram's place for two hours and outside in the backyard for ten minutes before he showed up. He usually sniffed out when I crossed the state line and came running as I pulled in the driveway. Waiting over 120 minutes to pop up and spread his joy meant he must be slowing down in his old age, that age being thirty-three.

Jackson sat on the half of the wicker couch I wasn't using. The cool steel-blue cushions looked out of place. Not a flower or sunburst pattern in sight, so nothing Gram picked.

I didn't have to look up to know Jackson started doing his staring thing. I did anyway. As usual, his scowl conveyed his disappointment in my life choices. He glided along, operating by a set of rules only he knew. I'd never been able to figure out what those rules were, but I clearly violated them.

"I heard you were here." He had the nerve to smile. "Did you get fired?"

It took less than two seconds for him to pick a fight. Surprisingly, that was longer than usual. "I'm starting to feel attacked."

"I think that's what you said after you lost the bank job and we dared to question you about it."

The brain-numbing bank teller job I took after the law school misfire. My dalliance with finance lasted less than two months. A short-term career stop, at least that's how I preferred to think of it. Hours of inactivity punctuated with screaming fits of rage by irate customers. One minute bored. The next paralyzed with fear that I'd accidentally honor a fraudulent check or complete a transaction and not notice a counterfeit twenty. Worst job ever.

"I quit. No one fired me." I took a long sip of ice water and didn't offer him any. He knew where the kitchen was.

He'd been coming to the house since before I moved in. At six, I'd been traumatized and scared when I walked in the big front door with my little suitcase. He'd just become a teenager and had taken an instant dislike to me for infringing on his precious territory.

He believed Gram and Celia liked him more than me both back then and now. They didn't. Couldn't. Not possible.

He stretched his arm across the back of the couch with his fingers almost touching my shoulder. "What are you doing here?"

Squirming. Being this close to him always turned me into a fidgety mess. I spent most of my energy trying to remain composed and keep my voice steady. "Sitting."

"I meant in the state."

"Same answer."

A small smile came and went on his lips before he settled back into his usual grumpy state. "So, you haven't changed."

Neither had he. Under the starched shirt and perfectly knotted tie lurked a hottie. Not that I would ever admit that out loud. Brown, almost black, hair. Brown eyes. That perfect face. The firm chin. Those wide shoulders.

Damn . . . He was far too attractive. Noticing had been a lifelong problem. No matter how much I tried, I couldn't shake the thing where my mind wandered in his direction. The weakness swamped me and drowned my common sense. I'd tried everything to crush the weird dance my stomach did whenever I saw him, including pretending we were blood related and he was off-limits. Neither of those things was true.

In addition to smelling good, and he did, he'd starred in most of my teenage daydreaming, but I was an adult now. I could control my bad decisions, including my unwanted lingering crush on him. I needed to stomp that out or at least ignore it. And I tried. Honestly.

We were complete opposites. My light to his dark. My charm to his moodiness. My flailing to his overachieving. My inability to hold a job to him making law partner before any of his classmates.

My taste in men changed as I got older. Now I picked losers who ghosted me after two dates instead of one . . . but Jackson's pull still kicked my ass.

I decided to speed up the conversation. The sooner he delivered whatever lecture he had planned, the sooner he'd leave. "I'm visiting my beloved grandmother and my aunt."

"*My* aunt and I'm surprised they didn't put you to work cracking eggs or sifting flour."

Same, but give them time. "Sounds like you're talking from experience."

He groaned. "So many eggs."

Okay, that was kind of cute. "They think I can't bake."

He laughed. "Can you all of a sudden?"

"Not even a little. No patience for the measuring." But enough about my long list of shortcomings. "What's going on with you? Don't you have a job you should be doing?"

"It's been months since we've seen each other."

Three months. Two days. "Not really an answer to my question, but okay."

He threw out one of those beleaguered sighs men did when women didn't immediately cede the floor. "You swung into town the last time you lost a job. I'm assuming it happened again and we're in for another touch down of Hurricane Kasey."

"When did everyone around here get so rude? Y'all are obsessed with my career status."

"We're trying to be prepared for the worst."

The words sounded testy, but his posture remained relaxed. He didn't appear to be in his usual hurry to race back to the office. That meant he planned to say something annoying.

As predicted, he continued talking even though no one had asked him to explain. "You tend to breeze into town, cause chaos, then run."

"I see your interpersonal skills are as stellar as ever." No surprise there. People had to want to change, and he didn't. "And 'chaos' is a strong word."

"Is it, though?"

That voice carried a hint of a smooth Southern drawl. The tone wrapped around me like a hug. "I was here last time because it was Christmas and—"

"Oh, I remember. You insulted that bigwig at the tennis club. A client of your grandmother and Celia's at the time. Thanks to you, they lost a contract for a New Year's Day brunch and a lot of money."

Yeah, that. "That's not how I remember it."

This twenty-something club jerk had lurked around a girl who couldn't have been out of high school yet. He followed her down the hall toward the club's bathrooms then moved in front of her and blocked her attempt to get around him. I stepped in and would do it again because that's what women did for each other. I also had a general *not on my watch* rule to uphold.

"I think I showed amazing restraint in only telling that loser off."

"I agree. If I had known about his amateur stalking, I would have told him off, too. But his father didn't see the situation the same way we did."

"That man had no sense of humor and a complete inability to see his son for the entitled walking disaster that he was. Not my fault." No one warned me about the harasser being the spoiled son of some rich dude who owned a company that sold rich dude things and didn't hesitate to throw around his rich dude influence in the form of threats.

Time for a subject change. One that put the spotlight on Jackson. "Where's . . . Lucy, Suzy, Dolly?" I followed the question with a nonchalant shrug meant to telegraph how little I cared about his love life even though I sort of did. "Whatever you girlfriend's name is."

"Anna, and we broke up."

Funny how Gram and Celia forgot to share that juicy piece of information during our weekly FaceTime calls. "She found someone else?"

"She moved to Atlanta."

"So, your personality is driving them out of the state these days."

His exhale drowned out the sound of the birds chirping in the trees behind us. "I seem to remember you asking Anna at Christmas if something crawled up her ass."

That totally happened. "Did I?"

"It was basically a direct quote."

"And a fair question on my part. She was very . . . clenched. I thought the poor woman might hurt herself doing that puckered-lip dismissal thing."

It wasn't my fault his ex-girlfriend lacked anything approaching a personality. Pretty but dull and her dullness turned out to be contagious. Jackson became positively humorless around her. She'd sucked what little charm he possessed right out of him.

"Your taste in women is weird." Since that seemed like a safe word to land on, I went with it.

He rolled his eyes this time.

"No. Don't. I should be the one making dramatic gestures, not you. Did you forget she ate a muffin with a fork?" He tried to respond but I talked over him because I had more. "If that wasn't odd enough, she didn't even finish it. A homemade applesauce muffin."

"Your point?"

Oh, come on. "Who does that? It's like opening a bag of chips and only eating one. I think she might have been a sociopath. Be happy I shooed her away."

"You didn't . . ." He stared at my almost empty glass of water as if wrestling for control before continuing. "What are you really doing here?"

Apparently we were done talking about his fork-using ex. That didn't mean I wanted to dance my way into a dangerous new subject. One that made me look bad. "A visit."

"I know you. Stop bullshitting." He leaned in closer. "Are you planning on pitching Mags and Celia a wild business idea?"

What the hell was that scent? Cologne? Shampoo? He always smelled like he stepped out of a shower of citrus and sandalwood. It was sexy in a concentration-zapping way.

"Of course not." I switched to a whisper just in case. "How do you know about pitching?"

Jackson being Jackson, he kept right on talking at full volume. "I work with companies like yours all the time."

Since when? "That's what you do for a living?"

"I deal with corporate assets and regulations. Draft agreements. Work on contracts." He didn't say *duh* but he looked like he wanted to. "What did you think I did?"

Boring lawyer shit. Just hearing him describe his job killed off most of my brain cells. "Sat in a room with a bunch of books and read documents."

"That's not far off except we use computers these days." He shrugged. "The point is I researched your job and company. I'm familiar with your responsibilities."

Was that sweet or overbearing? Hard to tell. "That doesn't sound stalkerish at all."

"You've been there for a few months. I'm sure you're getting pressure to produce."

He seemed to know everything all of a sudden. "What's with the overhyped interest in my work life?"

He stared at me for a few loaded seconds before shaking his head. "Can I offer you some friendly advice?"

"No." His advice tended to be more bossy than helpful. No, thank you.

"Whatever you're planning to do is a mistake."

"I guess you didn't hear me say no."

He kept right on talking. "Enjoy a few days of quality family time. Eat lots of baked goods. Forget about this pitch then go back to DC."

He sounded a little too excited about the part where I left town. Then there was the bigger problem. "It's not that easy."

"See, that's the thing, Kasey. You make things hard." His smile came roaring back. "This time, refrain."

•

CHAPTER FOUR

You make things hard. I continued grumbling about Jackson's comment all last night and from the second my feet hit the floor this morning. After a short caffeine break I intended to go back to grumbling.

First, breakfast. As usual, Gram beat me downstairs to the kitchen. No matter what time I got up, Gram got up earlier. She had an internal alarm clock that ensured she was the one to make tea and warm the muffins. I loved that about her. I also loved sleeping in. The crisp sheets and soft, but not too soft, mattress made the bed in this house my favorite bed in the world.

Gram stared out the window over the sink and across the backyard. "Why are you scowling?"

My butt barely hit the breakfast bar stool before Gram launched that one. "You're not even looking at me."

"I can hear you frowning."

"That's not a thing." Was it? I mean, she did always seem to know what I was about to do or say. She had all kinds of spooky skills.

She turned to face me, showing off her bright pink zip-up robe with the big yellow flowers. The thing was over the top, which was how I knew it was perfect when I bought it for her for Christmas. She sipped tea from her "Cool Grandmother Club" mug, another perfect gift.

The morning was one of the rare times she swapped out her beloved iced sweet tea for something warm. Morning and whenever she poked around in my feelings about something—first boys, now men, my career goals, my worries about paying the rent. Earl Grey was her go-to *let's have a chat* hot beverage and had been since I hit middle school.

On a regular day, starting at about eleven, no matter what time of year, hot or cold outside, she reached for sweet tea over ice, served in the same pitcher she'd inherited from her mother. She actually owned many pitchers. She had a group of clear glass carafes of different sizes with glass handles and rounded bottoms. We used those for company.

Her favorite, the family-only one, was a cheap plastic pitcher passed down from generation to generation. It had a simple green flower on the side and matching lid with a push button in the middle. You pressed that to break the seal and take the top off.

One of Gram's greatest disappointments came the day fifteen-year-old me suggested her favorite iced beverage basically consisted of a bag of sugar with a little bit of black tea mixed in. So, a liquid dessert and not a very good one.

I wasn't wrong. She liked her tea heavy on the sugar and didn't appreciate my pointing that out. She'd actually gasped at my audacity then insisted she had to leave the room because she *needed a minute*. We never spoke of my iced sweet tea betrayal again.

"Do you want me to help today?"

Gram eyed me over her mug. "With what?"

Honestly, I'd made the offer since it seemed like the right

thing to do. The whole *respect your elders* thing and all. Her skepticism made me double down. "Cleaning?"

She snorted.

Good choice since cleaning was not my thing. But I had to have a *thing* and it was about time I found it. "Okay, cooking."

Gram took a long sip then set her mug down on the bar with a clink. "You mean baking. We bake."

"Yeah, forget that." Me helping in the kitchen sounded like an invitation to food poisoning. "I could help with business paperwork. Gather up—"

"No."

Whoa. That answer came fast and hard. I'd been recruited to wash dishes, stir, and perform other baking assistant tasks over the years. By "recruited" I meant *ordered to do* certain things. This one time I initiated and offered to pitch in on a non-tasting-related chore and Gram shut it down. Apparently she loved paperwork and didn't want to share.

Still, I could be a team player. "I thought you might need—"

"That part of the business is handled. It's fine."

The odd snap in her voice didn't sound fine. It seemed like we were having one conversation out loud and one unspoken, only I couldn't keep up with the silent one. "Is everything okay?"

"Of course." She waved a hand in the air, which was Grandma code for *find another topic*.

Gram wasn't a yeller. She didn't need to raise her voice to make her point when she could pull out *the look*. It consisted of one arched eyebrow, a grim expression, and an unblinking stare. The kind of stare that bored through you and slammed into the wall behind you.

I'd spent most of my life trying not to tick her off and re-membered with painful clarity every instance where I'd failed. The time as a teenager when I crawled out my upstairs window and went to meet friends. The day I drove the car into the ga-rage door because I was texting rather than paying attention. The big misstep where I took twenty dollars from her purse without asking. In my defense, I was only ten during the last one and the guilt ate at me until I fessed up.

Gram's warm smile returned. "I made cinnamon muffins. Would you like one or two?"

If she wanted to divert my attention with food . . . well, it worked. I split the muffin in half and let the spicy aroma fill the air. I could swim in a bucket of these and eat my way out. That was the fantasy.

While I ate, Gram cleaned this and rearranged that. The years did nothing to tame her need for constant motion. She was this little ball of energy. Five-foot-one, though she insisted she was closer to five-three. Every inch of her determined and sassy and ready to defend. I was a solid six inches taller than her actual height, but she could outmaneuver me physically and verbally.

My theory was that she lived life at a sprint to keep the bad memories from catching up with her. If she stuck to her racing pace, she could outrun the pain and destruction that defined so much of her adulthood.

She'd lived long and survived some heartbreaking shit. Growing up with a father who spent most of his life sucking down whatever alcohol he could find only to escape to a hus-band who used his fists to carry his side of the conversation. The men in her life taught her to be on guard. Losing my mom, Gram's daughter, by her son-in-law's hand shaped everything that came after, including raising me to be bold, fight back, and detest violent men, especially the one who made my existence possible.

Gram buzzed around the room, keeping her hands moving. Once she wiped down the counter, she started taking baking pans out of cabinets. The bang of precooking preparations sounded like music to me. Familiar and comforting. Soon the house would fill with the delicious scent of some variety of cupcakes.

Most of the work for Mags' Desserts, the name of Gram and Celia's business, took place in here. The smaller room next to this one had once been a pantry. It now served as a supply area with two dishwashers that ran what felt like constantly.

The cooking space had been extended and updated several times over the years, swallowing up an office and the formal dining room. They'd invested tens of thousands of dollars in appliances and baking equipment, including a fancy oven that required reinforced flooring, updated electrical outlets, and a special vent hood before it could be installed.

A baking annex converted what had once been my grandfather's separate garage and workshop into the overflow area with a table for afternoon tea and recipe tasting as well as some offices. The multiple spaces helped the operation run at peak efficiency. Just like everything else in Gram's life.

I finished off a cinnamon muffin and reached for a second. "I can't get these in DC. Except that one time I found them in the grocery store, but they didn't taste the same."

Gram stopped moving. "You bought muffins in a grocery store?"

Shock. Confusion. The same tone she might use if I told her I'd robbed a bank. Gram had pulled out her *I am horrified* voice.

Laughter from the doorway saved me from answering. Celia walked into the room in her usual hanging-around-the-house outfit. An oversized long sleeve top and matching lounge pants. She had a set in every color and wore them because "North Carolina gets colder each year." Never mind that it was seventy-five today, warmer than usual for late March.

"Grocery store muffins? Honestly, Kasey. What were you thinking?" Celia gave me a hug before heading straight for the coffeemaker.

I hated to state the obvious but did anyway. "People usually buy food in a grocery store."

Gram's expression could only be described as grim. "Muffins should not be bought in the same place you buy garbage bags."

That wasn't a bad argument. But Winston-Salem was the home of Krispy Kreme doughnuts, which suggested pastries could be bought in all kinds of places. I decided not to point that out.

"You need to find an appropriate bakery." Gram rummaged through the catch-all drawer and took out a pad and pen. "Better yet, we can send you muffins and other items like we used to when you were in college. Maybe once a week?" Gram waved her hand in the air again. "We can come up with a schedule."

I never wanted to say yes to anything so much in my life. "If you do I won't be able to fit into my apartment."

Gram dropped the pen. "You worry too much about your weight."

Not anymore . . . or not as much as I used to. I'd been trying to break the *I'm not good enough* habit I picked up in college. My fellow students had been blond and beautiful, which by comparison made me look like an evil troll. The differences morphed into a defeatist attitude that pummeled me until *the hair debacle*. The day I looked in the mirror after dyeing my brown hair blond was the last day I wished for blond hair. Some people were meant to be brunettes.

It took most of my post-college years to silence the judgmental voice in my head. I decided my secret part-time job shouldn't consist of fussing and worrying as I counted every calorie like I was training for an Olympic event. Even as the real world pushed and pulled at me to be dissatisfied with my size, my face, my hair . . . my everything, I fought back.

The whole weight topic annoyed me, so I pivoted. "I feel like we've gotten off topic."

Gram snorted. The first of the day.

Celia slid onto the stool next to mine. "Which was?"

"Me helping out around here."

Celia stopped in mid–coffee sip. "With what?"

Not the elated and relieved reaction I'd hoped for, but I was in the conversation now and not backing down. "Business stuff."

Celia frowned over the top of her mug. "Which means?"

This sounded like an interrogation. "I don't know. Computer input. Paperwork. Filing."

This time Celia slowly lowered her mug to the counter. "Filing what?"

Gram delivered a fresh plate of muffins to the breakfast bar and put them in front of me. They were small. I could have at least one more.

Gram shook her head. "She wants to be our helper all of a sudden."

That tone followed by the second snort of the morning. Not a great start to the conversation. "What's happening right now? You two always wanted me to take an interest in the business and I am."

Celia stared at Gram. Gram stared back. I could almost see the unspoken comments jumping back and forth between them.

Celia put her hand on my forearm and gave it a squeeze. "We want you to relax, honey. Eat some delicious, healing food and enjoy the sunshine."

They wanted me out of their business. I didn't need a law degree to figure that out.

I'd taken for granted they had the money they needed. As a kid I never thought about it. Everything—clothes, food, books—just showed up. As an adult, I'd assumed the business expansion paid the bills, but it made sense they might be struggling financially and vowed to hide that struggle from me. They lived in a huge house. There were two of them, two incomes, but they shared the same job and keeping the lights on in this place couldn't be easy.

Whenever I'd asked about paying for the kitchen renovations or my undergrad education in the past, Gram changed the subject or shooed me away. I let her because she was proud and convincing . . . and it was easier on me not to know the details.

She'd once mentioned the inheritance she'd gotten from her terrible husband. That and life insurance. Sitting there, I questioned all of it. Would an abusive man really make sure the wife he regularly attacked had future financial security?

Celia and Gram stared at me now with their rosy cheeks and big eyes. Love wrapped around the kitchen like a warm blanket. But this time there was an underlying unease. These two were hiding something. Maybe they did need help and we'd all gotten lucky. NOI could swoop in and save the day . . . and my job . . . and their livelihoods.

The last time they hid something from me it was huge and nearly ended in a catastrophe.

We weren't doing that again.

These two cuties possessed James Bond–level skills when it came to sparing me from what they considered to be bad news. That left me with few choices, the most obvious being snooping, which sucked. The only thing Gram hated near as much as crappy men was anyone touching her stuff.

Over the years, I'd been accused of being a bit dramatic. Totally unwarranted, of course, but even I could admit my current *not right* feeling might stem from a combination of stress and an active imagination rather than any real problem. So, no searching. For now. I'd listen and watch for the next few days. I had to be careful and focused.

Unfortunately, I lacked both skills.

CHAPTER FIVE

A few hours later I wandered back into the kitchen. Staying focused and careful required food. Food in this instance meant a dessert.

Gram and Celia kept a supply of freshly made cupcakes in a sealed container on the counter. They'd set six aside. Well, they did when I was home. I rarely saw either of them eat any of the items they baked, so I assumed the easy access was for my benefit and appreciated the gesture.

Today's selection included cheesecake-stuffed chocolate cupcakes, the most glorious-sounding description in the world. I didn't like to play favorites, but this flavor had earned a spot on my Best Cupcakes List. Any dessert that didn't make me chose between cheesecake and a cupcake was a clear winner.

The ladies usually added colored sprinkles to the icing. During my freshman year of college, a woman on my dorm floor referred to sprinkles as jimmies. She grew up outside Philadelphia and jimmies were a thing there. When I told Gram about the different name, she told me I needed to switch dorms. Clearly, she was not a believer in jimmies.

Today? No sprinkles. To be fair, there were sprinkles in the icing, just not enough to make the decoration worthwhile. I didn't know how to bake and wasn't really interested in learning how, but I knew where to find important things like the sprinkles, tiny marshmallows, nuts, and other assorted cup-cake toppings.

I set my midday dessert down with some reluctance and headed for the pantry. Sealed cannisters lined the shelves. Different flours and sugars. Muffin wrappers. Pans, cookie cutters, and . . . a cabinet. A wooden cabinet with double doors. Possibly an antique. An inexplicably locked cabinet right where the containers of assorted sprinkles should be.

Why in the world would they lock up baking supplies? I refused to believe this choice was some sort of message or way to decrease my sugar consumption because Gram and Celia spent a good portion of my visits shoving food in my direction. Celia threw in a *you're too thin* every now and then. That delusion was one of the many reasons I loved her.

Maybe it just looked like . . . nope. It was a lock. I pulled and tugged. The thing didn't budge. I moved the cabinet around to look at the back and heard something rattling around in there.

Every shelf in the pantry looked the same as I remembered. This was the only change, but it was a weird one. It was almost as if they were hiding something.

Not again.

The words tumbled in my head and wouldn't leave.

The last time they acted weird, avoided conversation topics, and stashed things out of sight was two years ago and Gram ended up in the hospital. Crushing chest pain. Heart palpitations. Nausea. They'd waited until she went to the emergency room before filling me in on any of it. Even then, Jackson was the one who called. Since the news sent me into a tailspin, he also said I shouldn't drive and bought me a plane ticket then picked me up at the airport.

I came home, thinking she'd had a heart attack. At the hospital, the doctor told me the cause was a syndrome called Takotsubo cardiomyopathy. Jackson explained the nickname for the condition was broken heart syndrome, a weakened heart brought on by severe emotional or physical stress.

Gram refused to tell me what had sent her into the health nosedive. She waved off the concern and insisted she only needed rest. Celia divided her time between pacing and leaving the room to cry in private, thinking I couldn't hear her. I could. Jackson agreed with me that something bigger—something Gram and Celia were keeping from me—must have happened.

Yeah, my crappy father happened.

I'd been stumbling my way through law school when he popped up with a fresh-faced attorney and talk of newly discovered forensic evidence. He thought he deserved another trial and opportunity to prove he didn't kill Mom. Gram got paperwork and a call from the prosecutor then collapsed.

He'd been in prison for eighteen years at that point. On a rainy Friday night, while I was staying overnight with Gram and doing little kid stuff, he strangled my mom then set fire to the house to destroy any incriminating evidence. Not that he ever admitted to his crime. He'd wept on cue and talked about being innocent. He wasn't.

Once he got caught, he pivoted and blamed Mom for her own murder. *She was erratic. She attacked me. She was unstable.* It turned out she'd committed the ultimate sin in his eyes. She'd asked for a divorce.

My father had been the guy everyone liked. He seemed by all outward appearances to be a great family man, but he did have what his then-boss called *a bit of a temper*. That one Friday night it spiked, and he lost his usual rigid control.

Gram and Celia had hidden the news of my father's new court filings and claims because they didn't want to *bother* me while I was studying. That was the word they used. They didn't tell me details and wouldn't show me the paperwork until I threatened to use Jackson and his lawyer skills to track the information down.

My father never got a new trial. He eventually slithered back under his rock, but the memory of how far Gram and Celia would go to protect me lingered. They'd hide bad news even if it meant landing in the hospital. Their behavior, no matter how good-hearted, put me on a constant state of high alert.

The warning bell pinged now as a familiar dread welled up from my stomach. The two women who'd raised me and who I loved unconditionally were hiding something. The only questions were how big and how bad . . . and how hard it would be to pry it out of them.

I'd come home to fix a business mess I'd made. Looked like I was staying for a totally different reason.

CHAPTER SIX

My first stop on the *figure out what the ladies didn't want me to know* tour was the baking annex. I walked in, expecting to see Gram and Celia cleaning up. My plan was to pretend I was on an icing-tasting run then fire questions at them while their defenses were down.

The low rumble of voices didn't register until I opened the door and found Celia and Harlan, Jackson's dad, standing in the middle of the main room, locked in what looked like a top-secret conversation. Between Celia shaking her head and Harlan's nonstop talking, I couldn't figure out if I'd walked in too early or a step too late.

I also couldn't just back out of the room again without it being weird, so . . . "Hello."

Harlan smiled. Not a real smile. One of his fake lobbyist smiles. The kind that promised a ton of bullshit waited on the horizon.

He had what Gram called presence. He stood there, unmoving, and still seemed to take up most of the room. A man with a law degree and other academic accolades to his credit. He threw around his family's reputation and his place in the community every time he walked out the door. Successful and well-dressed. Wealthy and fit. Confident and handsome in a chiseled and chilly sort of way.

His actual business title was political strategist. He made a living getting other people elected to office. He schmoozed and told stories. He made deals and lured in big-money donors. He worked on state campaigns for local politicians and on national campaigns for politicians who needed votes and influence in North Carolina.

He was successful and, if his eight-bedroom house was any indication, loaded. Celia told me during one of our calls that after some big transaction Harlan had bought a ninety-thousand-dollar car with cash—one of four cars he kept in those big garages on his property. The expense sounded so absurd I dug around for more info about him.

The words "advising," "polling," "researching," and "financing" were all over the "About Us" section of his company's website. That and photos of Harlan with important figures. Athletes. Businesspeople. Politicians.

I could see hints of Jackson in Harlan's face. Jackson had his dad's nose and eyes. The same hair color though Harlan's carried a touch of gray. Both checked the *objectively good-looking* box but the similarities ended there. Harlan was always "on" and Jackson showed no interest in playing that game.

"Kasey. Welcome home. I heard you were in town." He nodded in the direction of the door. "Mags is in the house."

His voice sounded all shiny and charming. No way was that real.

"Did you need something, hon?" Celia asked.

I'd known Celia long enough to recognize her fake smile. The one she wore when talking with a particular lady from church who frequently took verbal shots that included the words *if you had children you'd understand*. With Harlan, Celia made an effort, which seemed like a waste of energy.

My gaze bounced from Celia to Harlan. Neither of them moved.

Harlan jumped in before I could come up with a good question to ask. "Is this a short visit to town or something else?"

The rumor network moved with amazing speed in this town. "Jackson told you I was here?"

"No."

Uh, okay. Not sure how to interpret the quick response. "I needed to speak with Celia."

"Of course." Harlan nodded but didn't leave.

I didn't think it was possible to find him more annoying and in-the-way than I already did. I was wrong. "I'm sure you're almost done. I can wait."

"You were in and out at Christmas." He nodded as if agreeing with his own comment. "We didn't get a chance to visit, but I know you're busy back in DC."

He didn't overtly attack. He'd perfected the art of looking and sounding engaged and interested. Still, I couldn't kick the sensation of being assessed and measured.

Before I could respond, Celia cleared her throat but didn't say anything else.

A warning. *Be nice*. Got it.

Be respectful and understanding even if the person you're talking to is a complete asshat. Celia hammered that basic rule into my head from the time I got into that fight with Taylor whatever-her-last-name-was when she tried to cut the line at the climbing wall. Being seven, a tactful approach wasn't my go-to response, but Celia told me to appease, not fight. Talk, not yell.

When it came to dealing with unpleasant people, Gram went with the more direct *tell the bastards to go to hell* reaction. I sided with Gram on this topic.

"I'll be here for at least another week. Visiting." There. Neutral. Not bitchy. Somewhat respectful.

Harlan kept on nodding. "Interesting."

Was it?

He finally stopped staring at me and turned to Celia. He shot her a huge smile that wasn't one bit more genuine than the ones he'd delivered up until now. "We'll talk soon."

"Of course." Celia followed Harlan to the door, as if she wanted to make sure he actually left.

I fought the urge to run behind him and lock him out. Something about him annoyed the crap out of me. Maybe I still blamed him for his treatment of Jackson's mom fifteen years ago. Maybe it was because Harlan possessed an *I'm barely tolerating you* vibe. Maybe it was because we'd never had a conversation of more than three sentences. Could be any of those or a combination of a few.

"What was that about?" Because if he was bugging Celia, I would not hold back.

Celia busied herself with the dirty baking dishes. Moving them around. Stacking them on the counter. "We meet now and then. Usually not here because Mags isn't his biggest fan, but he was my brother-in-law. So, I make the time."

Should that be past tense? He still was her brother-in-law . . . sort of. "Don't you find him a little—"

"Condescending? Fake? Annoying? Yes." She picked up a bowl that had cake batter remnants up the sides. "He usually keeps talking until I give in and agree out of exhaustion. I guess that's what makes him successful at work."

"He would fit in back in DC with that move. Not that I want him there." I rushed to add that last part. "He should stay here, taking people out for drinks or whatever he does."

"He thrives on power. Craves the attention and wants to be right in the middle of the action so he can take credit for it." That was more than Celia usually said about Harlan. For the most part, she tried not to talk about him at all. "It's all an illusion."

"He's not good at his job?" That sounded like cosmic justice.

"Oh, he is." Celia's smile came and went. "He's also a very limited man who thinks he's a great man."

That matched how I viewed him. "So, delusional."

"He's tried to convince me more than once that he's misunderstood." Celia rolled her eyes as she said the words. "He's also explained why he was a saint for staying with Savannah as long as he did. *Other men would have left because no man signs up to play nursemaid to a sick wife.*" Celia mimicked Harlan's speaking style. "And that's probably all I need to say on that."

Celia and Harlan had a longtime prickly relationship. He was the guy who cheated on her baby sister then counted down the minutes until she died so he could move on. "Isn't it tough to be near him without kicking him?"

"Of course." Celia sighed. "I keep the peace with Harlan because it's easier for Jackson."

Harlan didn't strike me as a man who would be supportive of Celia and her relationship with Gram. That was my biggest problem with him, but I picked an easier topic. "Isn't Jackson a little old to worry about what his daddy thinks?"

Celia hummed, as if contemplating the question, which meant she was about to make a point that would defeat my argument. "Are you too old to worry about what Mags thinks?"

Yep. Just as expected. Score one for Celia. "No."

She shrugged. "There you go."

After handing me a spatula covered in leftover cupcake batter, she headed for the sink. I could smell the sugary vanilla goodness and thought about sticking the whole thing in my mouth but held off. For now.

I leaned against the sink, facing her. "Are you sure everything is okay?"

Her focus stayed on washing the bowl. "In what way?"

More roadblocks. "You and Gram sounded unenthusiastic when I asked you about helping out around here. Now I wander in here looking to lick a mixing bowl or two and find Harlan lurking around."

"Visiting, not lurking."

"I prefer my description."

Celia set down the bowl and wiped her hands on the nearest towel. "He does throw business our way."

All I could do was snort. And lick the spatula. From my experience, Harlan operated on a quid pro quo basis. He likely stepped in here so Celia and Gram would owe him something.

"Let's just say there's a game I need to play to keep Harlan happy. I'm willing to play it because the returns are worth it. After a meeting with him I shut him out and return to the business and to my life with Mags."

I loved hearing that. Loved how her face lit up when she

talked about Gram even after all the years together. But I was here for another reason. Icing leftovers, sure, but the image of that locked cabinet wouldn't leave my head.

"Back to my question about being okay. The reason I asked is because things seem a little weird around here."

Celia stiffened. "How so?"

"Unless there's a sprinkles thief on the loose I don't know why you're keeping them locked up in the pantry."

"Ah, yes. We have equipment and supplies spread over the pantry, kitchen, and annex. We're trying to rearrange and organize." She waved her hand in the air. "Things are getting moved around."

Did that answer my question? "And the lock?"

Celia hesitated. "We had some spices and things that might have expired. We put them in there until we had time to check."

Huh. She acted like it took a long time to look at a date and throw something in the trash. No, not buying it.

"I could help—"

"It's taken care of."

Sure, it was. "Right."

She smiled in a way that reminded me of Harlan. "More icing?"

I took the second spatula. There was no reason to be rude, but I now had more questions than I did when I walked in the annex. I needed answers and I had less than two weeks to find them.

Time for a new strategy.

CHAPTER SEVEN

It took another day and a cupcake emergency to do the one thing that might silence the warning bell that had been bonging in my head since I arrived back home. A big thank-you to Mrs. Phillips for forgetting to buy a fancy decorated cake for her granddaughter's surprise sixth-birthday party tomorrow and to her furious daughter-in-law for demanding the older woman *fix it*! Gram and Celia rushed in to help their friend and frequent lunch companion. It was an all-out sugar-fest in the baking annex right now.

The controlled chaos provided an open lane for me to slip into Gram's office. It was a privacy violation. Absolutely. Not cool at all. Not something I'd do under any other circumstance, but they'd accidentally taught me that they hid terrible news. Asking questions and trying to weasel the details out of them hadn't worked. That left me with one choice. A search.

If it turned out my father had filed another motion I would drive to the prison and take him apart. That was the vow. He would not hurt Gram again.

I opened the door nice and slow to Gram's office. Her sacred place. A loud *this is not your business* warning chimed in my ear. Funny how the judgy voice sounded a lot like Jackson's.

The room hadn't changed in twenty years yet still managed to look crisp and new. Maybe the style had gone out then come back in again and Gram had perfect timing. Not my thing, so I didn't know except to say I found the green walls soothing. Beadboard on the bottom that ended at a chair rail and wallpaper on top. All in the same green.

The shade was tough to nail down. It wasn't dark green or light green or even mint. Celia described it as fern. Whatever shade, the wallpaper on the top had long vines with birds and feathers in shades of blue highlighted by big pink flowers. The result was both dramatic and colorful in a Gram sort of way.

My favorite part of the room was the small sofa that fit in the corner across from Gram's desk. Like, exactly in the corner. The piece formed a perfect ninety-degree angle. I'd never seen another one like it. The plush velvet fabric was a soft greenish blue. I'd spent hours as a kid, sitting there reading and making up stories while Gram worked.

The temptation to sit pulled at me now, but I went to the desk instead. Marveled that Gram hadn't replaced the oversized leather chair that carried the creases and marks of a life that seesawed between days of tremendous joy and days of crushing pain.

Behind the desk stacked with papers was a wall of photographs collected and cherished through the years. The most telling picture was the one I didn't see. Not a single photo of her husband, my deceased grandfather. Stratton Nottingham. A man I never knew because he died right after I was born. We didn't talk about him or honor him at holidays or on his birthday. Father's Day was just another Sunday at our house.

Gram told me she hadn't spent a second mourning her husband because he didn't deserve a single one of her tears. Most people agreed he'd been a nasty bully, but no one talked about his unsavory traits in public. Gram explained that's how abuse was handled back then. It stayed inside the house walls, seeping out only in whispers passed around as church gossip.

A heart attack took him before he reached fifty-five. Then Gram saved herself by starting over, only to lose my mom less than six years later. Through the pain Gram had needed a lifeline. For the bulk of her struggles, Celia filled that role. They'd met in church and bonded over talk of broken marriages. Celia's husband hadn't been hateful and abusive, but he hadn't been great either. He bounced from one get-rich-quick scheme to another, hiding all of it from Celia, then left her broke and vulnerable when he died.

For years, Gram shooed away anyone trying to take her picture, but she smiled in the pictures with Celia. The one of them on a picnic with the sun shining through the trees. Them baking in an older version of the kitchen. The two of them standing with me, so proud, at my college graduation.

Gram referred to Celia as her *dear friend*. I realized early that meant *love of my life*. I would fight anyone who tried to come between them or shame them. I didn't believe in much, but I believed in them.

The other photos, the ones that felt like they belonged to another family in another life, were of my mother. I remembered her in blurry bits and pieces. An image crafted more out of what I was told about her than a real memory. The few family photos that survived the fire my father started showed Mom smiling and me on her lap or holding her hand during some outside excursion. I strained to recall her touch—anything—but when my father killed her, he stole that from me, too.

The first thing you lose is the sound of their voice.

Gram told me that once. At first Mom's voice rang in Gram's head as a constant clanging reminder of her loss. She said she blocked the noise, devastating and brutal, for the sake of her sanity. Lost in the senselessness of it all, she clung to her anger. Fury and guilt drove her, forced her to keep going as she raised me. The months then years passed, and the grief eased enough for Gram to breathe again, but when she reached for the sound of Mom's voice it was gone.

I didn't have the memories or her voice.

The same hollowed-out, empty sensation that had chased me my whole life caught up to me again. Just for a second it surrounded and suffocated me. Most days I could forget all I'd lost because I never remembered having it in the first place. Gram and Celia filled in the holes. But standing here, looking at my mom's smiling face, knowing that her ending had been so tragic, highlighted the unfairness of it all.

I fell into Gram's big chair and closed my eyes. Waited for the haunting loss to pass but knowing it would likely wrap around me for a few hours. Mourning someone I didn't know and ached to remember stole a lot of energy.

When I opened my eyes again I saw Gram's dark computer screen. Without thinking through where this could lead, I tapped the space bar and saw a page of what looked like a list of orders. After a few minutes of debating how uncool this snooping was versus the memory of Gram in that hospital bed, I scrolled through the document. More like, I scrolled while peeking at the closed door every two seconds to make sure Gram hadn't launched a sneak attack.

I recognized some of the names and most of the businesses. There were addresses for locals, for people out of town and out of the state. Some neighbors. Some people from church. Some bigwigs, like the mayor and a senator.

This spreadsheet covered items already delivered. Every entry noted the person, general information, and the item sent. Coconut cream pie. Buttermilk pecan and strawberry rhubarb. Butterscotch, double peanut, and lemon icebox. So many choices. All of them sounded amazing. I hadn't had Patti's sawdust pie in years. The name had something to do with a lady likely named Patti. That was the extent of my Patti knowledge. But how had I missed out on a delicacy called grits pie?

Bottom line: they sold a lot of pies, and those pies weren't cheap. The pies were the lead seller at Mags' Desserts but cupcakes, scones, cakes, and muffins made a pretty impressive appearance on the list as well. Lots of people. Lots of orders. Everything here seemed fine.

Maybe the real problem was my imagination. It's possible I'd taken a few unrelated things and slammed them together to create a fictional problem. After all, doing that was easier than tackling the mess I'd made with the business pitch. Still, I couldn't shake the idea of Gram hiding something. Gram and Celia formed a rose- and jasmine-scented wall between me and the reality they didn't want me to see.

One final look then I'd get up and walk out. I clicked on a tab then scrolled the whole way over and saw the previously hidden column on the right side. A few of the entries had a star there. Not all of them. Not many of them, actually. Just an unexplained star and nothing else.

The most recent starred item went to Abigail Burns just a few days ago. The name sounded familiar, but I couldn't picture a face. I hope she enjoyed the gift basket with assorted goodies and the banana cream pie and whatever about it that made it star-worthy.

I didn't have a business degree, but nothing looked out of place. I took a photo of the delivered and yet-to-be delivered lists with my phone so I could study them later.

My phone buzzed but I ignored it. Micah had already left a voicemail asking for a status check "on the grandmas" and that meant my time was running out.

I was starting to regret leaving law school.

CHAPTER EIGHT

Hours later, my cupcake lunch had worn off. After studying those ledger photos, I was ready for dinner. Gram ate dinner at six. She said five was too early and seven was ridiculous, so exactly six. If you weren't there, you didn't eat . . . and may the lord help you if you complained about what was on the menu. Never argue with the person cooking the meal.

Five minutes until mealtime.

The intoxicating smell of roasting pork hit me before I walked through the doorway to the kitchen. Someone had already prepared the table. Four place mats and four sets of dishes. A bounty of barbecued pulled pork, cheese grits, and green beans in their respective serving dishes.

That combo could only mean one thing: Jackson was coming to dinner. He loved this meal.

Lawyers ate at six? That didn't sound right.

Before I could ask, he walked in with a perfect, smooth stride. All businesslike in his dark suit. A different dark suit from the one he wore yesterday. One that fit him like he was born in it.

He kissed Gram where she stood next to the refrigerator and Celia as she sat down at one end of the table. He stopped and looked at me with fake surprise. "You're still here."

I could play this game, too. "Is this what time you eat lunch?"

Celia clearly thought it was a real question and not a snide comeback because she answered, "He joins us for dinner at least once a week."

"What a good boy." Celia might not catch my sarcasm, but Jackson would.

He winked as he took off his suit jacket. "I'm a boy who enjoys great food and knows what time it's served around here."

Some things never changed, including Gram's pulled pork recipe. See, this was Carolina barbecue. That meant slow roasted with vinegar and spices. None of that inferior sweet tomato barbecue nonsense touted by other states. This was shredded and tender, and in our house served without a roll because that's how Jackson preferred it.

"He goes back to work after he eats, but he thinks we don't know," Gram said as she set the sweet tea pitcher on the table. "He works too much."

Even I had to admit the way Jackson kept up with the ladies was kind of sweet. He checked in. They fed him. It sounded like the perfect relationship to me.

"Did you hear Cash died?" Jackson asked.

What a way to start a meal. He could have at least let me fill my plate first. "That was a bit dramatic."

He shrugged. "I walked in, sat down, and started a conversation."

He also managed to bring dinner to a crashing halt before it even started, which I did not appreciate at all. "My description stands."

"When?" Gram put the platter of pork down instead of passing it. "I hadn't heard anything."

Celia shook her head. "What a shock."

Celia didn't sound all that shocked or sad. Her voice stayed steady, almost without emotion. Gram sounded the same. Neither asked a basic question. Like, *How did Cash die?* The look that passed between them was . . . well, weird.

I needed to keep up my end of the discussion and that required more information. "Is Cash a horse, a dog, or a person?"

Jackson almost smiled but buried it in time. "A person. Cash Burns."

Huh. Not any clearer but strangely familiar. "That's his actual name?"

Gram stared at me with that *you know better* expression of hers. "Cash is a good Southern name."

Interesting that the name thing is what bothered her and not me being flippant about this man's death. I didn't know how to respond, so I skipped ahead, hoping Jackson would cough up more intel. "Was he a friend of yours?"

"He and Dad were close. They met up for golf and talked politics." Jackson took a sip of tea before continuing. "You knew him."

"Did we go to high school together or something? Because I can only remember the names of people I didn't like. Those are seared into my brain." Speaking of which . . . "Whatever happened to that Brandy chick? The one with red hair. Does she still live around here because I have some unresolved issues with her."

"Cash Burns, or his household, is a client of ours," Celia said before sneaking another peek at Gram.

"He's the father from the tennis club incident." Jackson broke the food logjam and reached for the grits. "At Christmas."

Oh, damn. That guy. "The rich dad who yelled at me for outing his son as a creep?"

Jackson moved on to the pork serving dish and filled half of his plate. "Same one."

"I only met the guy once." It was probably wrong to ask if his rotten son did it, so I tried more nuance. "Heart attack?"

"That's not clear. It happened yesterday and was the talk of the courthouse all day. He was only fifty-six." Jackson moved on to the green beans, not letting a little discussion about death impact his appetite. "Some people are suggesting poison."

Celia dropped her fork.

Gram did a cough-spit while drinking her tea. "Wait, who is saying that? I'm sure it was health related."

She was on the verge of gagging and demanded more details. I noticed what wasn't happening. They still weren't asking the obvious questions. Like *why* would anyone think that? Jackson jumped from saying a guy died to talking about poison and no one but me seemed to think that sounded like a big leap.

This whole conversation confused the crap out of me. "Is that something the police would know already? Unless he was holding a bottle of poison when they found him . . . wait, was he?"

"Something at the scene—and I don't know what yet, so don't ask—tipped off the police and started the rumor. They're talking to his wife." Jackson hesitated before taking his first bite. "And to Austin, Cash's son."

Austin Burns. So that was the creeper's name. I could see his face. His snotty, irritating, creepy face. Forget nuance, time to ask the million-dollar question. "Did he do it?"

"Kasey." Celia's voice was back to full volume now. "That's not appropriate."

"Why would his son kill him?" Gram said.

Jackson shrugged. "Is it such a stretch? Cash was not a nice man in business or in his personal life. He had enemies. He and Abigail had—"

"Wait . . ." The name finally clicked. "Abigail Burns?"

That's how I knew the last name. I'd read it. I'd studied it and her banana cream pie purchase.

"Yes. That's Cash's wife." Celia put a comforting hand on my arm. "Do you know her, honey? I wouldn't think so."

"No." But I remembered Abigail Burns and the star in the delivery ledger.

It probably meant nothing . . . or it could be something. Hard to tell because Gram wasn't talking. She sat there, tight-lipped and rigid. She looked everywhere—around the room, over at the stove, at the pile of pork on Jackson's plate. Everywhere except at me.

That couldn't be good.

"I get that he was a jerk, but that doesn't mean his wife poisoned him." I mean, the guy had been awful during my one experience with him, but I didn't wish death on people. Not without more information.

"I'm guessing we'll hear details over the next few days. The Burns's house is being searched. That and his office." Jackson scooped up a forkful of grits and swallowed before talking again. "It sucks for Abigail because people will jump to conclusions."

The weirdness of the conversation shifted into overdrive. I didn't know what unspoken conversation jumped between Gram and Celia but tension choked the room. The ladies looked like they wanted to bolt from the table.

Not Jackson. He kept eating.

The strange behavior. The secrets. The locked cabinet. The

star in the ledger beside Abigail's name. The timing of the pie delivery. The reaction to the poison talk—on steroids at some points and suspiciously unsurprised at others. The pieces probably didn't fit together into a complete picture. Certainly not anything nefarious.

Mags' Desserts. Purveyor of coconut, buttermilk pecan, and lemon icebox pies. Poison not included . . . but could it be?

No, of course not.

But . . .

Jackson had referred to me as a cyclone or a hurricane or some other natural disaster that blew through town and up-ended their lives. Turns out he wasn't wrong.

CHAPTER NINE

Meal eaten. Death discussed. General chitchat handled.

I couldn't concentrate through any of it. Every teacher I ever had said I was prone to daydreaming. My wild imagination would take off and get me in trouble as I made up grand stories. I preferred to think of what I did as creative license or a healthy extrapolation of facts. Gram used the words "embellishing" and "exaggerating." Two things I clearly grew out of, but the name on the ledger was an actual thing.

Abigail Burns bought a pie from Gram and Celia. The pie had been delivered one day before her husband died. Gram and Celia were acting weird and getting weirder by the second. They had absolutely reacted to the news about the nasty husband being dead, and not in the usual town gossip kind of way.

I needed help to figure this out. An accomplice. An ally.

I settled for Jackson.

He put his dirty dishes in the sink, said his round of thank-yous, gave kisses to Gram and Celia, and headed back for what appeared to be the night shift portion of his legal job. I caught up to him as soon as he stepped out the door and into the warm night.

"Jackson."

He stopped at the sound of my whisper-yell. "Why are you talking like that?"

I grabbed his arm and pulled him a few more feet away from the house. You know, just in case. "We have a problem."

"We?"

He made everything difficult. "Gram and Celia."

His skeptical expression morphed into concern. "What about them?"

"Something is wrong."

"With dinner? The pork was delicious as usual."

"Not the cooking." I leaned in closer. Just far enough to smell him because I was human and weak and he always smelled amazing, tonight being no exception. "I need you to listen."

He made a weird, strangled sound. "I'm trying."

"This is about the poison. Well, not really. It's about Celia and Gram and their sneaky behavior. Their odd reactions. Secrets." I tightened my hold on his arm. Took a second to appreciate the muscle under my hand. "Actually, maybe it is about the poison. Not intentionally because I can't see Gram and Celia doing that but something. I can't tell what."

"What are you talking about?"

He genuinely looked confused and *how was that possible*? "Did you fall asleep during dinner?"

"I'm starting to think so."

Fine. I'd spell it out. "Cash Burns and his wife."

"Are you okay? You're acting stranger than usual, and that's saying something."

This time he did the touching. His hand went to my waist and stayed there. Those impressive fingers brushed over the hem of my shirt. I didn't need soothing, but I didn't hate it. We never touched in a non-sibling way . . . except once . . . and *oh, boy*.

For a second, nothing moved. The sound of crickets and wind blowing through the trees filled in the background. The air felt sticky, signaling impending storms. It was near sundown, but I could see Jackson's face.

I had to swallow three times before I could say a word.

"It's easier to show you what I mean." I pulled out my cell then flipped through the photos, landing on the one with the notation about Abigail. "Do you see that?"

His body circled around mine as he leaned in closer. My brain short-circuited.

"Is that a photo of a computer screen?" he asked.

Two more swallows. "It's the business ledger for the dessert shop."

He stepped back. "Why do you have that?"

"That's not the point."

He moved on to frowning. Big-time frowning. "I disagree."

He wasn't wrong but that. Right there. He killed the mood. Sure, I was the only one reacting to the mood or even noticing there was a mood, but whatever.

I put a few more inches between us as I struggled to explain without suggesting I'd been snooping, which I had. "I was in Gram's office because I was worried the business ran into financial trouble. I didn't know about Cash Burns's death yet. But the spreadsheet was there."

He looked amused now. "Magically?"

"I didn't use that word."

"You accidentally took photos of it?"

Yes, my behavior sucked. I'd apologize once I knew for sure nothing was going on with Gram and Celia. "We can argue about this later but—"

"Oh, we will. You may have forgotten but I'm a lawyer."

How in the world could I forget that? "I didn't steal the ledger and you're not a prosecutor. Calm down."

He shook his head. "Every conversation with you goes like this."

That seemed unnecessary. I was trying to help here. "What does that mean?"

"Kasey, you . . ." He visibly grabbed for control. The tension rolling over him eased. "Okay. Fine. That argument can wait."

I should have moved on but the need to defend myself, at least a little, pulled at me. "You know they hide bad news from me."

"The heart issue. Yes." He nodded. "I know that's a constant worry for you. I worry, too. I also agree Mags didn't handle the situation well, but it happened two years ago."

That argument didn't persuade me at all. "Do you think Gram and Celia have radically changed their ways in the last two years?"

"Good point." He blew out a long breath that sounded like he'd hoisted the white flag of surrender . . . for now. "Tell me why you think this spreadsheet or ledger or whatever it is matters."

"The star." He didn't react to my epiphany, which made me think my imagination had run a little wild on this. I tried again anyway. "Do you know what the star means?"

"Something that's none of your business?"

Fair but not helpful. "I'm serious."

"I'm not sure why you think I'm not."

I needed a new accomplice. Until I found one, Jackson was it. Unfortunately. "There's only a star on a few deliveries and it's on the delivery that went to Abigail. The next day her husband was dead."

Still nothing from Jackson but a blank stare.

"What if this all goes together somehow?" I didn't have the fancy law degree, but I had experience with Gram and Celia, and that poison talk at the table definitely made them jumpy. No question about it. True, the timing could be nothing. But it could also be something, and if it was something, Celia and Gram needed our help. No way they'd ask for it, so we'd have to insist. "Do you need me to walk through the facts again?"

I saw the second he understood my point. I also heard it because his eyes went wide then he laughed. "Oh, come on."

"I offered to help them with the business. To file, do books, whatever. Gram and Celia were adamantly against it."

"I wonder why. You're the obvious person to help." His flat voice telegraphed his sarcasm.

"Now you're just being rude."

His mouth opened twice before he actually said anything. "First, we don't know if Cash was poisoned. So let's not invite trouble."

Easy for him to say. "That's not really how I operate."

"No kidding." He smiled. "Second, Mags and Celia sell a ton of pies. Abigail is probably a regular customer, like a lot of people in town."

Every word he said made sense, but I wasn't in the mood for a rational argument. We were dealing with a very unlikely scenario here. My reaction probably grew out of my need for a distraction from my business mess, but sometimes shocking things happened. My life was a testament to that. This could be one of those times.

"What about the star? It could mean—"

"That Abigail has an allergy they have to be careful of. That she likes extra coconut in her coconut cream pie." He exhaled as if he'd given a big speech. "There are a million reasons why they'd use a star and none of them are about poison."

Logic. I recognized it but didn't appreciate it at the moment. Something—money, poison, health—had gone wrong with Gram and Celia. The gnawing panic inside me told me that much and they weren't talking.

"You are off on a wild tangent here," he said.

He really did suck the life out of everything and made it boring. "But the man is dead."

"Cash probably has a huge amount of stress because of his business and his son. That Austin guy would be exhausting to have in the family."

"You say that now. It would have been nice if you'd stepped up and defended me at Christmas." Back then he'd shot me a look that said *behave* and scurried off with Anna hanging on his arm.

"I did."

"What?"

"I backed you up at the club. After you left."

What he was saying didn't have any relationship to reality. "Again, what?"

He shrugged. "The club manager got caught in the middle. He didn't want to ruin his business relationship with Mags and Celia or upset the other members. So, I calmed down Cash and my dad. I demanded Austin apologize, and he did."

Look at Jackson being all chivalrous. "No way."

"It was a half-assed apology, of course, but the girl said she was satisfied. Cash made Austin leave and cool off. The club then suspended him for a month. Not a perfect resolution, but it was more responsibility than Austin usually took for his actions."

Backing me up was sweet and decent. But Jackson had hidden his help, which made no sense. "You never told me any of this."

"My negotiation skills come in handy sometimes."

I stared into his eyes, ready for him to make a joke or pull away. He didn't do either. He matched my stare. We stood there until the roar of a car engine passing by broke the spell.

Despite being unable to swallow, I cleared my throat. "Right."

"Yeah."

"Yep." What else could I say?

"Mm-hmm."

I heard the hitch in his breathing and tried to calm mine down. "Exactly."

We needed to stop before we ran out of useless words. I took a giant step back this time and inhaled nice and deep, hoping a flood of fresh air would help restart my brain.

"Look, I have to get back to the office and work for a few hours. Tomorrow is Friday. We'll have dinner and you can plead your case," Jackson said in typical lawyer fashion. "Then I'll poke holes in it, and we can formally put the issue to rest."

"You're mighty sure of yourself."

"Yes, and after we finish that topic you can tell me what you're really doing in town."

How did he circle back to that? "I told you. A visit."

"I've set out my terms."

Smooth. Impressive, really, but his look of satisfaction made me want to fight harder. "Fine, but it's possible I'll win the argument."

His smile hit full wattage. "There's a first time for everything."

I refused to let him have the last word. "You'll see."

CHAPTER TEN

Micah called at seven-fifty the next morning. I was not a morning person. He didn't seem to care.

He said he needed a *Friday status.* I hadn't done anything that required a status check so far in this job. If actually doing work meant wake-up calls before nine I might go back to eating my free bagel, playing games on my phone, and waiting to be fired.

After another half hour in bed and a cup of coffee, I went outside. Actually, I took a shower and ate a muffin before declaring I needed fresh air. A legitimate excuse in this household. Celia used the phrase all the time. She thought the whole world needed fresh air.

As a kid she'd kick me out of the house in search of sun and oxygen. That worked in North Carolina for most of the year. It's lucky we never lived in Alaska or somewhere equally frigid.

In addition to the riot of flowers and the raised vegetable beds, my favorite thing in the yard was the gazebo. It sat in the back corner framed by two flowering dogwood trees. A trail of pavers led to the white octagonal structure.

This wasn't just any old gazebo. No, Gram had gone all out. She claimed every Southern home needed one. Since none of our neighbors had one, I was skeptical about that being a rule.

Electricity. String lights. A beverage refrigerator. An enormous outdoor sectional sofa. A serving table. A buffet. An ottoman. This thing had all the trimmings, which made it the perfect place for me to sneak away and study the ledger I'd photographed.

Knowing Jackson, tonight he'd break out a lecture on privacy and appropriate boundaries. He'd likely add a shot or two about my supposed tendency to exaggerate. While all of that was valid, I had to hold my ground until we had more intel on the weird things happening with Gram and Celia. I needed to be ready. He was a *fact* guy. He couldn't be won over by charm. I knew because I'd tried that for almost a decade before finally giving up.

An hour and one bottle of water later and I found the smoking gun. Not really but I wanted to think of it that way. I'd only photographed a few months of the ledger. Two deliveries had stars in that last column on the pages I grabbed. One was for Abigail Burns. The other was for Delilah Rhine.

In addition to having a spectacular name, Delilah had a dead husband. He died of a heart attack. A heart attack that happened one day after the delivery of a chess pie and other assorted goodies from Mags' Desserts. Unrelated, but in case anyone wondered the key ingredient in that Southern classic was vinegar. Gram told me that once as if she were passing down a family secret.

Right now, I didn't care about the ingredients. I cared about the timing of Delilah's delivery. Having two pies with a special star next to them delivered to two households with recently dead husbands qualified as a pretty big coincidence. Okay, that was a stretch, but still. Even Jackson with his big brain and tendency to ignore what the rest of us called *a gut feeling* would see the possible connection. I hoped.

"Here's some tea."

"Shit!" On instinct, I threw my cell and nearly dove under the sectional. "You scared the crap out of me."

Celia laughed. "Clearly."

My heart thundered hard enough for the neighbors to hear it. "I . . . uh . . . yeah."

Where the hell was my phone? I remembered holding it, then she snuck up on me. Kudos to me for having the instinct to lash out when attacked, but the phone had the incriminating, totally inappropriate, gathered through snooping photos on it, so I needed to beat Celia to finding it.

"This is for you." The ice cubes clinked when she held out a glass. "Don't worry. It's herbal tea, not that sweet tea crap Mags likes to drink."

I closed the notebook I'd been using because I didn't want her to see my scribbles but mostly because I needed to put all of my energy into responding to that shocking statement. "Celia Windsor, have you been pretending to like sweet tea to make Gram happy? Like, for twenty years?"

"Of course."

I delivered my best fake gasp. "That's outrageous."

"She adds so much sugar my teeth tingle when I drink it, but I sip it anyway because it makes her happy." Celia sat down next to me on the sectional. "In return, she'll share a cherry pie with me even though she detests cherries."

"Damn." I made an exploding gesture with my hand. "I have to rethink everything I thought I knew about this household."

"I figured you were old enough to hear the truth." She reached down and picked up my phone.

The force of the adrenaline running through me threatened to knock me over.

"Here you go." She handed it over without looking at the screen. Of course she did. Celia was big on privacy. Fresh air and privacy.

That made one of us. "You could—and hear me out on this—tell Gram the truth about the tea. Like I did."

"Oh, no." Celia shook her head. "I remember that day."

Who could forget it?

"I have a good excuse. You see, right after we first met, Mags served me sweet tea and a piece of her lemon chiffon pie and, well, it was early in our relationship. I didn't want to be negative, so I drank two glasses of her tea."

That was pretty adorable. I could almost see Gram trying to woo Celia with baked goods. "You condemned yourself to a life of sweet tea misery because once, long ago, you were determined to get on Gram's good side."

"We never lie about the big stuff. Only cherry pie and sweet tea." Celia glanced at the notebook on my lap. "Are you writing stories?"

Was I . . . ? "What?"

She treated me to an encouraging smile like she'd done for most of my life. "You wrote your first story at seven."

In crayon on construction paper. Even designed the cover, which highlighted my complete lack of drawing skills. "'The Great Possum Race.'"

"I think you revised it four times. You read it to us over and over again."

"Well, it was a masterpiece."

"True." Celia laughed. "Mags bragged about it for a year. She bragged about all the stories you wrote. Talked about your potential."

Gram was supportive but she wasn't the type to hand out praise over nothing. I'd been chasing her approval since I moved in. "Does she talk about the part where I can't keep a job?"

"I'm afraid the law school issue was our fault."

Celia had alluded to this many times over the last two years. I dropped out of law school right after Gram went to the hospital. There was a connection of sorts. Almost losing Gram made me reexamine my priorities and law school didn't make the list. That wasn't Gram and Celia's fault. It was law school's fault.

"You've struggled because you've been in the wrong career," she said.

No one bothered to tell me that before. "Meaning?"

"With your vivid imagination you're a born storyteller. When you were younger Mags feared you'd become a con artist or something because of the grand stories in your head." She shrugged. "Happily, that didn't happen."

I hadn't moved off the job comment. "How does writing translate into a paying job? It would be helpful to know because I don't have a clue."

Celia stayed quiet for a few extra beats. Long enough for the hesitation to be obvious. "I know what I think you'd be happiest doing, but you have to figure that out for yourself."

Maybe it wasn't too late to try that con artist thing. "Could you give me a hint?"

"I already did." She sighed. "So, fried chicken for dinner?"

Crap. Right. I forgot to give her a heads-up. "Can we bump that one night? I'm supposed to have dinner with Jackson."

"Really?" The question consisted of one word but came loaded with an unspoken opinion.

"Is that a bad idea?"

She patted my knee. "I think it's a great idea."

Uh, okay. "Are we talking in code?"

"I'm happy you're home." With that Celia stood up.

I couldn't exactly admit that I was in town for a business deal. One that, without her knowledge or permission, involved her. But I couldn't forget her not-so-subtle hint that I hadn't found my *thing* in life yet, probably because her sweet tea admission threw me off.

It was interesting how Celia and Gram hid bad news but didn't shy away from offering their advice. They came right out with it whether, in the case of a safe sex talk at thirteen, it made me squirm, or it was a general life lesson. They believed in preparing me for the real world.

I'd listened to about a billion speeches about bad men over the years. Never accept a drink from someone you don't know. Walk home in pairs. Never let him get you alone in a car. Pay for the ride share. The list went on and on. Yet here, when I needed details and direction, Celia clammed up.

First job: tackle the business issue.

Second: figure out what I was supposed to be when I grew up.

CHAPTER ELEVEN

J ackson picked a brasserie in a downtown hotel for dinner. The building wasn't far from his office, which explained his choice. Knowing Jackson, he intended to return to his desk after we finished.

The clubby restaurant with its paneled walls harkened back to an old-fashioned private men's club. The only thing missing was the thick layer of cigarette smoke I assumed lingered in places with this vibe. Winston-Salem, the home of tobacco, would have been ground zero for that sort of thing. Not anymore, thanks to the modern-day inside smoking ban. Very grateful for that.

We'd been sitting at the table for six minutes when I whipped out my notebook with all the information from my recent research. Time to impress lawyer boy. "I have proof."

Jackson finished drinking his water. The look on his face didn't give anything away. Unreadable. Annoyingly blank.

When he didn't say anything, I tried again. "About the poison."

"Yes, I know what you're referring to." He set his glass down with precision, as if it might shatter if he hit it too hard against the table.

He wore his usual dark suit, this time with a green tie that made his eyes sparkle . . . or would have if I noticed that sort of thing, which I no longer did.

He didn't smile or frown, but his voice sounded tight. We were coming at this dinner from two different directions. While I was enjoying a work break, he'd sat at a desk and argued all day. It was only fair I gave him an opportunity to vent if he needed one.

"Bad day?"

"Not particularly."

Huh. I sat back in my chair, resigned to a fight. "I give up. What's wrong with you?"

"Maybe we could order before you start lobbying me with your theories."

My menu sat in front of me. I hadn't opened it. Hadn't really thought about food, which was not how I normally prioritized things. I'd been so excited to hit him with my findings that I'd missed something. Not sure what. "Are you angry?"

"Should I be?"

Not a fan of answering a question with a question. It reminded me of the office and Micah and *ugh.* Also, if I knew what was happening with Jackson I wouldn't be squirming in my chair, searching for a comfortable position. "You seem . . . distant."

He shrugged. "I'm hungry."

That sounded simple. Too simple?

I leaned in again, thinking to keep our conversation as private as possible. "Did something happen? It feels like something happened."

"Look around you."

Fine. I'd play along. For the first time I heard the faint background music. Saw the crowd. Tables filled with couples and groups. A few people milling about, waiting to be seated. Lots of laughter and chatting. Servers talking about specials. The clink of silverware and water glasses. Basically, a pleasant crush of after-work activity.

Okay. Done. "What am I supposed to see?"

He rested his elbows on the table. "We're having dinner."

Yeah, obviously. "I'm aware."

"Well, we aren't yet because you're diving right into your poison theory." He glanced at my notebook. "You're skipping over the food part."

Did he sound frustrated . . . disappointed . . . something? I took another look at the couple at the table next to ours. They were holding hands and debating which entrées to get. The woman giggled. A grown woman giggling. No wedding ring, so maybe a date?

Wait . . . Every thought in my head blinked out. For a few seconds, I couldn't remember how to put words together.

After a false start and a bit of sputtering, I leaned in even closer. "Is this a date? Us. Right now. It's not, right? Because . . ." *Oh my God.* "Right?"

Somehow my floundering questions, meant to be asked in a whisper, came out as a semi-shout. People at more than one neighboring table stared at me. The server who was headed to our table performed an impressive spin and roamed off in another direction.

Absolutely fantastic. I hadn't been embarrassed in this town in years. Mostly because I only came home for short visits. If I stayed longer this would be more of a regular occurrence.

"I'd like to think if this were a date you'd know." Jackson kept his voice at a normal, non-screaming, non-embarrassing level.

"Cryptic but okay."

He nodded. "Okay."

No, he didn't get to drop a curt reply without an explanation. He wasn't allowed to be ticked off and distant. He's the one who started the sometimes sarcastic, always noncommittal back-and-forth relationship dance we'd been stuck in for years.

"Because you made your position clear . . . on that. Back then. You scurried away at a flat-out run." Now I had too many words bouncing around in my head. I tried to force my mouth to stop but lost the battle. "You did, actually. Run. That time."

So much nonsense rambling. The dinner shifted from weird to awkward, heading straight for wildly uncomfortable.

He frowned. "Excuse me?"

That's all he had? "Did you not hear what I said?"

"I heard you."

Then the anger bubbling up from my stomach was justified. As if he didn't know what he'd done. Wrong. He knew. He remembered. If he didn't remember that would be worse than what actually happened because it would show my stunning downfall meant nothing to him. He should at least have some remorse for the way he handled the situation.

He fell back on his usual frowning. "Kasey?"

Argh . . . fine. "The kiss, Jackson. What else would I be talking about?"

That time I hit the whisper sweet spot. My voice stayed low. I didn't sound pathetic, needy, or angry. I aimed for nonchalant, but his frown said I'd missed.

"Are you kidding?" he asked when he finally spoke again.

Not the response I expected. "I know it meant nothing to you but—"

"That was years ago."

Yet I remembered it like it was yesterday. Searing shame did that to a person.

I'd kissed him. In the same gazebo I'd sat in most of the day. I reached up and put my arms around his neck, balanced on my tiptoes, and kissed him. He acted like I tried to set him on fire. His *no way* response made me want to dig a hole and climb into it.

He bolted. Ran away yelling. I didn't see him for almost a month after that. When we met up again at some shindig at Gram and Celia's house we both pretended the kiss never happened. For him, it apparently didn't, and it sure didn't mean anything.

Men really sucked sometimes.

He continued to stare at me. His mouth wasn't hanging open, but it wasn't closed. He looked two seconds away from shouting.

"Sixteen." That's all he said.

I whined about my flailing kiss. He threw out a number. "Are we just saying random things now? I guess I pick four."

His sigh telegraphed his frustration. "You were sixteen. In tenth grade."

"And?"

He clenched his jaw to the point of snapping. "The distance between sixteen and twenty-three is huge, not to mention obviously inappropriate and illegal."

Our ages? Okay, but we weren't doing anything gross. "Jackson, we—"

"I was in law school. You were in high school." He shook his head. "I thought the problem with the kiss was obvious."

Now that he said it, sure, the issue should have been obvious. Still, the way he'd reacted sucked. A little tact would have spared my teen heart and wouldn't have killed him. "It was just a kiss."

"Just a . . ." He blew out a long breath. Looked ten seconds away from delivering a scorching lecture. "Okay, let's try this for comparison. When I was sixteen you were nine."

More math. *Great.* "We can run these calculations all day."

"I was kissing girls by the time I was sixteen. Not you. You were totally off-limits and I had zero romantic interest in a child."

To be fair, I couldn't argue with that.

He put his hand on the table right near mine but didn't go the extra few inches so that our fingers touched. "You kissed me, and I panicked. We were in the big brother, annoying little sister phase of our relationship. No thoughts of anything else. No kissing allowed."

He'd said a few important things, but one line stuck out. "You think of me as a sister?"

"Not anymore."

Tension snapped around us. "Oh . . ."

"Not for years."

CHAPTER TWELVE

H ave you really been upset all these years because I broke off the kiss and left that day?" Jackson sounded astounded by the possibility.

"That's not what I said." But it's what happened. Only Whitney, my best friend back in the office and miles away, knew about my unrequited and persistent crush on a guy who was totally not my type . . . and annoying . . . but adorable.

"Are you sure? Because that's basically what you said."

Be cool. "'Upset' is a strong word."

"Apparently it fits the situation."

"Fine. Yes. Over the years I've thought about what happened between us and how poorly you handled it." Too far? I made it sound like I was pining away for him, so I added a shrug because it fit with the *no big deal* vibe I wanted to send. "None of that matters now. It's long over. Of course."

He smiled for the first time since we sat down. "It sounds like you thought the kiss and my reaction to it amounted to a big deal."

His damn eye sparkle returned. The way his smile lit up his face made him seem less starched and serious. His smooth voice. I hated that the long-ignored crush popped up when I least expected it. Now happened to be a terrible time.

Fall back on joking. Keep things light. That was my safe space with him. "Has your ego always been this big or did that come with the law firm partnership?"

"You're trying to change the subject."

Yes. Definitely. "You're the one with the attitude."

"You're the one who's been carrying around a big secret." He took a sip of water and managed to look pretty hot doing it.

How did he make that sexy?

"I thought you wanted to eat." Suddenly, I didn't.

He didn't touch the menu. "If that's what you want."

I wanted this conversation to end. He seemed to be enjoying himself too much to let that happen, so I took control. "I can call the server over."

I scanned the room looking for a much needed assist. Jackson lifted his hand. That's all it took for the server to come rushing in our direction.

"Are you sure you don't want to walk down memory lane again?" he asked.

I'd lost control of the evening. No question. "I want to kick you. How about that?"

"I'm not into that sort of thing."

The server's sudden presence prevented me from responding to the innuendo. Good, because I had no idea what to say. Jackson morphed from sullen to almost flirty. If he was anyone else I'd say clearly flirty. Where was the emotionally stable, never flustered, always serious man I knew? The drastic switch had me scrambling to keep up.

The next ten minutes included a lot of verbal fumbling, almost all of it on my side of the table. I'd never been to this restaurant before and hadn't opened the menu. I ended up ordering the first entrée I saw. I couldn't remember what that was.

As soon as the server left, Jackson folded his hands on the table. Looked relaxed and engaged.

This had to be a trap.

He gestured in my direction. "Tell me."

Maybe I missed part of the conversation. "What?"

"What did you figure out? Your text said you had the evidence that would convince me about the poison."

"I might have overstated." I could barely remember my name at the moment. He had me spinning in circles and beating back a surge of adrenaline.

He feigned surprise. "Shocking."

His cute smile annoyed me more than usual. "Don't be that guy."

"Sorry." He swallowed the smile but still looked amused. "So, impress me with your findings."

I mentioned Delilah Rhine and the star by her name. Jumped to conclusions. Made connections that might not be there. Oversold my case . . . but at least we weren't talking about kissing.

He followed along and nodded. "I know Delilah."

That was a bit sparse. A few more details would have been nice. "Like *know* know?"

He rolled his eyes. "As a client. She owns an event planning business. She . . ."

He winced. I saw it.

"What do you know and aren't saying?"

He looked wary now. "Don't get excited."

Too late. "Say it."

"She didn't just buy a pie from Celia and Mags. Delilah works with them frequently. Their businesses overlap. The three of them are . . . close."

This sounded like the perfect time for an *ah-ha!* but I refrained. Barely. "See?"

"No. That is not proof."

"Killjoy." Now for the harder part. "We need to check into this."

Jackson shook his head. "We let the police do their job and investigate Cash's death and see what happens."

A terrible idea and not something I intended to do. Rather than point all that out, I went with the one fact that would make a difference for him. "Gram and Celia could be in trouble."

"Or not."

Nice try. His guarded expression didn't fool me. "They would step in and help a woman with a husband problem."

"I don't even want to know what that means."

He did. He knew better than most what Celia went through to disengage from the hideous mess her irresponsible husband left her in. May he rest in peace.

"They might have meant well. Talked with Delilah. Then everything went sideways . . . and for some reason they made the mistake again with Abigail." Admittedly, the last part added to the confusion. How many times did poison play a role, how, and did they have some sort of poison supply I didn't know about? I almost got lost in the long list of questions colliding in my brain. "The bottom line is Gram and Celia potentially could be mixed up in all of this."

He sighed. "If there's even something nefarious going on,

which I doubt, so that's a huge *if*. All we know right now is two unrelated men died at different points in time."

So many words and none of them were *maybe you were right to question all of this and I was wrong*. But I was and so was he. Score one for the law school dropout. "That's not all we know. I might be imagining things but you're downplaying them."

"I can admit that. I'll ask around and—"

"Yes. But you mean *we*. We can look around."

"Wait." He held up his hands as if to extinguish any excitement that might be brewing. That was his superpower. "I can find out more about Delilah's husband situation on my own. See if there are any rumors. Make sure Celia and Mags aren't being mentioned in the conversation."

He didn't outright refuse. That was a good start. "You have to report back. You're not cutting me out of this."

"Understood."

We spent a few minutes talking about strategy. Well, I did. He listened but didn't commit to anything. After that the conversation naturally switched to non-poison topics. His job. Celia and Gram. What was happening in town. People we both knew. We avoided any additional kissing talk and fell into a comfortable back-and-forth.

Being with him both unsettled me and grounded me. Those sounded like opposites, but the words represented the clashing between my heart and my head. I liked him, though I would never admit that. He made me smile. We shared a past. Our lives intersected and wove together in so many places.

I also wanted to try that kissing thing again. As an adult this time. But not happening, so I buried the idea as deep as possible and focused on the friendly stuff only.

We finished our delicious dinner. I'd gotten flounder. A good call. An hour and a half and I'd scarfed down a salad, entrée, and we shared a dessert. The dessert just happened to be one of Gram's pies. Blueberry crunch. One I hadn't tasted in years.

I waited for the server to clear the plates. "You know you're paying, right?"

"I thought we agreed this wasn't a date."

"Technically it was a negotiation of sorts. I got you to listen and believe me about the poison."

"No." He drew the word out for a few syllables, as if he needed to emphasize it. "I'm not sold on your theory. I still think you're jumping to conclusions and letting that imagination of yours run amok. Some things are coincidences, you know."

"Whatever."

"But dinner is on me." He folded his napkin and put it on the table. "This time."

My heartbeat spiked. "Is there going to be another restaurant dinner?"

"That's up to you." His smile returned.

"What's happening right now?"

"I'd note the difference between sixteen and twenty-three was a problem. The difference between twenty-six and thirty-three is not."

More math. This time interesting math. I was smart enough to shut up and not ruin the moment . . . but I would eventually.

CHAPTER THIRTEEN

How was dinner?"

The question sounded innocuous. Sort of a throw-away thing people asked in the morning on the way to the coffeemaker. Coming from Celia, seeing her bright smile, and knowing we were talking about dinner with her nephew, made my defenses rise.

"Fine." No mention of old kisses or talk about kissing because those weren't the types of things Gram and Celia needed to know. I'd been embarrassed enough, thank you.

Celia sat in the kitchen with her laptop. Years ago, she'd insisted the home office was too dark. No amount of white paint and sheer curtains made her happy. Gram gave up and went with the green walls she wanted. Celia found other places to do her non-baking work. Today, the breakfast bar won.

Seeing her there, typing away and studying whatever was on her screen, made me wonder about what *was* on her screen. I'd sent copies of the ledger photos to Jackson right after I woke up this morning. He didn't respond, being a busy man and all.

Never mind that it was Saturday at nine in the morning. He probably popped into work for a few hours, which was a *totally* normal thing to do on a sunny weekend day.

I sipped my Earl Grey tea and watched Celia. Her fingers flew across the keys. Years ago, she'd done data entry at her husband's company before turning to baking. She had serious typing skills and a dead husband.

Isaac Boone. Literally a used car salesman and constantly in search of a big payoff. He talked about grand ideas for making money but couldn't back them up. He tried to buy a dealership, but that didn't work. He tried other careers, ones that paid more and were considered more prestigious. Those didn't work either.

When his father died, Isaac inherited the family's medical supply business. It took only a few years for him to run it into bankruptcy through mismanagement and bad investments. That came after he and Celia got married.

She'd worked there. Her age was a moving target, but she would have been in her late thirties when they met. She'd wanted a child. Isaac, always being one to over-promise and fail to produce, knew and proposed. She didn't love him but said he seemed "nice enough"—a very low bar she now admits wasn't sufficient for marriage—and she said yes. Then everything went to hell.

Thinking he could reverse the surgery without trouble, he "forgot" to tell her that he'd had a vasectomy. He tried to fix the problem without her knowing and managed to fail at that, too. When checks started bouncing and their house went into foreclosure, she realized he'd lied in ways that could destroy her. With the trust irrevocably broken, she wanted out. He died in a car accident right after she told him, leaving her with a load of guilt and unpaid debts.

She didn't turn to her siblings for help because Celia refused to burden them. She also knew Savannah's marriage and health were falling apart, and had been for years, and Celia wanted the family's sole focus on her baby sister. Gram and Celia knew each other from church. Gram stepped up as a friend at first, offering support and a room to rent for almost nothing. It only took a year for things to shift and now they'd been together for more than two decades.

"Do you need money?" Celia studied her computer screen. "I'm paying bills and can write you a check."

A curveball of a question. "Where did that come from?"

Celia stopped typing and looked up. "I know your apartment is expensive and you have that law school loan because you wouldn't let us help out with tuition."

They'd done enough by paying for my undergraduate degree. Condemning myself to a lifetime of monthly payments for my fizzled legal career fell on me.

"You're home, so I thought maybe you needed a little help. It's nothing to be ashamed of."

"I'm fine." Even if I wasn't I'd lie. I had no intention of being a money-sucking drain on Celia and Gram. I'd return to law school first.

"We all need help carrying the weight now and then, Kasey. That is nothing to be ashamed of."

The comment meant something coming from Celia. Her life turned upside down thanks to her dead husband. When she needed help, she couldn't ask for it. Gram forced her way in, saying *martyrdom is a road to nowhere*. I grew up with the comfort of knowing if I needed a lifeline, one would be extended without question.

"I'm assuming you have savings. We've talked about this," Celia said.

Yeah, once or twice . . . or a billion times. That was Celia's other life lesson: have the resources to leave when you needed to go and then go. Being financially independent had been a running lecture from the time I earned my first allowance by washing dishes after a big bake.

Celia specifically drummed into my head that a woman needed to have money set aside for emergencies. She hadn't and paid for that misstep, so she made me promise if I had a partner that I would keep a separate small account just for me.

"I'm good." Also, a little relieved because offering me money meant she had some. My wild fears about the business being in financial trouble might be unfounded.

That left my other theory about their strange behavior. Gram and Celia were in the poison pie business.

Jackson would call that a leap in logic, which was why I intended to ignore his opinion on the matter.

Jackson. A puzzle of a man and a cute one. He'd thrown me off-balance. The last comment at the restaurant about our ages had my mind spinning. I knew what I thought he meant. I didn't know what he thought he meant. And that summed up my relationship with Jackson. Always a step behind, rushing to catch up, and a little breathless from it all.

"Celia?" The call came from upstairs.

Celia downed the rest of her coffee and slid off the barstool. "Sounds like Mags needs me."

Celia pretended not to love being needed, but I knew she did. She also left her laptop behind. She'd closed it but, I mean, there it was. In front of me. Filled with information, including additional ledger pages and the answer to how many other stars next to customer names correlated with dead husbands.

All of Jackson's talk about coincidences might stop if I presented him with more examples. Not that the need for more information justified snooping around in Gram and Celia's business records. It didn't. The danger, the possibility of them getting sucked into a criminal case, the spotlight I'd put on their business, their past behavior in hiding bad news made me fear a huge disaster waited, ready to pummel them. The tension ratcheted up with each new piece of information until ignoring my worries became impossible.

One more search. I'd be quick. I'd limit my snooping to that one column with the stars. I would not look at anything else.

This would be the last time.

I slipped around the kitchen island and stood behind the chair Celia had been sitting in. Keeping watch, listening for footsteps, and snooping turned out to be a lot to do at one time. I managed but my heartbeat thundered in my ears. Nervous energy bounced around inside me, making my hands shake as I opened the laptop. The document on the screen was a list of vendors and not helpful to my informal investigation, but I spied the tab for the ledger.

A few clicks and I was back in Celia and Gram's private space, fighting off a final kick of guilt for going down this road. I didn't expect to see a footnote about poison. I wasn't that lucky. But I did expect to see stars. They were gone. I scrolled through pages. Nope, that final column no longer existed.

Abigail Burns and Delilah Rhine now were just two of the people who bought pies and received some sort of gift package from Gram and Celia over the last few months. Nothing indicated anything special about their pies or their deliveries. The evidence was gone.

The sunny kitchen felt tight and airless as the walls crashed in on me. I tried to stay calm, but my frenzied heartbeat had other ideas. The rush of my own breathing filled my ears.

One more thing to check.

I opened the pantry door and scanned the shelves. No locked cabinet anywhere. The containers of cupcake decorations now sat in rows like they always had before with the sprinkles on display. Organized by color. Right there for all to see.

Wrestling my imagination back under control would not be an easy task. Two pieces of potentially damning evidence had disappeared. To be absolutely correct, were erased. The stars and locked cabinet might not have been indicative of anything before but the absence of both now felt like a big deal. Like Gram and Celia were covering their tracks because the police were looking into the possibility of Cash's death by poison.

Now I just had to convince Jackson.

CHAPTER FOURTEEN

A cup of tea and two cinnamon muffins later I showed up at Jackson's house after a quick warning text. He lived in a condo in downtown Winston-Salem. A loft because of course. The love of lofts appeared to be entrenched in male DNA.

I hadn't been there since he moved in three years and two girlfriends ago. That time I tagged along with Celia when she dropped off something for him. I remembered white walls, high ceilings, and exposed pipes. Expensive with a fancy kitchen complete with stainless everything. He was on the third floor but still had decent views. I also heard rumblings about a rooftop deck.

He answered the door all sweaty and breathless. His wet shirt stuck to him, showing off broad shoulders. It was criminal to hide those things under stuffy suit jackets. His hair went every which way. Those legs . . . toned and muscular, especially for a guy who sat at a desk twenty hours a day.

He looked adorably messy, standing there holding his earbuds.

I forgot how to use words.

After being subjected to a few quiet minutes of his intense frowning, I coughed up the information about the ledger revision and the now missing locked cabinet in the pantry. At least I thought I did. I could have said anything. My brain was so fuzzy it's possible I gave him my usual take-out coffee order.

His frowning didn't ease. "Say that again."

I couldn't even if I wanted to. But he could prevent further blurry thinking if he did one little thing. "I can wait if you need to take a shower . . . or find more clothes."

"What?"

Moving on. I'd pretend he was wearing a clown costume or something similarly sinister. I closed my eyes and reopened them and . . . nope. Still hot and sweaty.

"The stars are gone." There. I'd said something comprehensible.

"What does that mean?"

Maybe not so comprehensible. "I went back into the ledger on the computer and—"

"Again?"

Interesting that even in his half-clothed, rumpled state he used a judgmental tone. "I needed more evidence to convince you."

"So, this is my fault?" He left the entry hall and moved into the kitchen.

I followed, which gave me an opportunity to check out his outfit from behind. Equally impressive.

"Let's try this again." He took two water bottles out of the refrigerator and handed me one. "I thought we agreed I'd check for information on Delilah's husband, and you'd stand down."

I twisted the bottle top but didn't remove it. Playing with the piece of plastic gave my hands something to do. "No. You said you would look into it. I never said I'd stop investigating. I certainly never agreed to *stand down*."

"You're actively investigating Mags and Celia's business?"

He stopped right before taking a drink. His hand and the bottle hung there. "We didn't discuss that."

"It was more coincidental than active. I was in the kitchen and . . . well, you get it."

"Okay, look." He sighed. "It turns out the heart attack wasn't a huge surprise. This guy, Delilah's husband, had a heart condition. High blood pressure and tachycardia."

Sounded familiar but I hated chemistry and biology as much as law, so my knowledge on health stuff was limited to what I knew about Gram's previous issue. "Which is?"

"A fast heartbeat. It's not fatal but it has to be handled or it could lead to huge problems. His medication wasn't working. He had a doctor's appointment scheduled for early the next week."

Now who was investigating? Not bad for a lawyer. "How do you know all of this?"

"I asked around." He eyes narrowed as he watched me, suggesting he wasn't impressed with my nonreaction. "What? I told you I would."

"I left you fourteen hours ago." When did he have time to look into anything?

"Does that mean something?"

"My point is we talked about the star issue last night. It's Saturday morning. You were obviously exercising, not slithering around searching for clues."

He stood in front of the counter, facing me. "I went for a run."

"Why?" A legitimate question.

We stood a few feet apart. Not too close but not at a safe, non-gawking distance either. He didn't smell as good as he usually did, but I wasn't complaining.

"Why do I run? Is that what you're asking?"

This conversation seemed to be stuck. I blamed his near-nakedness and my wandering thoughts about his near-nakedness. It wouldn't be hard to strip off that tee and . . . damn. I had to leave this town and fast.

"I can't understand why anyone would willingly run. If you're being chased by a bear or a crazed killer, sure. Otherwise, I'm stumped."

He relaxed against the counter. "I enjoy running."

Oh, come on. "No, you don't. No one does."

"I think I'd know if I didn't."

Apparently not. "Running is like kale and quinoa. You've all convinced yourselves you like these things because someone told you that you should, but there's no way any sane person would partake in any of those choices absent undue pressure or the threat of bodily harm."

I'd thought about running a lot over the years and felt comfortable with my assessment. No one could convince me otherwise. I ran exactly one time in my life outside of a high school gym class. Peer pressure motivated me. I worked at that awful bank and wanted to fit in.

The couch-to-5K challenge. The way my calves seized. The uncontrollable wheezing. That stabbing pain in my right side. Basically, I felt like I was going to die after running three blocks. That was the beginning and the end of my running career.

Another reason to hate that job.

"I run to clear my head," he said.

Looked like he had all kinds of reasons for the self-torture. "Why is your head so cloudy?"

He snorted. "I wonder."

"Meaning?"

"I'm not going to ask how or why you went back to the ledger but—"

"Celia left her laptop open." I screwed and unscrewed the top of my water bottle. Did it again and then one more time. "The computer was mostly open. I needed more evidence to convince you, so I had no choice."

He reached over and put his hand over mine. The move made my heart rate spike. I didn't have tachycardia, so I blamed the unexpected touch of his fingers.

The whole thing lasted a second. Then he held my water bottle and put it on the counter next to him. Now I had no idea what to do with my hands.

A buzzer stopped me. His version of a doorbell. "Are you expecting someone?"

He gestured down the front of him. "Would I be dressed like this if I thought people were coming over?"

Yeah, I wasn't touching that.

He pushed off from the counter and walked back into the entry hall. Harlan's voice boomed through the condo a second later. The deep sound bounced off the high walls and those big windows. I couldn't make out the words, but that wasn't a problem because he stopped talking as soon as he stepped into the kitchen area and looked at me.

"Kasey."

No matter what emotion his plastered-on smile was supposed to convey, he didn't sound happy to see me. That made me want to pummel him with niceness. Maybe add a little *bless your heart* into the conversation.

"It's good to see you again." It really wasn't but I said it to be nice.

His gaze moved over me in a *you shouldn't be here* kind of way. "I didn't know you were visiting."

"What's up, Dad?"

"I called and texted this morning. You didn't respond. We were supposed to meet up and . . ." Harlan's gaze switched to me for a second before going back to Jackson. "Discuss some outstanding business issues."

"We never set a time. Could we meet later?" Jackson asked.

Harlan's gaze traveled around the open room. Zipped to the couch then to the stairs. "Are you two going to be long?"

We were now. He would need a crowbar to get me out of this condo. "Possibly."

Jackson smiled at my response. "I can be at the tennis club at noon. We can talk over lunch."

Harlan still lived in the big house where Jackson grew up. That sounded like a better place to meet, but what did I know about dealing with a father?

"Fine."

Harlan didn't sound fine. He sounded pissed. He was accustomed to people jumping at his command. Jackson didn't look ready to move one inch in his father's direction.

Harlan shot me one last glance. Heated behind the fake smile with a hint of *you're in the way here*. Then he turned and left. Didn't bother to say goodbye.

The tension wrapping around the room eased once he walked out the door. Something about his presence made my confidence plummet. I second-guessed every word I said. I didn't want to give him that much power over me. That meant not letting Harlan see me back down. No overt cowering here.

"I bet he's not used to you scheduling an appointment to eat with him."

Jackson shook his head. "That's not what I did."

I borrowed one of Gram's snorts. "Okay."

"I need to shower and go deal with Dad." Jackson looked at his watch. Pressed a few buttons. "I have plans tonight but I can come to the house tomorrow."

My mind screamed with the need to ask if he had a date and with whom. Questions that weren't my business. The answers that could lead me to a dark and grumpy place.

No, I did not care. He could do whatever he wanted with whomever he wanted. If I repeated that ridiculous thought a few more times I might actually believe it, but probably not. When it came to Jackson my usual ability to stay emotionally detached faltered.

"I'll text you later and we can figure out a good time," he said.

Dismissive. That's how he sounded. The last time a guy talked to me like that, made those assurances, he ended up ghosting me. I couldn't remember that man's name or anything about him. I wish I could feel the same way about Jackson because this crush was beating stronger than ever.

If I didn't leave town soon I could be in trouble.

CHAPTER FIFTEEN

Jackson got to Gram's house the next day in time for breakfast. Smart man. A minute after he walked through the door Gram had a plate in front of him, coffee brewing, and muffins warming in the toaster oven.

Impressive service. Maybe Gram and Celia did like him better.

I eyed him from the opposite side of the kitchen table. Not my usual breakfast seat, but I wanted to be close to him to look for clues about his adventures last night. Sure, he was a grown man. His private life wasn't my business. *Blah, blah, blah.*

Before I could poke around with carefully crafted neutral-sounding questions, Celia walked in. She smiled at Gram then sat down next to Jackson.

She touched his arm. "I'm sorry about yesterday. I thought he was going to ease off the hard sell."

I'd missed something. "What happened yesterday?"

Jackson shrugged. "Dad's not great at being told no."

Still had no clue what the subject matter of this conversation was except that it had something to do with Harlan. "What are we talking about?"

Jackson and Celia looked at me but neither said anything.

I skipped any attempt to be stealthy. "You can hear me speaking, right?"

"Sorry, hon. It's just that Harlan can be difficult to deal with when he gets an idea and won't let it go." Celia dropped that like it was big news. "Everything is fine."

Jackson didn't chime in. I took that to mean I'd guessed correctly. Things weren't all that fine. It sounded like Harlan's pissy mood had continued during his lunch with Jackson yesterday. Not a surprise. Harlan only knew one speed and one way to operate—to verbally overrun anyone standing in front of him. He talked and lobbied until he convinced someone of something, no matter the topic. But the clipped conversation at the table now suggested yesterday wasn't about the usual *Harlan is annoying* stuff.

The idea of Harlan running around to Jackson and Celia, pushing for whatever he was pushing for, had me worried that on top of the business deal Gram and Celia didn't know about because I hadn't filled them in yet and the poisoning issue I was investigating without their knowledge, something else might be wrong. That called for multitasking. Not my strongest skill.

After they dropped the cryptic Harlan remark the rest of the breakfast ran smoothly. Gram's spread included homemade lemon curd, jam, and this fancy butter she got at the specialty store. Just enough calories to make me forget about being left out.

Retelling of neighborhood gossip turned to Delilah Rhine and her dead husband. I was about to chime in when Gram pivoted to a story about delivering a cake to a baby shower where the mom and mom-in-law tried to see who could be more passive-aggressive. The event ended with one of them storming off and taking her famous potato salad with her.

I loved having this back channel to behind-the-scenes behavior. The people best able to hold it together in public tended to flail around in private. Fake decency ran a close second to fake competency in some social circles.

With the eating done and the dishes cleaned, Jackson gestured for me to follow him outside. He held his third coffee of the morning in a death grip. Whatever he did last night made him tired today and wasn't that just spectacular.

We walked to the end of the patio and kept going. A path wound its way past newly planted rosebushes. "These are a nice addition to the garden."

"We put them in last week," he said.

"*We* as in you?" On top of everything else he was a gardener. Not fair. One person should not be blessed with so many skills.

"I can do more than review business contracts."

"I sure hope so."

We took a few more steps and passed the mini greenhouse Gram used for storage. Walked past the shed that housed landscaping supplies. Gram had it painted a shade of green that made it fade into the yard.

We ended our travels at a bench. This one sat under an arbor covered in early honeysuckle blooms. This type didn't have a scent like other honeysuckle, but the vibrant red tubular flowers would soon light up the backyard in the way Gram loved.

Jackson killed my good mood almost immediately. "Okay, tell me more about the missing stars. The locked cabinet sounds unrelated, so let's skip that for now."

I didn't agree about the cabinet and we'd get to all that soon enough. I had a bigger target right now. "First, tell me what happened with your dad yesterday that has you and Celia acting like you're at a funeral."

"Are we going to keep doing this back-and-forth without

either of us answering a question?" Jackson's expression suggested he'd be happy to do just that. "I can go round and round until you tell me why you're really in town and what's happening at work. Then we can move on to other topics."

Huh. That didn't go the way I intended.

"It seems we've reached a communication impasse." We always sucked at communication. Everything he said sounded like a judgment. I fought back with a mix of sarcasm and defensiveness. The immature byplay hadn't gotten better with age.

He smiled for the first time this morning. "You really think you can beat me at this game?"

"You underestimate my ability to deflect and ignore." Then the rest slipped out. I didn't mean to say it, but yeah. "Maybe you'd be in a better mood if you'd had a better date last night."

My comment hung out there.

He started laughing. Not a little guffaw or a giggle. A full-throated, lead-with-his-chest laugh.

So annoying.

Enough of this. "I'm going to get another muffin."

"Wait a second." He put his hand on my arm and stopped me from getting up. "Don't run away."

"I never run."

"You've made that clear." He looked at his hand then his fingers slid off my arm. "Why do you care if I date?"

I did care. So much, and being in the same city only intensified my caring. "Don't be ridiculous."

My phone buzzed. Because I didn't want to look at Jackson's smug face, I checked it. Bad idea. The name flashing on the screen made what was left of my muffin-induced good mood shrivel.

Jackson took a peek. "Who's Micah?"

I answered Jackson without thinking. "My boss."

"I thought his name was Michael."

"It's a long story." *Hold up.* "How do you know his name?"

Jackson leaned back, crossing one leg over the other at his ankles. He looked relaxed. Unfazed. Very cute in his jeans and polo shirt.

"I told you I checked out your company."

I ignored that before but not now. Time to circle back to that topic. "Why?"

"Honestly?" He glanced away for a second then looked at me again. "Because I worry about you."

"You worry." I turned the words over in my head. He sounded like my keeper, or worse, a brother. That was not how I thought of him at all.

He exhaled nice and loud, as if to say he was taking back control of the conversation. "We have three topics up in the air and seem to be spinning in circles. We need to handle one at a time. You answer then I'll answer then we'll see where we are. Very easy."

That sounded reasonable but we could blow this without much effort. Simple things tended to go sideways when we talked.

My cell buzzed again. I meant to give it a quick look then tuck it back under my leg and ignore it while I verbally dug around in Jackson's private life. The text message stopped me.

"Oh, shit." *Shit. Shit. Shit.*

He frowned. "Not the response I expected."

Panic raced through me. I stood up then sat back down.

Blinked a few times hoping the message would disappear. I swear the font got bigger.

"Hey, are you okay?" Jackson's hand went around my shoulder and his voice turned soft. "Did something bad happen?"

"Terrible. The worst, actually."

"What is it?"

I could barely say the words. "My boss is doing something that will make my life impossible."

Coming to town. He wanted to meet Gram and Celia.

I couldn't think of a worse idea.

CHAPTER SIXTEEN

Jackson left fifteen minutes later. We didn't resolve anything or tackle the open questions we had for each other. Hearing from Micah flipped everything upside down. I didn't have time to sit around and discuss Jackson's dating life or even poison. Not when my worlds were about to collide. That meant rushing Jackson out of the house and promising we'd talk as soon as I *handled this one thing*.

Now I had to figure out how to handle that thing. That meant I needed a strategy. That would require more muffins.

I slipped back into the house and headed for the airtight container holding the sugary goodness. I removed one and eyed the coffeemaker. A second cup couldn't hurt.

"You're not ready."

Gram. She walked into the room wearing her Sunday finest. A sky-blue dress and matching sky-blue jacket. I couldn't see her shoes or purse from this angle, but I would bet the house they shared the same color palette. The woman never actually ventured into a clothing store, so I had no idea how she found these ensembles. They just appeared and she stepped out looking put together and ready to socialize every single time.

She glanced at the clock on the stove. "The service starts at eleven."

Let the arguing begin.

She considered Sunday church service sacred. She had to be sick and near death to miss the sermon. She loved the music and the community. The rituals and the promises. She attended because she'd been raised to go but also because she wanted to be there.

I wasn't going and she knew it.

Devout described her, not me. I believed. Gram's guidance and years of church classes guaranteed that, but the institution of the church didn't bring me any comfort. Not like it did for her. All too often I ran up against the way people acted at Sunday service versus who they were in the real world. The hypocrisy kept me at home.

"Kasey?" Gram set her—yep, sky-blue—purse on the kitchen counter as she glanced at my uneaten muffin. "Did you plan to drive separately?"

"Gram."

She snorted. "It's one day a week, Kasey. You can make the time."

Here. We. Go.

I loved this woman with every breath in my body. I would fight for her. I'd rescue her, even if that meant wading into the bizarre world of men poisoning. I mean, she'd have a good excuse, right? A righteous, churchgoing woman wouldn't poison men just for fun.

Bottom line: I owed her my life. She saved me when things were the bleakest. She reached out from her hurricane of grief and made me feel loved and wanted. But she couldn't sell me on this topic. She'd tried, and usually I caved to her stronger will, but today I would hold firm on this.

Her mouth stretched into a thin line. "We've discussed this

many times. Edmund Dennison is not indicative of people of faith."

The man who was more sperm donor to me than father. She never referred to him as my father. She spelled out his full name most times she was forced to use it, and she made sure that didn't happen very often. I got it. I wanted to separate from every part of him, too. His last name, which I dropped in favor of Gram's years ago. My eyes and chin that looked like his. His bloodline. His supposed love for the church.

The man who burned the house down with my mom's lifeless body inside had sung in the church choir, served on church committees, and volunteered for church activities.

He destroyed everything he touched. Being in prison for the last twenty years removed him from society but his legacy continued to screw up my life in big and small ways.

I swallowed a sigh. "You know how I feel about this subject."

"Raising you and going to church were the two things that saved me after Nora died."

My mom. Gram's only child. My heart ached for Gram. I mourned the memories I never had a chance to create with Mom. Gram mourned their stolen future as the memories of what little time they did have together slowly faded.

"I'm happy the church brings you peace or solace or whatever you get out of it."

"But you're still reluctant to come with me." Gram snorted a second time, which was a good sign because it meant she was ticked off, not sad. "I'd hoped you'd outgrow this."

Not the first time I'd heard that. The guilt nearly dropped me to my knees whenever she said it. Time made the comment easier to take but disappointing her, doing or saying anything that wiped the smile from her face, was my nightmare.

"You're an adult." She snatched her purse off the counter. "You make your own decisions."

She didn't really mean that. It was the line she used when I did something she didn't like. It basically meant I was screwing up and she'd wait to fix whatever mess I made.

"This isn't about me, you know," she said.

Oh, Gram. "Maybe a little?"

She made a noise that sounded like *pfft*. That signaled an end to the argument. Some of the tension left her shoulders. She still held her body stiff but the strain around her eyes eased. Then she snorted. Number three. Three in a matter of five minutes, which might actually be a record.

"I just want you to think about one thing." She stared at me until I nodded. "That man took so much from you. Don't let him steal your faith as well."

She kissed me on the cheek then called out for Celia. A few minutes later she was in the car, driving to the place that meant so much to her.

"I wondered if you'd cave."

I squealed at the sound of Jackson's voice. "What the hell?"

My stomach lodged in my throat. At least it felt that way. It took a second for my wild heartbeat to stop thumping in my ears.

Jackson stood in the kitchen doorway. He had the grace to look sorry. "Didn't mean to scare you."

"I thought you left."

"I forgot to drop some paperwork off for Celia."

Interesting . . . or maybe not. Could just be boring legal stuff. "What kind of paperwork?"

"She can tell you if she wants you to know." He shrugged. "Honestly, I was sneaking back in here to grab a muffin."

"No church for you?" Funny how only I got interrogated for not going.

"I usually work on Sunday."

Much more of that work schedule and he'd lose all of his personality. "That's healthy."

"I'm headed to the office now."

He hadn't changed out of his jeans. I liked the look but doubted his partners did. "Kind of business casual today, aren't you?"

"I'll be the only one there." He held up a muffin. "This will help me concentrate."

"Carbs have the opposite effect on me."

"Running would help you with that."

"Again, am I being hunted in this scenario?" He didn't respond because we both knew the answer. "Exactly. Not going to happen."

"There are still a lot of questions between us. Want to deal with them now?"

Wasn't he chatty all of a sudden? Curiosity poked at me, but I had other activities in mind for the next few hours. "No, I'm good. Go put in ten or twelve hours of Sunday work time and we'll handle the questions later."

He didn't leave. He stood there staring at me. "I know you'll be alone in the house but don't snoop through laptops and business paperwork while they're gone."

He knew. Of course he knew. "I can't promise you I won't see something while I'm in the house."

The service lasted an hour. Including drive time and a buffer for gossip, that gave me about ninety minutes of uninterrupted time to look around for the previously locked cabinet and whatever Gram and Celia hid inside.

He shook his head. He turned away but then turned back to face me again. "One thing."

Comments prefaced with that never led anywhere good. "Okay."

"I didn't have a date last night. I dropped off a friend at the airport. A guy I work with who was going out of town on business. He was giving me the status of a case."

"Oh . . ."

"Thought you might want to know that." He headed for the door but delivered one more gem on the way out. "Try not to sell the place or break anything while everyone is gone."

I'd be too busy trying to figure out why he told me what he did last night . . . and why the whoosh of relief almost knocked me over.

CHAPTER SEVENTEEN

Yes, I'd vowed that the previous peek at Celia's computer would be the last time I crossed a line into Gram and Celia's personal space. I meant it back then but my thoughts kept spiraling. This invisible edge loomed in front of them. I needed to pull them back before they fell in and I lost them, too.

I didn't care about how much they made or who they sold to, their expenses or their bank balances. I cared about them hoarding and possibly using a toxic substance that could kill people . . . and be traced back to them. I wasn't sure what I was going to do if I stumbled over evidence, but I'd deal with that mess after I made this new mess.

To start? Looking for the bottles Celia claimed she originally locked up in the pantry because they'd expired. I should be able to find them or a trace of them . . . maybe? Hunting down clues got a bit sticky when you didn't know what to dig around for or where you should be looking.

I had time to play James Bond before Gram and Celia returned from church but the fear of being caught nagged at me. If Gram walked in and saw me pawing through her property . . . *oh, boy.*

The most logical place to look, and one with less risk of getting caught, was the baking annex. The building wasn't an obvious hot spot for top-secret information because Celia and Gram weren't the only ones who worked in here. A student from the culinary school in Charlotte, about an hour away, came in every week to help out and get experience. Two women from town worked part-time, mostly when the operation got slammed with orders, like around the holidays.

The shop also had a rotating group of people who helped with the packaging, distribution, and marketing. They shared the glass-walled office at the end of the building. Gram once told me she preferred baking to paperwork. Celia used to handle the boring administrative stuff, but since the business had taken off she worked mostly with Gram on the floor.

All of those bodies, everyone in and out, required the annex to be clean and organized at all times. Well, semiorganized. The desk in the office looked like the employees shuffled everything together, threw it in the air, then walked out the door. I gathered the slips of paper and tried to decipher the comments jotted down on sticky notes. Someone had plastered the yellow squares on and around the computer monitor.

This looked to be their system for double-checking that they'd handled everything. A sort of master checklist that included future projects with customers and information like birthdays and anniversaries. Marketing. Customer reminders. It was all mixed together with feedback and bakery notes, which made me question how usable this business filing system was.

I had a bachelor's degree in English with a concentration in creative writing. The combination sounded very Jane Austen, but it didn't translate into a steady income. It hadn't for me yet, but I kept hoping. My skill set did not include business, finance, or accounting. Still, even I could tell this system needed work.

Determination kicked in. Poisoning intel could wait a few minutes while I came up with a streamlined and more intuitive way to handle this information. That caused one problem. Gram and Celia would know I was in this room when I presented them with my idea, but I could cover that by saying I went looking for leftover icing in the annex fridge. They'd buy that because I'd done it before.

In the end, I hoped to help, to make their lives a bit easier. If they didn't want that, at least I tried.

Gram's secondary pair of plaid slippers sat in a basket on the floor. Seeing the frayed and faded hot pink and white pattern made me smile. So subtle.

I took the scattered notes and reminder stickies and compiled everything then moved to the whiteboard. It started out clean, without a stray mark on it. After reading and shuffling and thinking, I had sketched out two separate but related systems—one aimed at future marketing and maintaining customer goodwill.

The other combined all the already available information into one easy-to-find place. Different employees, as they came in and out, would be able to see what was done and what needed attention without trouble.

After some amount of time, not sure how much, my neck stiffened. My lower back ached. I glanced at the clock. No, that couldn't be right. I never got lost in work, but I'd been at this for almost two hours.

How was that possible?

A familiar scent hit me. Gram's perfume. I spun around. Gram and Celia stood there in their fancy dresses, gawking at me through the glass wall. I could tell from their expressions that . . . nope. I had no idea what they were thinking.

Surrender. That was the only option here. "I can explain."

In my head they stormed into the office, yelling and demanding an explanation. In reality, they wandered in, looking dazed and confused.

Words. I needed words. After a few false starts I got there. "I moved things around. That's all."

Celia went to the whiteboard. Studied it.

"Okay, yeah. I also mapped out a system of organization for keeping track of everything without having all these slips of paper hanging around."

Celia continued to stare at my notes. Gram joined her.

Was the not talking good or bad? Unclear at the moment. "That part on the right is a general list of everything that needs to get done, short- and long-term, who is assigned to handle the task, and the status. A tickler system."

They turned to face me. In unison.

No, that wasn't scary at all.

"I know you've been operating the same way for years. I wasn't trying to interfere, just help." The words ran together as I raced to explain before they could pummel me with their special Sunday purses. "You're super successful and all, but the sticky note method made my eye twitch."

Still nothing.

Disappointment swamped the room. I waded in knee-deep without moving an inch. "I can erase the board and put everything back. I kept all the sticky notes. They are more or less on the same part of the desk."

Celia cleared her throat.

The panicked screaming in my head grew louder. "Or we can pretend this never happened and go have lunch."

Celia nodded. "This is very good."

The crashing sound vibrating through me stopped. "It is?"

She scanned the whiteboard. "This is a complete system with safeguards."

Approval? I didn't expect that. I actually didn't expect to get lost on an organization tangent or be found in their workspace. The goal had been to snoop and run, and I blew that.

"Implementing this would cut down on the frenetic search for information that Mags and I do whenever the assistants aren't here to answer questions."

No yelling . . . so far.

I wasn't sure what to say, so I stayed quiet. The urge to fill the void poked at me. Clamping my mouth shut and repeating *shut up* a thousand times in my mind helped. I needed Gram to talk. Any signal would do. Her unreadable expression slowly chipped away at my resolve.

"This is unexpected," Gram said.

Finally. But the comment didn't say all that much. Any minute she'd commit to an emotion and spill it.

"I'm intrigued by the part where we send out special-occasion reminders and get people to order when they might otherwise have forgotten the occasion or holiday or done something else to celebrate." Gram nodded. "How did you come up with this?"

No anger in her tone. Maybe a bit of surprise. She wasn't alone in that. I was dumfounded. "We use something like this at work. This is a modified version. Honestly, I tried to think of the smoothest way to put all of this together without need-ing a pile of sticky notes."

"Maybe your job isn't so terrible after all," Celia said.

No. It was. It totally sucked. "The computer ledger you have for deliveries is great but it's not thorough enough to cover the work not yet completed and keep track of bids and events you're trying to book."

I'd done more thinking in the last two hours than I had in months at my new job. Then I remembered. The job. Micah coming to town. I needed to tell them. Yeah, I should tell them.

Gram's eyes narrowed. "How do you know about the ledger?"

Oh, shit. What had I said?

"What?" That was a stall. My brain needed a second to re-wind and figure out how I messed up so I could fix it.

Gram returned to her previous staring. "As you pointed out, the ledger is on the computer. It's not on display in here. So how do you know about it?"

All good points. Wish I had a good response.

"I figured you had some sort of computer program to track things. You know, for taxes and stuff." Words flowed out of me. Not sure if they were the right words. They sounded more like a jumble of random thoughts.

"Basically, yes. The business accountant correlates all the information for our general ledger. The computer spreadsheet Mags is referring to mostly deals with accounts receivable. It's a way for us to keep everything straight. But, as your suggested system highlights, there might be a more efficient way to com-bine data."

A huge thank-you to Celia for the semi-assist. "Okay. Sure. A ledger is a different thing."

I acted like I knew the definition of "ledger" and what one was used for. I would have guessed a ledger and a spreadsheet were the same thing. Now I had no idea what I was talking about except that my proposed system didn't have anything to do with my previous snooping, poison, or dead husbands.

"I didn't actually redo anything. Moved some notes, but that's not a big deal." I hoped that was true.

Gram and Celia looked at each other. They hadn't said much, though Celia sounded more open to the idea of me digging around in their business paperwork than Gram did.

"I'm impressed." Celia smiled. "I like it."

Gram walked over and kissed my cheek. "Well done."

She put a hand on the side of my head in the same loving gesture she'd done since I was a kid. I leaned into her touch because nothing matched love from Gram. I didn't know what had happened at church to cause this change in attitude, but I liked it. I certainly wasn't going to question it.

"I told you I could be helpful." I felt the need to point that out.

Celia laughed. "We should have had more faith in you."

Contentment flooded through me. Then it shut off. This was great but it would all come crashing down when Micah got to town.

My time was almost up.

CHAPTER EIGHTEEN

Meet me at the hotel.

Five words you never want to hear from your boss. Apparently when Micah said he and Brock were coming to town he meant *on the first plane with available seats.* They provided two days of lead time before their arrival, which was far too fast. They took an early morning flight and cut my prep time even more.

There would be no reprieve. No way to hold them off. No time to plan or fix my mess.

I'd barely finished a muffin this morning when Micah texted over the details of where he and Brock were staying. The whole scene would have been bad enough without Brock. His presence guaranteed a bloodbath.

They'd checked into the historic Graylyn Estate, minutes from downtown. No bargain hotel for these two. They shot right for the top and snagged two suites because of course they did.

The estate included numerous buildings and acres of beautiful grounds with a stone mansion at the center. Talk about a flawless pedigree. The manor house had been built and owned by a tobacco millionaire. Though, to be fair, those words described many places in Winston-Salem.

I'd been there on a few occasions to help Gram and Celia

with deliveries and itched to get upstairs and look around. Now that I might have my chance I didn't want to go anywhere near the place.

When Micah texted a second time, I raced to get to him. He expected that reaction to his presence. He opened his mouth and people scurried about to make him happy. Me included.

I met them at a table under an umbrella on an outside patio. They both drank wine, the perfect beverage for eleven in the morning. Micah looked at home here, surrounded by waitstaff and expensive furnishings.

We quickly moved through the welcome chat. Micah made sure to mention that he was staying in the same suite Oprah had used on visits to Maya Angelou when she taught at nearby Wake Forest University. Micah's name-dropping hit expert levels with that one. I didn't have much to offer after that revelation, so I waited to see what verbal grenade Brock would launch in my direction.

He didn't wait more than three minutes to throw it. "You've failed to keep us informed of your activities and progress."

Micah signaled the waiter for more wine before focusing on Brock. "Progress?"

I hadn't missed Micah's question thing at all.

Brock continued. "I'm not sure where we are. She hasn't returned my calls."

"I told her she had two weeks to get the company under contract, so she's still within the time frame." Micah switched conversation targets without taking a breath. "Where are we, Kasey?"

Absolutely nowhere. "It's taking some time, as you would

expect. These women are savvy and don't trust everyone who promises to make them rich."

Brock's satisfied grin telegraphed incoming trouble. "When I didn't hear from you, I did a little investigating about the company and the women who own it. You forgot to tell us you were related to these ladies. That's pertinent information we should have been privy to up front."

Micah waited for the wine refill before chiming in. "Was that an oversight?"

I really didn't have an answer to any of these questions. I bought myself a few seconds by drinking water, but the glass was almost empty.

"Business is business." Nothing about the sentence made sense in the context of the conversation. Hell, it wasn't even a sentence. I didn't have anything more productive to say but the phrase made Brock's jaw clench, so mission accomplished.

Micah nodded. "True. To be successful you need to keep your heart out of these decisions."

Is that what I said?

Brock looked like he wanted to roll his eyes at Micah's nonsense. "I've known about your conflict for days. You should have disclosed the information when you made your pitch. You know that. It's a pretty basic business principle."

"Conflicts?"

If Micah kept asking insipid questions this talk would either take all day or he'd burn himself out and I could escape. Not sure which way we were leaning, but I hoped the latter.

"Her grandmother. Magnolia Nottingham." Brock gestured in my direction as if we didn't all know who he was talking about. "I have to wonder if you treated us to an actual business pitch or if you launched a desperate Hail Mary."

That Yale education of his had paid off. He was right on target here.

"Well, actually"—Micah enjoyed a good *well, actually* and fit one in here—"I've thought about this since you filled me in, Brock. The familial relationship should make it more likely for the women to agree to sign on and eventually sell. Doing so would guarantee the owner's granddaughter's happiness and financial future. A clear win."

Wrong. Nothing about this would sit well with Gram. Even ignoring the business deal, she would hate Brock and find Micah ridiculous. She might even tell him that. Would probably use that word because "ridiculous" was one of her favorites.

"But we don't have an agreement, tentative or otherwise. We don't even have a statement of interest." Brock's fingers wrapped around the stem of his wineglass. Much tighter and the crystal would shatter. "That's why we're here. To prevent this deal from exploding."

It's cute he thought there was a deal to blow up.

"The ladies have been unavailable due to their workload." The only truth in that sentence was the part about Gram and Celia having a workload. Everything else was meant to shore up my stall. I needed these two satisfied enough to leave. Up and gone.

No way could they talk to Gram before I could get a handle on the poison issue. If she heard the pitch and didn't agree, and I hoped she didn't, it was time for a new job. Those law school loans weren't going to pay themselves.

"We'll need to see the business assets. Equipment. Buildings. We'll also need to review the financials. Sales records. Loan documents, if any. Profit and loss statements, corporate documents, and those are just to start." Micah nodded, clearly satisfied with his assessment.

No way was any of that going to happen. Ever. My only option might be to come up with another pitch, this time with a business I had no relationship to and turn Micah's attention there.

Sure, no problem.

"I'd like to tour the bakery tomorrow," Brock said.

This just got worse and worse. "Tomorrow is a problem because of a large order they have to produce and package."

"A large order?" Micah looked entirely too happy. "Then we could watch them work."

Yeah, no. "I can arrange for another day, but it might be more efficient if you went back to DC then returned once everything is set up."

Even I was impressed with that suggestion. I worked in a variation of one of Micah's buzzwords—"efficiency."

"I'm not leaving town." Brock's smug expression suggested he knew he had the upper hand.

Micah looked at his watch. "You two work this out. I have a call on the Simpson project."

I had no idea what that was, but I secretly thanked this Simpson person or business for the distraction. "I don't want to keep either of you. I can text with more information once I have it."

Micah nodded, clearly no longer paying attention to anything except the message on his watch. He got up and left without saying anything else.

Unfortunately, Brock stayed.

"I know this is a ruse," he said.

Yes. Totally. "Of course not."

"Then I'll expect a written status report tomorrow. The two of us will go over it together, before approaching Micah. If you're lying, and I think you are, there will be consequences." He stood up. "Enjoy your day. You'll be busy."

He had no idea.

CHAPTER NINETEEN

I spent the rest of the afternoon driving around, wondering how I was going to get out of this NOI-related mess. A side trip to the Krispy Kreme with the drive-through helped. Hot doughnuts served through your car window and meant to be eaten immediately. Pure magic and one of the best things about this town. The weather, Gram, and these doughnuts formed the perfect Winston-Salem trifecta.

Celia was the only one in the kitchen when I walked in. The bulk of the baking appeared to be done. I picked that up from the flour all over the floor and the stacked, mostly empty mixing bowls with just enough homemade whipped cream left inside the top one for a taste. They cleaned as they baked but food carnage happened. Very tasty food carnage.

Celia held out the spoon covered with exactly one lick left on it. "For you."

I sat down at the breakfast bar and dug in. "Was there a flour war while I was gone?"

"I dropped the bag." Celia didn't take a break from wiping down the counters and cabinet fronts. "Where have you been all day? You tend to hide from people you went to high school with, so I doubt you were out with old friends."

"I'm happy to say I continued my avoid-the-former-mean-girls streak." I refused to be lured in by social media's promise of "finding old friends" online because no, thank you. If these people really were my friends I'd still be in touch with them.

"I studied your organization suggestion in more depth over lunch." Celia nodded, clearly satisfied with her cleanup job. "You've really been hiding your business skills."

More like I tripped over a stray skill by accident. "We can set it up if you want. Maybe work out the bugs."

"Will you be in town long enough for that?"

By tomorrow at this time I'd likely be fired, so yeah. "I can stay at least another week."

"You should have made her do the cleanup. Builds character." Gram made that announcement as she slipped in the back door, carrying a tray of muffins.

She put them on the counter in front of me. The move destroyed what little concentration I had left. I knew a banana chocolate chip muffin when I saw one.

I reached for the plump one on the right side as Gram started talking. "Were you at Graylyn today?"

I tried not to smash the muffin into crumbs, but I couldn't make my fingers unclench. I also forgot how to breathe. "Why, were you?"

Gram snorted. "No. I worked all day."

What kind of trick was this? Instead of rushing in and bumbling around—my automatic response—I waded in nice and slow. "I'm not sure—"

"Charlotte was there and saw you."

I had no idea who Charlotte was. Gram frequently threw out names, expecting I could follow along with some story about some person she talked about one time ten years ago. *Elma moved into the condo her son bought her. Shyla finished chemo. Larette ran over her husband with a car.* Those were just examples from last week. Okay, maybe not the Larette one but that was the kind of hometown news I wanted to hear. More of that.

I'd gotten the lowdown on Paula, Annabelle, Maxine, and Cheryl before I arrived in town. Gram had a never-ending list of people, some friends and some not, who had things or did things she thought I should know about *because you were in choir with her goddaughter in sixth grade* or some other such thing.

Who were these people?

Whatever was happening, Gram had Celia's attention now. "I thought Charlotte went to Maine."

Maine sounded like a nice diversion from whatever Charlotte usually did. I'd love to be there right now.

"No. It's too early. She goes in summer, but that might be off," Gram said.

Gram and Celia both made sad humming sounds.

Poor Charlotte.

"I think she's afraid to leave that husband of hers alone." Gram delivered another snort. "You know what happened last time."

They did. Charlotte did. I didn't but I wanted to. For now, I was content to sit there with my muffin crumbs and listen to the details.

"That man." Celia shook her head but didn't add anything else. Her tone made her feelings clear on Charlotte's husband. Not a fan.

Without warning, Gram and Celia both turned to me.

My stomach did an Olympic tumble. "If you're asking me,

I think Charlotte can do better. I don't even know her, and I think she could do better."

Gram frowned. "She's the one who helped me plant tulips last year."

That information did not help my memory one bit. Gram looked so cute, standing there holding an oven mitt, that I pretended. "Oh, right."

"Were you really at Graylyn?" Celia asked.

I'd hoped we'd moved on and found another topic but apparently not. They would not let this go. If Celia decided to back Gram up on the interrogation I would fold before I could shove this destroyed muffin, liner included, in my mouth.

It was too risky to deny being at Graylyn. For all I knew this Charlotte person took a photo of me sitting there, trying to ignore Micah. But I had to hit the conversation sweet spot because an avalanche of details only invited more questions.

"Are your movements a secret?" Celia froze. "Oh . . . I didn't . . . Was it a date?"

That came out of nowhere. "Who would I be dating here?"

Gram and Celia glanced at each other but didn't make a noise.

"Hey. That's enough of those looks and all the silent communication." I pointed at both of them. "You've been doing that secret mind meld thing for years and I still can't decipher it."

"I don't know what you're talking about." Gram's smile suggested she did.

Celia unwrapped another fully intact muffin and put it on a plate in front of me. "If not a date then why were you there?"

Plying me with food. Smart. But did they know? It felt like they knew, but how could they?

Now would be the perfect time to come clean. Admit that I'd messed up at work and dragged them along with me. Be mature. Apologize and stem the bleeding. Get this handled and done in an adult way then start looking for a new job.

I didn't do any of that.

"It'd been a while since I'd been at Graylyn. I decided to have coffee and take a walk on the grounds."

Gram frowned. The *take a walk* part might have tipped her off to the lie. "You got coffee at noon by yourself?"

I could handle this. Coffee and food sat solidly in my conversation wheelhouse. But Gram referenced the time I left Graylyn. Very specific. She could know other stuff. She was a sneaky one.

Step carefully. "I picked up the habit at work. I now drink coffee all day."

"Honey, no." Celia winced. "That's not good."

"Sweet tea would be a better choice," Gram insisted.

Not the way she made it. "I wonder if there's science to support that claim."

Gram moved on from her usual snort. This time she went with her famous *pfft* sound.

"We have a big day tomorrow. We have to prepare for a charity brunch." Celia sighed. "It needs to be perfect because a lot of potential customers will be there."

They bought the coffee thing. At least they pretended to. "We could get takeout tonight so no one, and by that I mean you two, have to worry about cooking dinner."

"Don't be ridiculous." Gram believed food should come from her stove, not a bag.

Her comment touched off a whole *nothing compares to homemade cooking* discussion. With that, the energy surging through me eased. Balance restored. I could handle food prep chatter.

The main problem was that this reprieve wouldn't last forever. Brock wanted a showdown. I feared he was going to get it.

CHAPTER TWENTY

The summons arrived before nine the next morning in the form of a text. Brock picked the restaurant and set a time to meet, leaving no room for argument. Unfortunately, he had good taste or a phone app that told him about local eating spots because he chose one in Reynolda Village, Gram's social hunting grounds. That guaranteed I'd see someone I knew, or Gram and Celia knew, when Brock lost it and fired me.

The reality of impending embarrassment didn't make me rush to get dressed, but I did have a clear path to sneak away from the house. Celia and Gram were in the annex, finalizing their baking for that charity event. I left a note saying I had to run some errands. They'd need to depend on Charlotte, or some other person Gram knew, to be lurking around and report back about my real activities.

Ten minutes before the set time of the grand showdown, I walked into the Village Tavern wearing the only halfway-work-like item of clothing I brought with me to North Carolina, a short navy-blue dress with three-quarter-length sleeves and pin tucks in the front. It was cute and kind of casual and the best I could do on short notice.

The luring scent of cheese and all sorts of food goodness hit me when I walked into the place. The sights and smells threw me back to all the times before I left for college when we'd eaten here. My teenage mind found it fancy and special. Gram really wasn't a go-out kind of gal except for her regular lunch with the ladies, but she knew I loved the place and made excuses to take me there.

Reynolda Village consisted of a group of buildings that used to be part of a bigger estate owned by a tobacco-rich family, though a different tobacco-rich family from the one that owned Graylyn Estate. The main house now operated as a museum. The former barn and other outbuildings had been turned into an upscale eating and shopping destination.

I was a big fan of all of it but mostly this restaurant. The white building with the green shutters. The outside tables with the big umbrellas. Those amazing homemade potato chips served warm with a ranch dipping sauce. I'd eaten about a million of them over the years.

The good memories screeched to a halt when I saw the one bad thing about the restaurant—Brock sitting in it. He'd picked the lunch rush to meet—the more people to see my downfall the better—because everything about him was annoying.

I waded through full tables filled with lively conversation to get to him. He glanced up but didn't say hello. Just nodded at the empty chair in front of him. Not the cheeriest of welcomes but then, we didn't like each other, so why pretend.

He studied me for a second. The kind of studying an old-time executioner might have done before sharpening his axe.

He jumped in without preamble. "Where's your status report? I asked for it in writing. It's due today. Right now."

Oh, right. That. It didn't exist because what the hell would I write? "I told you I'd experienced unexpected delays."

After a few beats of tense silence, Brock leaned forward with his elbows on the table. "You mean you needed time to invent a scheme that would cover your lies."

Exactly. "I don't know what you're talking about."

I'd already lost the thread of the conversation because a server went by carrying a tray. Every meal on those plates looked delicious. Interesting how Brock had both menus on his side of the table.

"Maybe you think it's okay to have your employer pay for a trip home and an unnecessary vacation, but it's not. It's unprofessional." He set his water glass to the side. "Even you should know that."

Even you? I fell back on fake outrage to avoid admitting he had a valid point. "This is an intricate deal with a lot of moving parts. My deal. There are emotions at play but there's also an opportunity for a lucrative ending that benefits all of us."

Kudos to me for using a firm voice and projecting confidence. I'd been clear, no-nonsense, as I spouted bullshit. Mostly I wanted to know if he'd ordered and if he intended to buy my lunch.

Brock shook his head. "How do you think this is going to end, Kasey?"

Excellent question. "It's possible this deal won't work. I suggested it. I didn't guarantee its success."

"You're wasting time and I'm about done."

In his defense, he wasn't wrong. He was the boss, and we all needed the firm to make money. I was the one lying and making the mess. That didn't mean I had to like the words or him.

He placed his napkin on the table as the crowd noise swelled behind him. "I'm going to use the restroom. When I get back we're going to discuss how you intend to present the truth to

Micah and what that will mean for your continued employment with NOI."

With that not-so-veiled threat, he and his expensive sneakers stomped off.

"Kasey?"

The unexpected male voice made me jerk and smack my hand into Brock's water glass. I caught it right before it tipped. "What the—"

Jackson stood, looming over the table, looking kind of pissed. "Who was that?"

"Have you always been this sneaky?" I looked around. "Where did you come from?"

"I just finished a business meeting. I was sitting a few tables away." He pointed somewhere behind me. "You walked past me when you came in. I guess you didn't see me."

Only because I'd been so focused on Brock and my dislike for Brock and how much the meeting with Brock was going to suck.

Jackson sat down in the unused chair next to me. "Answer my question."

Tension thrummed off him. His face had this clenched look to it, like he planned to bluster around and not listen to anything I had to say.

"Are you okay?" If he got this stressed at work then he needed to find a new job. When I said the law sucked, people should listen to me.

"Your friend?" he asked without context or more information.

I didn't understand the question. "Brock. He's not really a friend."

"Boyfriend, then."

Talk about a nightmare scenario. "Do you really think I'd like that guy? Blowhard jackass is not my type. Not on purpose. Sometimes I find out too late, but you get it."

Something in Jackson's expression changed. Something unreadable. "I'm trying to figure out—"

"Excuse me."

Oh, good. Brock returned.

Brock took his seat and stared at Jackson. "I'm assuming you're an old friend of Kasey's. Now is not a good time. We're in the middle of a meeting."

The mood at the table flipped from uncomfortable to hostile. I thought the energy was negative before Jackson got here. Now it felt like a toxic swirl of angry dudes and chest thumping.

Time to shut this down before the other diners noticed a problem and went running to Gram. "Jackson Quaid, this is Brock Deavers. Brock and I work together."

"I'm her boss."

Not the way I would say it, but yes.

Jackson relaxed back in his chair. "Interesting."

"We were . . ." What did I say next? I stopped talking and hoped neither of them noticed.

"Why are you in town, Brock?"

Brock's eyes narrowed at Jackson's familiarity. "Well, *Jackson*, Kasey and I are in Winston-Salem about a business venture."

Jackson's eyebrow raised. "Even more interesting."

That got my mouth moving. An offensive strike. That was the only play here. This one time I needed Jackson to play along and not make my life more difficult. "Jackson is the attorney for the, uh, enterprise."

Jackson slowly turned his head and shot me that deadly stare of his.

I rushed on, hoping Jackson had somewhere else to be and would go there now. "He's been clear it's too early for any status or commitment discussion. The ladies need more time to think about the potential and rushing them only guarantees they will decline."

Jackson blinked a few times.

Embarrassment hovered right in front of me, ready to pounce.

Then Jackson turned to Brock. "Kasey's assessment is correct. The hard sell is detrimental to your interest. That statement is not personal or targeted. My clients simply are skeptical of claims to grow their business that involve them giving away a share of their profits. They've been hugely successful without assistance or the worry about conglomerate politics."

That sounded real. Jackson had some skills.

"I understand the hesitancy. That's why I'm proposing a meeting so we can pitch our services. Spell out what we have to offer and the type of investor clients we cater to."

Jackson nodded. "Lobby them, in other words."

"Educate them," Brock said in a louder voice.

The conversation had my head swiveling back and forth as if I were watching a tennis match. They both seemed to be winning, though Jackson had inched ahead. Maybe.

"Fair enough." Jackson continued to use his serious lawyer voice. "I'll talk with them and get back to Kasey with an answer."

"That's not usually how—"

"That is the only option I can offer. You won't get a shot at my clients without me being present and, right now, I can't in good conscience recommend a business deal. Not without due diligence and more information." The words flowed. Jackson was in control and acting the part. "I'm sure you understand that while you're assessing their business for a possible future relationship, they're assessing yours."

"I can provide any information you need." Brock pulled out a business card.

Jackson waved it away. "I can go through Kasey. After all, this is her project, correct?"

Brock hesitated. He had that could-explode-at-any-minute expression on his face. The man did not like being told no. He really didn't like being told I was in charge.

That crush on Jackson? It kicked stronger than ever. I couldn't deny it this time.

After a few stressful minutes, Brock relented. The fight ran right out of him. "Of course."

Really? That worked?

"I'll be in client meetings in South Carolina for a few days." Which was code for *playing golf with my buddies*. "Then I'll be back, Kasey. I'll need to see some progress."

Then he was going to be disappointed. "Sure."

"Jackson." Brock nodded.

Jackson nodded back.

I had a first-row seat to the odd male ritual.

A punch of relief hit me as soon as Brock stomped off until I realized that meant I was stuck paying the bill for anything he'd ordered. I was about to thank Jackson for jumping in and playing along when he ruined it.

"Tell me what the hell is going on."

It looked like my procrastination days were over. Time to come clean. Maybe being in a public place would prevent this from being as terrible as I feared.

Knowing Jackson, probably not.

CHAPTER TWENTY-ONE

He seems like a big fan of yours."

That was some expert-level sarcasm by Jackson. He'd honed his satire skills since the last time I was home.

"Picked up on that, did you?" I scanned the table for the menu but didn't see it. Did Brock take both of them with him?

Jackson folded his arms in front of him, looking far too satisfied with himself for comfort. "At least we've answered one of the open questions between us."

"You've lost me." Probably because it was now clear no one intended to buy my lunch.

"You're in town for exactly the reason I predicted."

"It sounds like you want to say *gotcha* or some equally immature thing." Didn't blame him. I would have in his place.

"Care to explain what just happened?"

"That's annoying. That tone. The words you use."

Jackson exhaled loud enough for the people in the next building to hear. "Is there anything about me you do like?"

Not answering that. "Fine. Brock recently caught me off guard during a boring meeting. He demanded I make an on-the-spot pitch, clearly hoping I'd fail. I didn't want to give him the satisfaction and, honestly, I panicked and talked about Gram and Celia's business."

Jackson nodded. "What I'm hearing is you sacrificed Mags and Celia to save yourself."

Damn. My behavior sounded so much worse when Jackson described it. "I wouldn't put it like that."

"Of course not."

Much more of this and I'd forget he helped me out of a jam by backing me up. "Thank you, by the way."

Jackson shrugged. "No problem. The idea of that guy winning an argument pissed me off."

"I feel that way every day I step into the office." Now what? The steady buzz of conversation around us grew louder the longer we sat there not talking. "Don't you have to get back to work?"

"I have a few minutes. You can use that time to explain how you intend to get out of this and still keep your job."

If I knew the answer to that I would have done it already. "Well, you're the new business attorney . . ."

He smiled. "Nice try."

"Jackson."

His smile vanished. "Dad?"

Harlan pulled out the chair across from us. "How did your meeting go?"

Sure, sit down. We'd love to eat with you.

Harlan didn't wait for an answer. "I assumed you'd want me to attend but then you moved the time up without letting me know. I only found out about the change when I called your office earlier."

"I had a work conflict this afternoon. It seemed better to get the meeting done over lunch. It just ended." Jackson fiddled with the knife at his place setting.

The flash of nerves was a surprise. Jackson tended to glide through life without showing much emotion.

Harlan's attention shifted back and forth from the knife to Jackson's face. Harlan looked ready to grab the utensil and throw it across the room. "Was the short length indicative of a problem?"

Really, Harlan? Who talked like that?

Jackson shook his head. "More like my lack of interest. But you know that."

A very cryptic response. Also, a little snotty, but in this case Jackson's sharp tone didn't bug me. Throwing up a boundary when it came to Harlan struck me as both smart and necessary.

I should have excused myself and ran out of there. Let them have some privacy before Harlan started asking me questions. But this was my table, so no. I'd sooner give up eating chips than make Harlan happy.

He seemed hell-bent on chasing Jackson all over town. As far as tactics went this persistence thing bordered on unsettling. So was not knowing the subject matter of the conversation bouncing around me. I understood the words but not the context. Jackson's meeting sounded important to Harlan. To Jackson? Not so much.

"We can talk about the details later." Jackson flipped the knife end over end, letting it thunk against the table each time.

"Kasey. This is a surprise," Harlan said in the least welcoming tone ever. "I didn't know you planned on attending Jackson's appointment."

Appointment? "I didn't."

Harlan made an odd sound. Like he was mulling over the timeline of events. "I'm confused. I helped to arrange the get-together and, except for the unexpected scheduling issue, intended to be here for it. You just, what, happened to be in the same restaurant as Jackson?"

"Dad."

Harlan lifted both hands in mock surrender. "No judgment. Just a question."

Oh, there was judgment all over his question. I didn't need Jackson's help to reply to this one. "I love this restaurant and stop in whenever I'm home. Have you tried the homemade chips? I dream about those back in DC."

Harlan didn't look impressed by the food talk. "You understand how important this consultation was, right?"

Interesting how the meeting had morphed into a consultation. The new description might fit. I still didn't know what was going on.

Jackson sighed. "It actually wasn't."

Harlan continued talking as if Jackson hadn't piped up and contradicted him. "This is an excellent opportunity for Jackson."

"Dad. Kasey doesn't care about this. That's enough meeting talk."

Not for Harlan. He had more. "He's being vetted. Reputation is everything. I'm sure you understand."

Not even a little. Harlan talked in sound bites without actually saying anything. Maybe that's how the political world operated. I tried to jump the conversation over this part. "I was here for a business meeting."

Harlan didn't miss a beat. "That's why you came into town? To attend Jackson's discussion?"

Wait . . . what? Now it was a discussion and not a consultation? "I have no idea how to answer that question because I don't know what you're talking about."

Jackson finally put the knife down. "Not my meeting, Dad. She was here on business related to her job."

"I do have one." At least for the next few days.

"None of this matters because the lunch was a formality only. And it ending means I need to get to the office." Jackson pushed his chair back.

For some reason that seemed to tick off Harlan. "We're not done."

Oh, I don't know about that. It felt like we were done.

I stood up when Jackson did. Harlan didn't take the hint. He continued to sit there. The look he shot me carried a chill. I got it. He didn't like me very much. I didn't know why or what I'd done, but the feeling was mutual.

Jackson turned to me. "We can continue our conversation at dinner."

When did we agree to another dinner?

He'd supported me with Brock, so I supported him here. "Okay. Sure . . ."

Jackson nodded at someone behind me before looking at me again. "Be at my place around seven."

Seven? I'd finished dinner and moved on to dessert by seven most nights. But Harlan's presence killed my ability to shoot smart-ass replies in Jackson's direction. I also didn't hate the idea of dinner with Jackson at his condo. If he cooked as well as he did everything else I might lose it and kiss him again. Make it a once-a-decade thing.

Jackson stepped around me to talk with someone. Harlan used the conversation interruption to push his case.

He stood. "Can I be honest with you?"

That sentence starter didn't sound good. "Sure."

"Jackson has a bright future."

Interesting how Harlan managed to make that sound ominous. "Okay."

"Naturally, with my connections and expertise, I stepped up to marshal his aspirations in an appropriate direction. To provide guidance and focus."

If Harlan wasn't careful his overinflated ego might pop.

"*His* aspirations?" Because it sounded like Harlan was using the wrong pronoun.

"The timing of these exploratory meetings is crucial."

We were back to calling today's event a meeting. Still clueless but fine.

"As it is, I've had to push Jackson and insist on his attention to get this done. I'd hate for him to lose out on this opportunity because he got temporarily distracted." Harlan packed a lot of posturing into the words he didn't say.

I was getting blamed for something, but I wasn't sure what.

"I'm here to offer him support. That's the extent of my involvement," Harlan said.

Sure.

"I promised Jackson's mother I would remain actively involved in his life." Harlan delivered a solemn nod. "She was only days away from dying, and I wanted her to know I'd heard her. That I would make Jackson my life's priority, and I did."

Damn. Talk about overplaying his hand. Harlan's words came wrapped in a thick layer of bullshit. I wanted to ask if his then-girlfriend had been in the room when he made this supposed promise to his sick wife, but I refrained.

Jackson had been nineteen when all of this allegedly happened. He was a lot older now. A fact Harlan conveniently ignored. "Jackson is a grown man and a pretty smart one."

"About most things but not everything." Harlan hesitated just long enough to hammer home that he was trying to make a big, important point. "Not everyone."

There was nothing subtle about that.

"Just think about what I said." Harlan dropped the line and walked away.

The man did like a dramatic exit.

The crowd in the room parted to give him a straight path to the door. No wonder his ego was so big. People treated him like royalty.

Harlan. Harlan. Harlan. So deluded. I'd only been in town for a few days. Even I couldn't ruin Jackson's future in that short amount of time.

I had so many questions. Jackson was stuck with me for dinner now because I intended to show up at his condo in search of answers. We had a lot to talk about.

CHAPTER TWENTY-TWO

I dressed up for dinner. By that I mean I didn't wear lounge pants, though I was tempted. This time of night called for napping on the couch, bad television, and a gooey dessert. I went with a T-shirt dress. It literally looked and fit like an overly long tee. It matched the bargain white sneakers I'd picked because heels were an unnecessary burden placed on women by the fashion industry.

My life got much easier and less painful once I came up with that justification for dumping uncomfortable shoes.

Jackson, of course, beat me at this adult game, too. He out-dressed me. He'd taken off his navy suit jacket and rested it on one of the dining room chairs. A chair at the table with dishes set and a candle burning.

This guy knew how to woo. Not that he was wooing me, but I could see from this setup that he'd perfected his *dinner with the ladies* game. Not bad for a man who worked twenty hours a day.

He set a glass of white wine on the kitchen island in front of me and turned back to the stove. From this vantage point I saw the way his white dress shirt tugged across his shoulders as he fiddled with a pan. He moved around, flipping this and adding that, showing off his cooking skills and a few other attributes.

That running nonsense worked for him.

Both the promise of food and the man lured me in. Speaking of dinner . . . The feast smelled like pan-fried chicken was the star. A salad peeked out of a bowl on the counter. I approved of the combo.

We'd known each other forever but being here, at his house like this, unsettled me. Not in an uncomfortable way. More like diving into the unknown. My tongue felt too big for my mouth. Every move I made came off as fumbling and awkward. The chance of me tripping or falling or doing something else equally ego-deflating increased with each second.

This was Jackson. The guy I grew up around. The one who rolled his eyes at me and viewed me as a natural disaster making landfall on his turf. Yet, I wanted to be here. That said something about my personality. I would unpack and assess that later, back in DC. Away from his pull.

A thousand conversation starters flipped through a Rolodex in my brain. Without thinking it through I landed on the one sure to mess up the peaceful calm of the kitchen. "I have a question for you."

Jackson smiled at me over his shoulder. "Shoot."

Was the dimple new? The cute butt, impressive shoulders, and adorable face already kicked my ass. I didn't need new reasons to conjure up an image of him in my muddled mind.

I took a fortifying gulp of wine. "Why does your dad think I'm a nuisance?"

Jackson laughed. "Well, as long as it's an easy question."

"I'm serious." The conversation hadn't started that way. I'd asked to break the silence before it had the chance to turn uncomfortable. The quieter the room, the more likely I'd rush in and say the wrong thing. But this suddenly mattered. I wanted to know what I'd done to make Harlan put on a fake smile to hide a snarl every time he saw me.

Jackson switched off the burner and moved the pan off the residual heat. When he turned, the starkness of his expression said I wasn't going to like his answer.

"He's not an easy man. He doesn't always come off as genuine," Jackson said.

That was not a Quaid family secret. "No kidding."

"If it's any consolation, he's annoyed with me right now, too."

I had experience with a shockingly bad father, so I knew how devastating that could be. But Harlan wasn't a killer. He hadn't abandoned Jackson.

"He's not warm. He doesn't like many people, though he pretends to. Most of what he says and does is aimed at getting everyone to do what he wants. The political world, with all its compromises and competitiveness, suits him. Father-son bonding? Not so much."

Jackson acted like he'd delivered another news flash.

"Dad has these goals for me. He doesn't care if I share the same goals. Protecting the family name is more important to him. His public persona." Jackson walked over to the table and scooped up the plates. A few seconds later, he brought them back into the kitchen and began filling each with food. "As an only child all the pressure falls on me to carry the legacy he thinks he's handed down."

That was a lot. "Wow."

"He uses Mom's memory as emotional blackmail but insists he doesn't. *Do it for her. She would have been so proud.*" Jackson looked like he wanted to say more, but he stopped.

All of that fit with the bullshit Harlan tried to sell me about how he'd been such a considerate and loving husband. "He told me you had a solid reputation and a bunch of opportunities, and I was going to ruin all of it."

Jackson fumbled the plate. It tipped in his hand, but he straightened it before major food wreckage occurred. "What? When did he say that?"

"I'm paraphrasing, but he dropped a few hints at the restaurant."

We divided the salad and sat there as if we'd done this sort of domestic thing forever. Like this was a regular occurrence. Wrong. We'd eaten together about a billion times over the years, but the two of us, sitting alone in his condo by candlelight, never happened before. I wasn't clear why it was happening now. Jackson had extended the surprise dinner invitation to throw Harlan off . . . or so I thought.

The signals coming from Jackson since I'd landed in North Carolina made my mind race and all my good intentions flee. What did he want? Did all of this mean anything? His throwaway lines. Those comments he made that crossed into a gray area. Flirting? Placating? Was he being supportive or setting me up for a fall?

So many questions. So much fear in digging around for clarification. Right now, our relationship hovered in the safe and sarcastic, joke-around, we-both-love-the-same-people sphere. If I said the wrong thing, asked the wrong question, I could tip my hand and expose the lifelong crush I tried to destroy, bury, and ignore on a daily basis. No one could withstand that much embarrassment.

Stay focused. That was the key. "So, back to the reputation thing. What opportunity does he expect you to capitalize on?"

"Right." Jackson hesitated for a few tense seconds. "Dad wants me to run for office."

If he'd said his dad wanted him to join the circus I would have had the same, stunned reaction. "Politics? You?"

"Dad's proposal came with a PowerPoint presentation. Be happy he didn't whip that out at the restaurant and show you all of his hard work."

"That's not weird at all."

"His plan is for local office and eventually the governorship." Jackson performed a wildly out-of-place shrug. "That was the point of my lunch at the tavern. Dad set it up. I was meeting with connected types who would help run and finance a campaign if they thought I was worthy of their investment."

Jackson wasn't phony. If anything, sometimes he was a bit too honest for comfort. He wasn't the *put on a fake smile* type either. I tried to imagine him attending potlucks and kissing babies and . . . nope, couldn't see it. I'd never heard him talk about politics or raising money, which made the whole idea even stranger.

"Is this your secret dream?"

"No."

Jackson didn't yell but came close.

CHAPTER TWENTY-THREE

Neither of us said a word following Jackson's stark denial. He said no in a way that suggested he'd been shouting it from the rooftops for a long time, but no one was listening.

If he needed to be heard, needed to talk it out, he could count on me. That meant he needed to answer one obvious question. "Have you told your dad how you feel?"

"Many times." Jackson followed up his answer by moving food around on his plate. He took a drink then picked up his knife, set it down, and picked it up again. "Mom asked me to give him a chance. To maintain a relationship with him after she was gone. She was so sick . . . I would have promised her anything at the end."

I could hear the pain. Time made it bearable but didn't erase it. Jackson carried it with him. Harlan took advantage. There was no way to make it sound pretty. He used Savannah's death to control Jackson.

"She wouldn't want you to forfeit your future. Your dad is wrong on this." I felt pretty confident with that assessment. Savannah and Harlan were very different people. Very different types of parents.

"Dad isn't easy to impress. In his mind, despite him being the perfect father, I haven't been the ideal and obedient son.

I've failed to live up to his expectations or jump on the path he generously set for me."

I waited for the punch line because *come on*, but Jackson stopped there. No other explanation.

"Is it your Ivy League education he's disappointed about? Maybe the way you excel at everything you do? Making partner by working your tail off?" By any measure Jackson was a stellar parental success story. "If you're failing, the rest of us should just wrap it up and slink away in shame."

"It's not . . ." Jackson performed an uncharacteristic word fumble.

He looked like he was searching for the right way to say whatever he wanted to say. If the idea was to deliver a comment to make his father look like less of a self-important windbag, Jackson could relax. I knew who and what Harlan was.

"He thought I'd join his consulting firm after college. That we'd be in business together. Hit potential clients from two directions, and I would eventually take over what he'd built," Jackson said. "But I went to law school instead, which he didn't love because it wasn't his idea, but he eventually agreed my choice made sense. He talked about how passing the bar would 'up' my profile."

"It's interesting how he expected you to sacrifice your life for his dream."

"But I didn't. My choice to land at a law firm that had nothing to do with him amounted to a significant betrayal in his mind."

Jackson, ever the overachiever, had pushed through the trauma of his mom's death while juggling college and the burden of his father's expectations and boorish behavior. Jackson excelled as he buried himself in billable hours. Words like "failure" and "disappointment" never popped into my head in relation to him. The idea that Jackson viewed his life in those terms made me want to punch Harlan more than I usually wanted to punch him.

I set my fork down. Eating could wait. "You've done everything your dad could have, and never should have, dared to ask of you. It's not your job to match your life to the way he wants it to be."

"Agreed."

But did he? Jackson sounded more resigned than won over to my view.

He must have seen my confusion because he continued. "I'm not arguing with you, but I do have a hard time ignoring Dad. He's the only parent I have. He's imperfect and flawed. He treats women as disposable. He believes he knows everything and that he can argue his way out of any disaster. All of that sucks, but he's also my father."

The longing. I could hear it in every word Jackson said. Heard but didn't really understand it. "I don't have a dad other than biologically, so you're going to need to explain."

"Do you want Mags to be proud of you?"

With every breath I took. "Of course, but—"

"That's your answer. We both have these big personalities in our lives, and we want to please them." Jackson shrugged. "In my case, I'd like to fix him, make him better, but I've learned that's not possible. He can't, at his core, change who he is, mostly because he doesn't think there's anything to change."

I got stuck on the part of the argument where Jackson compared Gram and Harlan. The thought that they were alike in any way made me want to pick up a metaphorical sword and shield and rush into battle.

I loved Gram for many things. In that moment, I loved her for accepting me for the messed up, uneven, perpetually-searching-for-something person that I was.

"It's asinine to sacrifice your whole life so Harlan can ruthlessly chase the power he craves." Worried I'd gone a little overboard, I stepped back a bit. "Or whatever this is."

Jackson smiled. "No matter what my dad says or does, no matter how much I want to please him and fulfill the promise I made to my mom, I'm not leaving my law practice. I won't let Dad ruin the career I chose."

Like he ruined Jackson's mom. Neither of us said it but we didn't have to. The truth sat there, spinning in the silence. Harlan destroyed most of the people who loved him. Savannah. The women who came both after and during his marriage to Savannah. Now, he was going after Jackson.

"I actually enjoy what I do for a living," he said.

I was with him until right there. "If you say so."

The tension that had wrapped around him the second he divulged Harlan's political ambition crap eased. "Some of us liked law school."

True, and I worried for those people. "Now you're just making things up."

Jackson didn't fight a smile. His words no longer sounded forced. He wasn't backing his father down or telling him to go to hell, but this still felt like progress.

"So, you're playing along but have no intention of being governor?" He'd be North Carolina's cutest governor, and I would vote for him if I still lived here, but I kept that to myself.

"Dad wanted to attend the money meeting to convince me to say yes. I didn't want him there for exactly the same reason."

That sounded clear. Final. I heard Jackson's intentions even if Harlan didn't. The reality that Harlan had lost this battle and didn't know it yet made my night.

"You rescheduled the meeting, which was an awesome display of passive-aggressive behavior, by the way, to make a point. To maintain control." Nicely done, lawyer boy. "Kudos."

"Thank you." He leaned forward and reached a hand across the table. "Look, I'm sorry my dad dragged you into this."

An inevitable result of our tangled families and confusing relationship. Jackson's life and mine had crashed and ricocheted off each other since the day we met. Still, this time Harlan acted more hostile than usual when he saw me. He could usually hide his distaste, or at least stay out of my path.

"Your dad thinks I'm a bad influence." And he might not be wrong about that.

"That's not new."

Not a surprise but not what I thought he'd say either. "Rude."

"I don't feel that way. He's . . . well, he forms opinions of people and then getting him to shift is tough."

Okay, but that didn't fully explain Harlan's rabid reaction to seeing me near Jackson. "That's his loss because I'm lovely."

Jackson's fingers brushed over mine and I felt the touch down to my knees. No guy ever made my insides shake . . . except for him.

He rubbed his thumb over the back of my hand. "You are."

The gesture stole my breath. I tried to inhale, exhale, and nothing. Somehow I forced out a few words. "I didn't expect an agreement."

He lifted his eyebrows. "It surprised me, too."

"Admit it. You like me." I tried to keep my tone light and carefree, but I really needed him to say it.

"That's not new either."

Oh . . .

He winked before he pulled his hand away. "We should eat before the food gets cold."

I'd forgotten about the food.

No one made me forget about food. Ever.

The rest of dinner fell into an easy back-and-forth. We joked and drank. Ate then bickered over the best dessert pie. The clear answer was coconut cream. His vote for traditional apple pie showed misplaced dessert priorities. Politician or not, he needed to work on that.

It wasn't until I got back to Gram's house about two hours later that I realized we'd never talked about dead husbands or worked on my self-created work pitch disaster.

If that was a date, it was a good one. And I was in deep shit.

CHAPTER TWENTY-FOUR

I filled Gram and Celia in on Harlan's political aspirations for Jackson the next morning over peach scones. We sat in the formal dining room, sipping our preferred morning beverages, and neither of them showed even a twinge of surprise about my intel.

"You knew." My real complaint was that they knew and didn't tell me. We talked at least every Sunday and texted nearly every day and they never dropped this big piece of juicy gossip.

"Of course, dear." Gram sounded surprised that I was surprised.

Celia sipped on her coffee. "Harlan hasn't been subtle. He's been all over Jackson, trying to wear down his resistance while building him up as a possible candidate to potential financial backers across the state."

Gram responded with her famous *pfft*. "He's also been working Celia to get her to side with him and put additional pressure on Jackson."

"That's not . . ." Celia sighed. "Okay, it's true, but Harlan hasn't been successful. I support Jackson and whatever he wants to do. I'd prefer his goal not be politics, but that has to be his choice."

"That's why Harlan has been sneaking in here and bugging

you." An interesting and annoying tactic, so exactly what I'd expect from Harlan.

Gram shot me her confidence-destroying I'm-on-to-you grandma look. "You think *he's* the one sneaking around here?"

An unexpected shot across the bow. Gram had been holding that in and now she launched it when I had nowhere to hide.

Do not take the bait. Do not take the bait. Do not . . . "Are you saying I have been?"

Celia put her coffee mug down as if she needed all of her strength for whatever bit of wisdom was about to come out of her mouth. "Honey, we know something is going on."

Another opportunity to come clean came . . . and went.

I switch to stall mode. "What do you mean? What kind of something?"

Gram snorted. "You tell us."

"The surprise two-week vacation." Celia looked at Gram before continuing. "You've danced around questions and given half answers, but did you get fired? It's okay if you did, but not telling us makes it hard for us to know how to help you."

"I have not been fired." Yet. It was coming but right at this moment I was not overtly lying. To my knowledge.

Gram and Celia did that mutual staring thing. I wasn't always the subject of their unspoken communication, but this time I was. No question.

Gram was the first to use actual words. "Maybe not fired, but not nothing. Your visit with only two days' notice is not a leisure trip."

She always knew when I hedged and then pulled the truth out of me. That history chipped away at my resolve. I still hadn't told them about the pitch and the lying and Brock for many reasons but mostly because I didn't want them to be disappointed in me. I'd had so many restarts and do-overs. I needed them to think I was capable. Not a burden.

Jackson would tell me to spit it out. Come clean.

So, it was good he wasn't here today.

Not that he was wrong. He wasn't. I knew the right thing to do. The expedient and mature thing to do. But—and this was a big "but"—if I did come clean Gram and Celia would see me as someone they needed to educate and save. Worse, to protect.

With the poison question hanging out there, I needed them to see me as competent and able to handle difficult news. As an ally. For me to help, they needed to share. I toyed with negotiating a communications truce—they tell me their secret and I would divulge mine. If only I knew how to do that without having one overtake the other.

I needed advice from Jackson but the uncertainty with him on a personal level had me floundering. Him, us, the dinners, his comments . . . it was a whole messy and confusing thing. As if I needed one more unexpected twist in my life.

I stopped my mental wanderings long enough to focus. Celia and Gram continued to look at me. None of us had talked for a few minutes. That made me think I'd missed something. Maybe I'd blacked out in panic and didn't hear whatever else they said.

I smiled.

They didn't smile back.

Panic flooded through me. I had to do or say something. Straight-out lying exhausted me. Also made me feel shitty.

"Things are up in the air right now. I hate my job. I'm not sure I like DC. I'm rudderless and it's very frustrating." I didn't intend to verbally vomit the truth—a truth but not *the* truth they were searching for—all over my loved ones. But none of what I did manage to spit out was a lie.

My tenuous employment might be ending soon, whether or not I wanted that to happen. But between the poison and Jackson, I had enough questions to dump them in a pile and build a wall around the house.

"Take all the time you need," Celia said.

Gram snorted, earning a side-eye from Celia.

"We're here for you." Celia smiled at me. "Always. No matter what has happened or what you've done, you just need to tell us."

Every word made it harder to carry on with the lie of omission. They were wearing me down, those adorable evil geniuses. "What if I said—"

A beeping noise interrupted my near-confession.

"Sorry. I set an alarm." Celia took out her cell phone and put it on the dining room table. "We need to make desserts for the film festival's pre-event party."

The RiverRun International Film Festival. Ten days of screenings and talks. It kicked off with this pre-festival party thrown by the organizers for volunteers and town bigwigs. Having a regional movie festival in town was pretty cool. It had been around for nearly three decades, but this early party was new and a good gig for Mags' Desserts.

"No cupcakes or cake of any kind. Cherry, apple, and peanut butter pie in copious amounts," I said. All three sounded delicious. While cupcakes were my favorite Gram-made dessert, the pies were the shop's staple and quite delicious.

Gram frowned. "What?"

A question I could honestly answer. Finally. "Those are the pies that were ordered for the event."

"How do you know that?" Celia asked.

"The information was on one of those sticky notes in the office." That set off a new round of Gram-to-Celia glances and I was about done with those.

"And you remember which pies were for which event?" Gram sounded skeptical.

"Let's not act like I don't collect all relevant dessert information whenever possible. But yeah. You have six substantial orders for big-ticket special events this week plus orders via the website and your usual deliveries to restaurants and regular customers." That sounded big. Not NOI-wants-to-sell-you big but enough to grab Micah's attention. Unfortunately.

Celia made a humming sound. "Impressive memory."

Was it? I'd never had trouble memorizing things. It tended to happen when I wasn't even trying. Give me a list of things and I'd remember it for days. "I'm not totally useless."

Gram nodded. "Clearly not."

"We never thought so," Celia said at the same time. "In fact, with your organizational skills and memory skills there's always a place for you around here."

Every word stabbed into me. She was offering me more business responsibility while I was putting them in the headlights of people who wanted to buy all their hard work.

That's it. I needed Jackson's advice. It would come with

a lecture and step-by-step instructions on how to do what I should have done more than a week ago. I'd at least have a little help . . . and the fact I had a new reason to see him so soon after our dinner didn't suck.

Having a plan should have given me confidence. Not yet, but I hoped it was coming.

CHAPTER TWENTY-FIVE

Jackson showed up at the house a little before eight that night as promised. He was many things, including dependable. I texted him after talking to Gram and Celia. He texted back about an associate and a memo along with a promise he would "swing by later."

Later had arrived.

Celia and Gram sat in the family room, watching a police procedural and complaining about the poor choices the police, the victim, and the attackers made. They claimed to be big fans of the show, but they hid it well.

I caught Jackson as he opened the side door to the house and shoved him back outside. He grumbled about being rushed away from the kitchen, but clandestine meetings needed to be held in secret. Otherwise, they were just boring meetings. This situation called for something special.

I dragged him to the gazebo. Didn't face him until we stood under the lights.

Another suit. Another opportunity to look all tall, dark, and thoroughly put together. Had he gotten cuter? Could that sort of thing happen? Maybe only to men because the older I got the more television commercials harped on my undereye circles and thinning lips that needed puffing. I loved a good moisturizer as much as the next gal but hearing the *you need to buy this new lotion or potion* spiel exhausted me. I refused to believe I'd run out of time to save my skin at twenty-six.

Jackson looked awake and engaged. Still pressed and impressive in that navy suit and aqua tie. He'd worked something like twelve hours already today and would likely put in a few more after our talk. Always the overachieving hottie.

"What's the big rush? I wanted to steal a cupcake."

"I have you covered." I lifted the plastic container I'd been hiding and held it in front of him. "Black velvet with cream cheese icing."

As if I didn't know his favorite cupcake. I also knew his favorite pie, favorite meal, and favorite restaurant. He liked his food straightforward, not fancy. No need for swirls or sprinkles.

It was possible I knew an unhealthy amount about him.

He opened the lid and looked at the two cupcakes I'd packed for him. Not that he couldn't go inside and grab his own. He could, but I'd come up with this contingency plan to keep his attention.

"Nice." He dipped a finger in the icing and brought it to his mouth. "So good."

He licked it off and something in my brain sputtered. I could almost hear the series of tiny explosions.

"What?" He frowned. "Did you want some?"

I never noticed the way he spoke in innuendos. Now, it's all I heard, which could mean I was the one with the innuendo problem.

"Tell me how to admit to Gram and Celia about Brock and the pitch and the mess I made."

"Easy." Jackson closed the lid but looked reluctant to do so. "You sit them down and tell them."

Not helpful. "I'm serious."

He snorted in a way that made him sound like Gram. "So am I."

He was the worst wingman ever. "Forget it."

"Okay, wait." He caught my arm before I could bolt. His fingers wrapped around my elbow. He used the other hand to set down his precious cupcakes.

I now understood the concept of erogenous zones. What they were and how they worked. His hand. My bare skin. The dizziness that had my body falling into his.

Think of Brock. That would kill any sexual feelings and shift my focus back to my never-ending work mess.

"What exactly are you asking?" His eyes narrowed. "Because my advice is simple. Tell the truth and end this before it blows up on you."

I didn't even want to think about how this work situation could get worse. "They're going to be mad."

He winced. "It's more likely they'll be disappointed."

The comment stabbed through me. "Don't say that. My behavior sounds so much worse when you use that word."

"They're also going to understand your panic and how that led up to the pitch disaster. They aren't going to let NOI near their business, but I sense you didn't want that to happen anyway."

Such a smart hottie. "Right."

"But the longer you wait, the worse this will be. If they find out from someone else what—"

"Who?" The traitor. "You?"

I pulled back and he immediately let go. So fast that my balance wavered and my body tipped. He caught me before I did a header into the post. To be technically correct, he grabbed on and tugged me closer . . . and my work priorities took a violent nosedive.

"Are you okay?" he asked, sounding more concerned about me than usual.

No. This whole treading-water-at-work thing I'd been doing zapped my strength. Being close to him shut down my brain. The combination of the two had me flailing and jittery and a whole bunch of other words that sounded like wading into dangerous territory.

I looked up at him, ready to launch into a renewed *I need a plan* whine when something shifted. In the air. Inside me. In the gazebo. The place I kissed him all those years ago and sent him running. We stood in the same position, under the same lights.

A miscalculation . . . or was it?

My stomach performed the same tumble it had back then. I might be older, but I appeared to be not one inch wiser when it came to Jackson Quaid.

"I think . . ." What did I think? My brain put up an *out to lunch* sign.

His gaze went to my mouth and lingered there. It's possible I stopped breathing. Who the hell knew.

He lowered his head just a fraction. "Tell me not to kiss you."

Those words were not coming out of my mouth. Ever.

His head moved another inch, bringing his mouth within a breath of mine. "If you don't want this . . ."

Warnings fired in my head and logical questions filled my brain but mostly I thought: *Do it!* I'd lost the power to speak and all sense of self-preservation. That was the only explanation for my next move. I shifted. Just a bit, but a definite shift, until I stood in the circle of his arms with my hands pressed against his chest.

"Good." That's all he said.

Then he lowered his head and kissed me. Not a gentle, exploring kiss. Not a testing-the-waters kiss. No, this was *a kiss*. He didn't hold back. He didn't play coy. He kissed me as if he'd been waiting forever for the chance.

His mouth crossed over mine and his hands went to my waist. The touch of his lips and his fingers set off a blast of energy. I curled into him. Up on my tiptoes, arms wrapped around his neck, heat pounding through me. Every shield I'd erected to protect myself from this attraction fell.

Need and desire washed through me. The incessant craving I kept at bay leapt to the front of my mind. I wanted to jump up and wrap my legs around his waist. To tell him I'd been dreaming of this for years as he cycled through girlfriends and women who weren't me.

When he lifted his head . . . nope. Not yet. I drew him back in. I wasn't ready to stop or to move on or, worse, to pretend the kiss didn't matter. I put every ounce of the affection, arousal, and need I'd stored up over the years into the kiss. I kissed him like I'd never be allowed to do it again and wanted the memory to last.

When we broke apart a second time, he rested his forehead against mine. Heavy breathing filled the air between us.

"Wow."

He wasn't wrong. "Yeah."

"That was . . ."

"Yeah." I couldn't seem to come up with another word.

"I didn't mean to—"

"Nope." *Oh, no.* Not so soon after what was unquestionably the best kiss of my life. "If you're about to say you're sorry for kissing me I'm going to smash those cupcakes before you can eat them."

He smiled. "That's a serious threat. It sounds like you mean business."

I waited for my usual awkward rambling to start. For the regret to settle in. Both seemed to be tardy because all I felt was the need to kiss him again.

He glanced at the lights and the darkness outside the structure. "I really like this gazebo."

I laughed. I couldn't help it. The bizarre and untimely turn in our relationship amounted to a lapse in judgment—his—but I ignored the doubts and focused on his comment. He really could be adorable.

"Apparently I'm going to kiss you in this very place every ten years." Or, you know, again in three minutes.

"I know you wanted to talk about what to say to Mags and Celia."

It took me a second to catch up to the topic change. "Originally. Sure."

When he stood there, holding me, I began to panic. He really was going to say something very Jackson-like and annoy the crap out of me. Then I would smash those innocent cupcakes because I had no choice.

"This was better."

He said . . . *wait, what did he say?* His thumb gently brushed across my stomach. How in the world was I supposed to concentrate when he did that?

"You mean the kiss was better than talking?" I asked, trying to keep up with all the unnecessary chatter.

That smile of his grew wider. "Yes, Kasey. The kiss."

My entire world flipped upside down. Things I thought I knew, the crush I tried to kill with fire. Nothing made sense.

Now what?

I looked up at the house and saw the light in the kitchen and thought about the ladies yelling at the television. My hands slipped down his arms. My brain sent a message to my legs to step back but my legs ignored the desperate order.

I inhaled because I wasn't sure I'd actually breathed since we entered the gazebo. "Maybe we should take a minute."

His smile dimmed a bit. "Is that what you want?"

Hell no. "There's a lot happening."

"True."

"Our emotions are all over the place." Mine were scattered to Alabama and back.

I ended the babbling by resting my head on his shoulder. I could smell him. Feel him. A woman could only take so much before she caved to her bad judgment.

He rubbed my back, soft and reassuring. Sweet, even.

I wondered how fast I could get his shirt off.

"On the work front, think about what you need to say to explain what happened. We'll pick a time and talk to them together. Consider me your backup."

My head shot up. It missed knocking into his chin by a fraction. "Really? You'll be there for support?"

"Of course."

He finally stepped back and I hated it. Touching him was so much better than not touching him.

He picked up his container of unharmed cupcakes. "One other thing."

Jackson, no. He could still ruin the moment.

"My emotions are just fine."

It took me a second to figure out what he was saying. It wasn't a struggle since he went ahead and filled me in.

"When it comes to you I know exactly what I think and feel. And I'm sure as hell not going to wait another ten years to kiss you again." His smile came roaring back as he stepped out of the gazebo. "Sweet dreams, Kasey."

When he winked I doubted I'd ever sleep again.

CHAPTER TWENTY-SIX

The next morning did not go well. It started with calls from Micah. He tried twice before eight. Either he didn't own a watch or he didn't care about my sleep schedule. Brock then texted to say he was back in town and: **We need to talk today.**

In addition to destroying my post-kiss buzz, the warning also started an alarm clock bonging in my head. The time for avoidance and denial had run out. I was being called in to explain. An unavoidable and, frankly, deserved ultimatum hovered on the horizon.

I'd had plenty of warning and time. From Brock. From Jackson. From that little voice in my head that recognized when I was on the cusp of tripping over my own feet. But knowing an explosion waited behind the closed door didn't keep me from running headfirst into it. Unfortunately.

Confronting the mess days ago would have been the wise and mature thing to do. At every opportunity I'd chosen a different path.

In a feeble attempt to prolong my Brock-free time and inevitable firing, I left the house. If I couldn't save my job, I could at least try to save Gram and Celia from a potential prison term. Not that I had a definitive answer about the poison, but I had a pile of things that seemed not quite right, a few *that's never happened before* events, and a load of suspicion fueling my imagination.

That was the point of this errand. Gather intel.

With that special column in the business's ledger gone, I lost the ability to link stars with the town's recently dead husbands. That meant backing into the evidence by determining how many men had died unexpectedly in the area so far this year then cross-referencing to see if their wives or girlfriends ordered from Mags' Desserts around that time.

Sounded simple, but no. How many local men over the age of thirty—an age I randomly picked—died? So many for so many different reasons.

A smart-thinking person might have stopped there. Not me. I dove into a new round of bad planning, which explained how I ended up standing in the bushes on the side of Abigail Burns's house. An oversized SUV sat in the driveway, probably Austin's, but he never showed his jackass face. If Abigail was in there she had some pretty stealthy skills because I didn't see her either.

It's amazing how much attention sneaking around draws. A woman chased me away by asking fifty questions about who I was because I looked familiar and "Do I have to call the police on you, young lady?" The neighborhood watch was alive and well in Winston-Salem, which was a good thing but not helpful for my informal investigation.

My next step . . . a scone. Possibly a cupcake after the scone because I'd walked to and from Abigail's house. Not miles but I'd racked up far more than my usual zero steps of morning exercise. I was a treadmill-after-work kind of gal. Any machine that allowed me to burn calories and watch television at the same time was my favorite.

With exercise checked off for the day my sole focus became working out a time to meet with Jackson and unload the twisted truth on my unsuspecting Gram and Celia.

Talking to Jackson. That part made me ridiculously happy and a little jumpy, two things I never was. Putting off the inevitable *let me tell you about my work pitch* talk with Gram might prolong my time with Jackson, but I could accidentally make an even bigger mess. Increasing mess size had been my greatest skill for several years now and I needed to break the habit.

I heard voices as soon as I walked into Gram's kitchen. Gram and Celia and someone else. Another female. I shuddered to a halt when I saw who—Abigail Burns. I recognized her from my hours of online research. The starred pie lady stood right there next to a plate of blueberry muffins.

Blame Jackson. That kiss kept me up late. Reading about poison and information on the Burns family eventually helped me to sleep, but it took longer than expected.

Cash's death, or murder, depending on who you talked to, had set off an explosion of press. News articles touted his intellect and business prowess. A few mentioned his son's shady background. Austin liked to drink and drive, and why wasn't that a surprise? A big-time jackass move performed by a big ole jackass.

Abigail and Cash married right after she graduated from college. He was older and had already launched business ventures, thanks to Daddy's checkbook and a family loan he liked to pretend never happened. That made Abigail forty-something, but she looked more like a teenager. Petite with perfectly styled blond hair that landed just above her shoulders. She came off as fragile in a floral-print dress that fell past her knees.

"You're back." Gram could not have sounded less excited about my return.

It looked like I was interrupting something. Not hard to guess what. No one offered an introduction, which I mentally added to the *yeah, they sold a poison pie* evidence I'd been collecting.

Abigail rubbed her hands together in front of her. "You must be Kasey."

She might know about my run-in with Austin, but she might not. Asking if he'd been arrested for anything lately lacked tact, so I skipped that in favor of a boring response.

"I am." I extended my hand and Abigail took it. My fingers swallowed hers. This close she looked even smaller. The rounded shoulders. The tension pulling around her eyes. Panicked. Grieving. Guilty. I wasn't sure which description fit.

"Abigail stopped by to say hello," Celia explained.

Yeah, sure she did.

What exactly was the proper etiquette for broaching the topic of a dead spouse to the woman who probably killed him? I had no idea. I went with a comment that sounded perfectly fine in my head. "I'm sorry about your husband."

Maybe not so fine because at the mention of him a suffocating tightness gripped the room. Gram made a grumbling noise, which was never a good thing.

Abigail's gaze darted from Celia to Gram. When Abigail finally did speak her voice sounded weak and small. "Thank you."

I had a million questions and no ability to ask even one. Gram stared at me. I took that as a warning to be careful. That warning hadn't worked for the first twenty-six years of my life. It wasn't clear why she thought it would now.

"Did you come to get a pie?" Every word I said came packed with unintended questions and condemnation.

Abigail went back to the hand-wringing. "Uh . . . I . . . no."
Yep. Nothing suspicious about that response.

Celia delivered one of those fake smiles she'd perfected over the years. "Abigail needed to get out for some fresh air, so we invited her here."

That sounded like a friendly thing to do. Funny how Gram and Celia forgot to mention this special friendship before now. "Of course. Would you like—"

"I was just leaving." Abigail stepped away from the counter.

She was this flaming ball of nerves. All anxious and unsure of herself. She shuffled her feet and shifted her balance from side to side. The constant movement made me feel bad for her and a little dizzy.

Since I wasn't a total asshole I skipped all husband-related questions and any comment that strayed too close to death talk. This woman looked like she'd been through it. I refused to add to her pain. "I didn't mean to interrupt your conversation."

A light red stained Abigail's cheeks. "You didn't. No."

Her voice carried a hint of uncertainty mixed with an unnecessary apology. The right word to describe her finally hit me—"lost." She looked as if she'd spent her entire life jumping to commands and waiting for people to tell her what to do.

I'd gotten a taste of her husband's pointing and shouting. Dealing with rude and condescending behavior would take a toll. If the home version of him was as terrible as the public one, I'd continue not to mourn him or hope for him to have a peaceful rest because he didn't deserve either.

"Okay, well . . ." Abigail looked down at her shoes and then to Gram. "I should be going. I promised Austin I'd make his lunch."

That guy. He was old enough to make a sandwich. "I'll walk you out."

My comment made all activity in the room stop. Honestly, this was the least subtle crowd ever. If Gram and Celia were in the business of men poisoning they'd better work on their poker faces.

I motioned for Abigail to come with me before Gram or Celia could step in. We walked to the door in silence. A death march. That's what it felt like.

Abigail stopped right before touching the doorknob. I waited for her to talk again because the hesitation felt like something. Not sure what, but something.

"They're happy you're here." She whispered the comment.

It took a second for her words to sink in. Not a confession. More like a friendly reminder not to take Gram and Celia for granted, which solidified my belief about Gram and Celia having a personal relationship not only with the other woman with a surprise dead husband, Delilah Rhine, but with Abigail.

I needed to know how many more women had special pies delivered around the time of unexpected family deaths. I also needed to respond to Abigail because the way she looked at me with that vacant stare made me sad for her.

"I missed them." That wasn't a lie. I did. "Very much."

Abigail treated me to a slight smile as I opened the door . . . and saw Brock standing right there.

CHAPTER TWENTY-SEVEN

B usted.

Of course Brock would pick this one time in his life to step away from a golf course earlier than expected. He played in the rain. He played when it was freezing outside. He played on public and private courses. He played in tournaments. He played then insisted the playing was really a business meeting. He played so often I wondered if his useless ball-hitting obsession explained his broken engagement two months ago.

I'd already forgotten her name because Brock never talked about her. She was an . . . architect or accountant. Something with an *a* but not assassin because I would have remembered that. Congrats to whatever her name was for being smart enough to run.

Brock's arrival on Gram's porch was a power play. I'd hoped Jackson's lawyer puffery would have prevented this. Jackson told him not to drop in. I told Brock the same thing. Despite all the warnings to the contrary, Brock plunged ahead with his *you can't tell me what to do* plans.

I ushered Abigail around Brock and watched her scurry down the walkway to her car. That solved one problem, though it would boomerang eventually.

On to the next issue. Dead husbands should trump general boss asshatery but not today. Good job, Brock.

"Are you stalking me?" Because stumbling over him every few days was not my idea of a good time.

Brock crossed his arms in front of him, sending a clear I'm-not-open-to-discussion message. "Do you think this situation is funny?"

"I don't think anything about my job is amusing." The most truthful comment I'd ever uttered.

"You are on a work trip. I'm your boss."

As if he ever let me forget that. "I'm aware."

"Then you also know we expect results, not roadblocks."

I deserved his anger but ignored it anyway. "I'm trying to make the deal work."

"By hiding in North Carolina?"

Time to bring out the big guns. "The business lawyer told you to back off or risk blowing the deal."

Brock scoffed. "That guy?"

The punch of anger surprised me. Jackson didn't need me rushing to his defense, but he didn't have a choice. "He's a respected lawyer."

"He's been handled."

What kind of mob talk was that? "Meaning?"

"Your sole focus should be on me. On getting this deal done." Brock leaned in as if he needed to emphasize his words with a bit of intimidation. "I've been very clear about this. Your continued employment depends on your being able to deliver this deal. You are out of chances."

More stuff I already knew or at least guessed.

"Micah sees something in you. I don't get it. I think he'll soon regret giving you an opportunity and realize that his storied ability to read people was off this one time." Brock shook his head. "Lucky for you, and since Micah believed this deal could be lucrative, rather than waiting on you I started the financial health assessment on the business with what little information has been made available so far."

Gram would love that. "Why?"

"This project has legs."

Brock said nonsense stuff like that all the time.

"Because of that, I need to step in before you blow this." He finished his speech and made a move toward the house.

Not so fast. I performed the perfect block. I also caught him off guard and dragged him off the porch to the space under the maple tree out front. The trunk should block anyone from watching from the road.

"Kasey?" He sounded more stunned than angry but give him time. "What the hell are you doing?"

Touching him and not enjoying it, so I stopped. "Keeping you from making a mistake."

He brushed his hands over his arms. Right where I'd touched him, as if I'd given him girl germs.

This guy.

"I don't get it, Brock. All the directors are cultivating clients and making deals without your interference. They're on calls, out to lunch, visiting sites." I had listened just enough in work meetings to know those things happened. "For some reason I don't get the same respect."

"You haven't earned it."

"I'm trying to." Not really, but still. This conversation called for an indignant response. I aimed for fake indignation. I could pull that off. "You are the problem here. Micah gave me a deadline. I'm still inside of it."

Barely, but I had a few days.

"The difference between the other directors and you is simple." Brock crossed his arms in front of him. "I don't trust you."

Wise. That Yale education really did come in handy. "You've made that clear from my first day in the office."

His mood shifted. The abrasive guy with his own agenda—gone. A choking whiff of smugness filled the air. "You're not going to like the way this ends, Kasey."

Okay . . .

He continued. "Remember when this implodes that I tried to help you and keep this from becoming an embarrassing disaster. You've been warned."

The chilling words haunted me as I opened the door and stepped back inside. Celia and Gram stood there with dire expressions reminiscent of mourners at a funeral.

"Uh, hi." Because, really, what else could I say?

Did they hear Brock? See him? All the unexpected visitors made me want to install a better alarm system and locking gate to the driveway.

"Kasey Adelaide Nottingham."

Oh, damn. Gram pulled out my middle name. She didn't weaponize it often but when she did it was a clear sign of terrible things to come.

"Kasey." Celia going with the usual name she called me was

only a little less terrifying. "Is there something you need to tell us?"

So many things. "Like?"

Gram sighed. "Do not make me use your full name again, young lady. Start talking."

Shit.

CHAPTER TWENTY-EIGHT

B rock and his booming voice caused this. He'd stomped around, demanding attention, and he got it. Now I had to deal with the fallout.

Gram and Celia possessed a unique ability to ferret out egomaniacs then avoid them. Their rabid dislike for men who yelled or used their size to intimidate often ended with a side comment from Gram like, *It wouldn't be a loss if someone ran over that man with a car.*

That sort of thing used to sound like a joke. Now? Not so sure.

Four minutes into this awkward assembly and the ladies hadn't moved. They formed a perfumed wall of stubbornness in the middle of the entrance hall. Their angry little faces made one thing clear: my dodging and weaving days were over. These two would not take a step until they had answers. If that meant we stayed there, rooted in the spot, as summer came and went, so be it.

"I can explain." I could and should have days ago. Now I didn't have a choice.

"That would be a nice change," Gram grumbled.

She wore the same stony expression she used whenever anyone at a group meal in a restaurant took out a calculator instead of just evenly splitting the check. She found that sort of thing "unseemly"—her word, not mine.

Celia, always the peacemaker, put a loving hand on Gram's arm. "Let's give Kasey a minute to sort out whatever she needs to sort out in her head."

Gram snorted. "We've given her days and now this."

I'd never wanted to crawl under the couch and hide as much as I did right now. Unfortunately, adults weren't supposed to do that sort of thing. "I was planning to tell you."

Gram's eyebrow lifted. "When?"

"Why are you involving Jackson?" Celia asked at the same time.

Gram barely let Celia finish. "That wasn't a way to make this man jealous, was it? I can't imagine you doing something deliberately hurtful."

I needed roller skates to keep up with these two and this conversation. We'd only ventured a few sentences in, and I'd already lost control of the topic. What were they talking about and why did it include Jackson?

Brock's unwanted visit ran through most of my reserves, but I couldn't show weakness here. The ladies would be all over that. "I think we need to back up."

"Kissing one man in the gazebo one day. Hiding under the tree with another the next." Celia shook her head. "This behavior isn't like you."

Panicked sentences rolled through my head. She did not just say "kissing." Please have her not have mentioned kissing. No kissing. "Did you—"

"Balancing two men is dangerous, not to mention exhausting and unnecessary." This time Gram sighed. Not a quiet, subtle sigh. An everyone-listen-to-me sigh. "I know you think you can handle anything, but—"

"I wonder where she gets that from," Celia mumbled under her breath.

"I don't blame her for being skeptical or feeling confused. Men are a nuisance." Gram never skipped an opportunity to recite her general view on men and slipped it in here. "I can only think of a few likable ones other than Jackson."

Round and round they went. Jackson's name kept popping up and not in a way that made sense. Most of the bickering happened between the ladies. They left me out of it, which was a relief but only a temporary one. The temptation to sneak out of the room pulled pretty hard but I stayed put. Mostly because these two would hunt me down if I took one step in any direction.

Just as they entered a new back-and-forth, I clapped. The move was strategic and a little dangerous. I'd clapped in the car exactly one time as a kid. Gram immediately pulled over and delivered a lecture in her serious Gram voice about why that was never going to happen again.

They viewed clapping as disrespectful. They also insisted the noise gave them a headache. The unforgivable sin? Clapping in church. Gram exploded every time it happened. *Do you remember ten years ago when Cynthia clapped after the children's choir sang "Silent Night"?* More than one of our weekly FaceTime calls included a church clapping rant.

I had their attention. Good, because they sure had mine. "How do you know about the kiss in the gazebo?"

Celia shrugged. "We saw you from the house."

We'd entered nightmare territory. "You did . . . *what*?"

"We had to go upstairs and move some furniture around to get a better look." Gram acted out the movements while she talked. "The trees blocked the view but when we sat on the bed and ducked down, we could see you two."

They . . . but we were . . . *oh my God.*

Celia shook her head. "Poor Jackson."

Wait a second. "Hey, I'm not that bad at kissing."

He hadn't complained. Not to me. If he'd given them a critique he'd better be damn good at running because I would go after him.

"The other man is the issue." Gram treated us to another dismissive snort.

There's no way I'd heard them correctly. "Back up. You two were sneaking around, watching me with Jackson?"

Gram gasped. Actually gasped. As if this conversation wasn't dramatic enough. "I do not sneak around in my own house."

"Well . . ." Celia winced. "We did hide behind the curtain when she looked up at the window."

I could almost see them shushing each other as they moved through the house, jockeying for a better view. Running here and there, slinking around, peeking out windows like a nosy crime-fighting duo.

"Jackson and I have shared one kiss." Well, two, but precise details would not help here. They'd only make the explanation cloudier. "You don't approve? Is that the problem?"

There was an offensive answer here and they better not say it.

"It looked like a big kiss." Celia sounded excited about that.

Gram nodded. "I'm impressed Jackson has it in him."

Celia and Gram were off again. Celia took the lead. "He's had practice with those girlfriends, though the last one was incredibly serious."

Gram nodded. "I couldn't imagine her kissing anyone or anything."

Okay, that was enough of that topic. "Ladies. Can we pick a subject and stay on it?"

Gram's stiff stance eased a bit. She leaned into Celia but didn't relinquish the barricade and let me pass. "Fine. Tell us about your boyfriend."

"My *what*?" So, they hadn't overheard Brock talking about business crap. Instead, they'd created a horrifying scenario about my nonexistent dating life and gave me a fictional boyfriend. Brock.

I'd rather scramble to find their hidden poison . . . then drink it.

"The man in the yard." Gram gestured in the general direction of outside. "The squirrelly looking one."

"Don't say that. What if she really likes him? Although I can't imagine." Celia went back to wincing. "Do you?"

"We recognized him from before," Gram explained without an ounce of guilt. "Charlotte snapped a photo of him during that visit to Graylyn."

That unwanted business meeting kept biting me in the ass. "She did what?"

Celia wasn't done wincing. "Charlotte texted Mags about seeing you with a man. Mags asked for a photo."

Of course she did. "It's interesting how you forgot to mention Charlotte's private investigator skills earlier."

Their spy network had been working overtime. They'd sent out their minions to collect information and report back. The realization was enough to make me stay inside forever.

"We're even because you forgot to tell us about the boy-friend."

Gram's fluffy pink-and-blue plaid slippers made it tough to take her ire seriously.

"Did you and your man have a fight? Is that why you're here? He did something to upset you and you ran?" Celia reached for my hand. She cradled it in her palms in a soothing touch. "I'm not judging. You should run if you're not safe."

"Some people might think a man following you across state lines is romantic. It's not. It's a warning sign." Gram nodded as if to punctuate her comment. "It's a hint of controlling be-havior to come."

Wow. I loved them and appreciated their concern, or what-ever this was, but . . . wow. "He's not . . . okay. We'll circle back to Brock."

Gram graced us with her third snort of the conversation. "That sounds like one of those California names. Brooks. Now there's a good Southern name."

Celia shot Gram a look. "Mags, be supportive."

"California." Gram acted like the state name was a swear word. "He's not the right man for her. He had those beady little rat eyes. I know a bad man when I see one."

I'd never again be able to look at Brock without thinking of a giant rodent. "I feel like we're having eight different conver-sations and I'm miles behind in all of them."

"We're talking about the rat-eyed man at the door just now."

As usual, Celia went with a calmer approach. "And the kiss with Jackson. There was some flirting, too, but mostly the kiss."

"About that. Why are you lumping Jackson and Brock together?" They didn't belong in the same universe, let alone the same conversation.

Celia pressed a hand against her chest. "We're not the ones trying to balance both men."

"Dealing with one is bad enough." Gram sounded pretty sure about that. "With apologies to Jackson, of course."

The haze cleared. This bizarre showdown was about my nonexistent love life. They believed I was dating Brock. I couldn't think of anything more vomit-inducing. "I've told you about Brock. He's my boss."

Now Celia looked as confused as I felt. "But you call your boss Big Ego Man."

"I do but that's not the name his parents gave him. It's Brock. Same guy."

"You're dating your boss?" Gram whispered the words like some people did when they talked about cancer or something equally horrible.

"Oh, Kasey." Celia sounded disappointed. "What have we always told you about men in power?"

Time to kill and bury this conversation. I could not endure another round of this. "We aren't dating. I promise. I will never be that desperate."

"Your conversation with him looked a bit heated. We were about to come out and hit him with a plate," Gram said.

Celia nodded as she dropped my hand. "Mags originally suggested using the vacuum cleaner, but we agreed a smaller weapon would be less awkward."

It was nice to know they had a boundary. "He's in town because of golf. He was with friends and decided to swing by."

"Good gracious, no." Gram shook her head. Wagged her finger. Even stomped a foot. Her full *absolutely not* repertoire. "I do not appreciate anyone just *swinging by*. Honestly, what is wrong with this younger generation?"

Gram opposed any and all visits without an invitation. Courtesy demanded you get permission before you showed up at a person's house. I'd always believed this was more of a Gram rule than a general society rule, but she really got pissed when people violated it.

She continued to vent. "When did schools stop teaching manners?"

I didn't have the energy for an etiquette discussion. "Probably in the eighteen hundreds."

"And that strut of his." Gram's finger kept wagging. "It was off-putting."

"The point is she isn't cheating on Jackson." Celia smiled at Gram. "I knew she wouldn't."

This might be the most confusing family conversation in the history of family conversations.

"I'm not sure what you think you saw, but Jackson and I aren't together." A sharp pain stabbed my chest. I pretended it was from heartburn and unrelated to how hard it was to say that sentence out loud.

Celia's smile fell. "But for years—"

"Celia, no."

After all the back-and-forth they stopped talking. "Now you two clam up?"

"If you're not . . ." Celia visibly swallowed. "Why kiss?"

"It just happened. We didn't plan it." I couldn't give a better answer because I still didn't know what the kiss meant or how it fit into the rest of my life. If I could get ten minutes of peace I might be able to figure it out.

Celia's questioning stare hadn't eased. "And the dinners?"

"I like to eat."

"I thought Jackson would . . ." Celia stopped talking when Gram touched her arm. "Never mind."

They thought they could just throw those words out there and not follow up. Nope. We babbled about Brock for fifteen minutes, which was fourteen more than necessary. This topic—Jackson—needed more attention.

"It's your life, dear. You'll figure it out." If Celia thought she'd sold that as an offhand remark she was dead wrong.

"Let me get you a cupcake." Gram said something to Celia without using words and they scampered off toward the kitchen.

Weirdly enough, I didn't want a cupcake.

CHAPTER TWENTY-NINE

"A bigail was at the house." Jackson repeated my point for the third time. "Standing in Mags's kitchen?"

We really needed to move this along. He told me he'd arranged to meet his father at the condo right about now. Jackson tried to call a few minutes ago and wave his dad off but couldn't reach him. The clashing of our schedules was my fault, not Harlan's. I'd stopped by without warning. I hoped to be long gone before Harlan arrived in all his glorious splendor.

This was why Gram had those call-first visitation rules. I got it now.

We stood in Jackson's quiet family room with the television turned off. No music. Not a pillow out of place. Not a dish or cup on the kitchen counter. Not a stray scrap of mail floating around. The place had a show-home feel. Classy not flashy. Streamlined with soothing colors. Basically, it looked like no one lived there.

My initial plan didn't include rushing through my new Abigail information. Drawing out the visit, testing the attraction, maybe working in another kiss before talking about poison—because kiss before poison was the right order—sounded good. Then Gram and Celia unloaded on me, and a hundred topics jumbled in my brain, all of which had to be sorted before Harlan showed up.

Celia and Gram knew about the kiss. Hell, knowing them they might have photos of it. They'd danced around their concerns about it happening but the fact they had any concerns was confusing. Did they really have a problem with the kiss?

Jackson slipped off his suit jacket and tie and sat down next to me on the couch. "Abigail being with Mags and Celia doesn't necessarily—"

"Jackson." No. We were not playing this game. "Don't even try to make it make sense."

"She's a client."

Why were we debating this? The woman probably offed her nasty spouse. Thanks to seeing Abigail in person, talking with her, I grew more confident about my conclusion the more I thought about it. The open question was if Gram and Celia's fingerprints were all over this mess. "The woman just lost her husband and is under suspicion for his murder. Instead of grieving in private, she's running around town, visiting Celia and Gram."

Jackson lounged, looking calm but engaged. "People handle death in different ways."

"I get that. I'm not a fan of competitive grieving or telling people how they should act when they lose someone."

As a person who waded knee-deep in family trauma for most of my life, I understood how complex and complicated grief could be. Pain could sneak up and drop you to your knees at unexpected times, often after years of being tucked away and cordoned off. Seeing a mother and daughter walking in the park. Standing in line behind a woman with the exact shade of brown hair that you'd seen in family photos.

Smelling chocolate cake, my mom's favorite.

Riding out the alternating waves of fury and agony was a job society demanded survivors perform in private, behind thick walls where sound and light couldn't penetrate. Mourning was fine but once the body of this precious person was laid in the ground your grieving needed to find an outlet, a quiet one that didn't make other people uncomfortable. It was your job to transform, rise above, be brave, and move on . . . or pretend to.

Living that lie ate up an enormous amount of energy. So did keeping the despair at bay. The hard fact was that you didn't overcome a loss of that magnitude or grow to accept it. If you were lucky you found a way to survive it. Even then, rage could burn uncontrolled, begging for an outlet.

Dragging out those murky memories and dissecting them had a time and a place but this wasn't it. So many issues fired around Jackson and me. So many ways to trip up. We needed to talk this through, and "this" meant one of many open topics.

I focused on the most obvious one, and the supposed reason for my visit. "We can make up excuses but why was Abigail at the house? Because she wanted a cupcake? The cupcakes are great, but I doubt that's the reason."

He opened his mouth then closed it again. Whatever lecture he planned to give seemed to vanish. "I don't know."

That is not where I thought he was going with that windup. "You never say that."

"I'm not an asshole. I don't pretend to know everything."

His fingers slipped into my hair. The light touch kicked off a yearning I didn't have the strength to lasso and subdue. "No, you're not an asshole. Confusing. Frustrating. Hotter than you have a right to be, but not an asshole."

"Want to talk about the 'hotter' part?" He flashed a smile that said *who cares about any issue but this one?*

"No." Didn't need to. The thought played nonstop in my mind these days.

"You once told me I looked like a car ran over my face."

I laughed because younger me had been quite the charmer. "I was nine at the time and you deserved it. You tattled to Gram about my eating a chunk of Celia's birthday cake before the party."

"You did eat it."

Not quite. I ate three chunks then had to deal with a different type of chunk. I threw up for an hour but was that the point? "No one likes a teenage narc."

"My job was to lie and take the blame for you?"

"Nice of you to finally admit it. Yes. And you've grown into your face. It's cute now."

He pretended to weigh those words. "I think that was a compliment."

"I kissed you last night, didn't I?" Yep. I brought up the topic I'd planned to avoid until absolutely necessary. Dragged it out and set it on the table in front of us.

Smooth.

"Technically, I kissed you," he said.

I saw it that way, too. "It was mutual."

"And amazing."

His fingers dipped deeper into my hair and his thigh pressed against mine. That uniquely Jackson scent wrapped around me, knocking out what little common sense I still possessed.

"Are you flirting with me?" *Please say yes.*

"The fact you can't tell is very frustrating. How exactly do men in DC date?"

Talk about killing the mood. My mind flipped to my last few dates, and I renewed my vow never to pick a blind date over a night in, watching a *Housewives* TV marathon, again. "You don't want to know."

"I'd like to kiss you again."

My heart took off on a wild roller-coaster ride. He'd barely touched me while he whispered the words I longed to hear. My self-protective shields crumbled.

Still, a woman could not be too careful. Rushing in—my lifelong method of doing anything—was the wrong choice here. Our lives were too bound up and interconnected for that. "Why?"

His eyes widened. "*Why?*"

"It's a legitimate question. You've spent years being annoyed by me. You've never shown any interest before now." I refused to describe our first kiss again as an example, especially after his mouth dropped open like that. "What's with the face?"

"For a smart woman you can be pretty clueless."

His thumb brushed against the skin on the base of my neck. The shiver that ran through me almost knocked me off the couch. He had to have felt it.

I didn't even know what we were talking about anymore.

"What if I kissed you right now?" he asked.

No thinking it through and weighing the consequences. "I wouldn't stop you."

That sexy smile of his made another appearance. "Interesting."

He cradled my head in his palm. The pull between us tugged

until my body leaned in. My mouth hovered an inch from his. "I'm a complex woman."

"That you are."

Then his mouth was on mine. This kiss, scorching and fierce, made the same demands as the last one. Stop worrying. Lose the inhibitions. Don't think about what could go wrong. Dive in and feel. I mentally said yes to all of it.

The kiss raged on. He lifted his mouth long enough for his breath to brush over my cheek, then our lips met again. The couch cushion dipped, bringing his body tight against mine. My hands roamed over his shoulders. His arms wrapped around me.

When his mouth moved to my neck every nerve ending kicked to life. My eyes begged to close so my body could savor the moment. My brain started to shut down. I fought to remember why I came to the condo and what mattered so much that I had to see him that night.

Oh, right. "We're supposed to come up with a plan for me to come clean with Gram and Celia."

I sounded breathless and blamed that thing he was doing with his tongue. What was that? If his mouth skimmed over my ear one more time he'd find me on his lap.

"That's definitely a later problem." He sounded equally out of breath as his hand slid down my side. His fingers slipped under the hem of my shirt. "I suggest we table any conversation about other people and deadly concoctions."

He pressed gently, pushing our bodies down deeper into the cushions. I pulled him in close. Brought his body tight against mine as my back hit the couch.

"I suppose you think that's sexy lawyer talk."

He lifted his head just long enough to wink at me. "I can give you sexy talk, if that's what you want."

That deep voice was going to be the death of me.

I wanted his suit off and to somehow get to his bedroom. He had one, right? Who the hell knew at this point.

"Dad won't be here for . . ." He glanced up at the clock. "Oh, shit."

Harlan. Yep, the mention of his name killed the moment. I relaxed into the pillows stacked behind me and sighed because sighing seemed like the right call.

"Gram and Celia saw us kiss." The words popped out. It took me a second to realize I was the idiot who said them.

Jackson froze above me but didn't get up. "What?"

I was in it now. If we were going to kill the mood, we might as well stomp on it and bury it as well. "They were lurking at the upstairs window. We really need to find them a hobby."

He frowned. "They told you they saw the kiss?"

His body slipped over mine in a way I'd dreamed about for years, but we were talking about the ladies. An unsettling combination and pretty much the norm for us lately. "They thought I was cheating on my boyfriend with you."

"What boyfriend?" He didn't shout but got really close.

"Brock."

Jackson shook his head but that didn't clear the confusion in his eyes. "That guy?"

"Now you know how I felt during the entire conversation with them."

"Okay . . ." He lifted his body up on his elbows.

I detested even that small distance between us. "They're very up in our business."

The familiar sound of the doorbell rang out and Jackson lowered his head in what looked like defeat. "I can't catch a break here."

"It's been that kind of day."

"I'm sure it's Dad." Jackson exhaled. "I'd say his timing sucks but I'm the one who invited him tonight. This is on me."

I could smell Jackson's hair. Run my fingers through it. Breathe in the scent of him.

Then I thought about Harlan and how Jackson had to be adopted because they were too different to be blood related. "I wanted to be long gone before he got here. Then you lured me to the dark side with that hot mouth of yours. I forgot about Harlan because I never think of Harlan and kissing at the same time."

"That last part is especially good to hear."

Jackson sat up and took me with him. Our arms and legs tangled. Neither of us rushed to separate or open the door to Harlan.

The doorbell rang again. As if I needed another reason not to like Harlan. "I don't suppose you have a window ledge I could hide on."

"You're afraid of heights."

"It was a joke." I stared at the window, trying to figure out how high off the ground the third floor actually was. "Mostly."

He brushed my hair off my face. "You could—"

"I'll hide in the bedroom." I didn't wait for his vote. I jumped up and nearly dropped again when my knees buckled.

He stood up in time to catch me. Didn't miss a beat. "Or you could be here when Dad comes in because we're adults. You're allowed to be in my house. In fact, I want you in my house."

Those strong hands against my back. That cute face hovering above mine. A woman could get used to this. "You're the only Quaid man I'm interested in spending any time with."

He wiggled his eyebrows, which was both cute and the least Jackson move ever. "We're going to talk about that after Dad leaves."

"I'm about talked out for one day. Gram and Celia were on fire."

Banging this time. No more doorbell. It sounded like Harlan had switched to pounding his fist against the door. I could hear him calling out for Jackson.

"Let him in before he ticks off the neighbors. I'll be in the coat closet, so make his visit short." Not the most adult thing I'd ever said, but not the worst either. "You don't want to disappoint him."

Jackson's smile fell. "But I always do."

CHAPTER THIRTY

The closet barely had room for coats let alone a grown woman. I crouched between a distressed-leather jacket and what looked like a proper black raincoat. I didn't own that type of coat because that's what umbrellas were for, but I'd bought one for Gram. It had a green background with huge yellow and pink daisies all over it. I got a headache just looking at it, which was how I knew she had to have it.

Standing there regretting most of my life choices lately, including the choice to hide, I waited to hear the welcome chat I assumed happened between parents and their kids when they saw each other. Hugs, pats on the back, that sort of thing.

Harlan jumped right to complaining. "I'm happy you finally made time to see me."

"I work, Dad."

Seemed obvious but probably not the real reason Jackson had put his dad off. Harlan should have been smart enough to know when his kid was avoiding him, but maybe not.

"I'm here now and ready to talk. Despite your waffling, your meeting went well. At least it did according to the team."

The team. Harlan's team. I'd never met the team but questioned every person handpicked by Harlan.

"As predicted, you haven't offered up details. That's why I'd planned to sit in at the restaurant. It was for your benefit. To skip the step where you had to remember every word and relay it to me," Harlan said. "Why did you lead me to believe the financing people were no longer interested? They were very impressed. Praised your presentation and speaking skills."

Jackson sighed and was pretty loud about it, too. "This isn't about what they thought. This is about me. My goals."

I peeked through the thin crack at the edge of the door. Not the best angle but I could see two figures, standing in the kitchen. Their posture looked anything but relaxed and comfortable. I knew how they felt because the hanger poking into my back didn't feel great either.

"Jackson, you can't waste this golden opportunity. People would steal and kill to have the spotlight you're getting. The meetings might not be your favorite thing, but they're a road to a better position. To power."

"I don't care about any of that."

Good for Jackson. He wasn't backing down. He was handling the situation like he might handle a difficult client. Clear voice. On his feet and ready for battle.

"Son, come on. Don't let her visit derail you," Harlan said.

Oh . . . wait.

Every part of me clenched. The muscles across my upper back and shoulders tightened and strained to the point of cramping. I put a hand over my mouth because my breathing echoed and pinged in my head. So loud that I waited for Harlan to throw open the closet door and find me standing there.

"I know you . . ." Harlan visibly weighed his words before starting again. "Listen. She's a lovely girl. She's from here. Constituents love that, but the compatibility ends there. She's not going to help you get the life you want."

"*You* want. Not me." The edge in Jackson's voice grew more pronounced.

Where was a window ledge when you needed one? Hiding out there might have blocked the memory of Harlan calling me *lovely* in a tone that sounded anything but. Putting unnecessary pressure on his son. Dragging me into this politicking nightmare. The list of Harlan's loving-father violations grew longer by the second.

This conversation could take a nasty turn but I couldn't look or walk away. Literally. The small closet space didn't allow for any maneuvering. Forfeiting all sense of self-preservation, I pressed my head tight against the door's seam and waited for Harlan to say more shitty things disguised as compliments. Since I was stuck in there without an end in sight, I didn't want to miss a syllable of the conversation.

"You were on board with the plan. The financial team put together a strategy. I lined up a series of informal get-togethers with some of the state's more influential power brokers."

Harlan didn't come up for breath.

"All to ease you in before you have to make speeches and design a platform." Harlan's smooth voice was aimed at convincing and maybe a little shaming. "It was a lot of work, and I was happy to do it, but then she came to town and—"

"Stop." Jackson's voice shook with defiance.

"I understand. I enjoy a pretty woman, too, but you need the right pretty woman. One with gravitas. Speaking ability. The right hobbies. Poise. Elegance. Position. A woman who can charm for donations and act concerned and interested when necessary."

"You make this perfect woman sound like a computer in a nice dress."

Harlan blustered right over Jackson's smart-ass comment. "I'm sure if you contacted Anna you could work out your relationship issues and get back on track. Her father being a judge would be a huge help to you."

Anna. The one from the Christmas muffin incident. How could I forget. I tried, of course, to block her memory. To not to see her perfect blond prettiness and the way she hung on Jackson's arm. Meeting her ruined last Christmas for me.

My general grumpiness heated up. I hadn't reached full-on-hostility level yet, but hovered right on the edge. Anger slipped through my defenses, drowning out my curiosity.

"I've listened to you. Heard you out and thought about your proposal to help me in politics, but you're not listening to me. You're not hearing what I want. I'm a lawyer and a good one. The law firm is where I belong."

Harlan laughed and sounded smug doing it. "You wouldn't be the first lawyer turned politician. It's a logical next step."

"It isn't for me." Jackson sounded done. Frustrated but still in control. "And let's be absolutely clear. The relationship with Anna is over. Forever."

I counted on Jackson's even disposition. He worked under a lot of stress. We bickered back and forth but he never crossed the line or yelled or did anything scary. I joked that this was part of his boring side, but really, that consistency earned my trust from the time I was old enough to understand that many men operated under a very different set of personal rules.

"Are you really going to throw away all this progress, all

this potential, because of a woman who doesn't even live in this state?" Harlan's voice went in and out as he moved around the kitchen. "Again, she's . . . sweet. But that's not good enough for the life you can have."

"We're done talking about this."

"You know I'm right. Kasey lacks her grandmother's drive. Honestly, I've often wondered how someone as successful as Magnolia raised a granddaughter who is so unfocused."

The conversation volleyed back and forth. Neither seemed happy and both referenced me. Forget listening and biding my time. I did not want to be at the center of this discussion. I didn't want to be here at all. If I could slink out and slip away I would.

I put my hand against the door, ready to shove it open. Jackson's stern tone stopped me.

"Enough." The word echoed through the condo. "I'm not going to listen to you berate Kasey. I feel—"

"I know exactly how you feel about her. You haven't been nearly as successful at hiding it as you think. And that mess at Christmas? A complete embarrassment and a forewarning of what life would be like with her."

Jackson made a strangled sound. "I'm a grown man. I'm not doing this with you."

"I hear you." Like that, Harlan's voice returned to normal. All the heat ran out of his tone. He spoke like they'd never disagreed. "I have a business dinner tonight, but we can meet for breakfast tomorrow. Let's sit down and talk this through. No anger. No insults. No talk about Kasey. We'll focus on you and your needs."

"Can't. I have a brief due."

That sounded bogus. I couldn't blame Jackson for putting off a future meeting with his dad, but he needed to up his excuse game.

"I know you're angry and think I'm interfering, but you're too close to this. You can't see what's happening. I really am doing what's best for you."

Correction, best for Harlan. Jackson had to see that. Right?

"We'll find a time tomorrow." Harlan walked toward the door. His expensive dress shoes clicked against the floor. "I know you don't want to hear this and saying it doesn't bring me any satisfaction, but she is going to leave town again. She can't be part of your future equation."

I really disliked Harlan. In that moment I hated him because he was right. My life wasn't here. Jackson wasn't mine. All of the sparks between us amounted to a quick, confusing fling that could derail our long-term relationship and drag in Celia and Gram as collateral damage.

I slipped out of the closet when the front door closed. Instead of turning and going to Jackson, I headed for the entry. I'd wait to avoid a run-in with Harlan, but I needed to get out of the condo before the walls closed in.

"Kasey, don't go."

The pleading. That voice. None of this was Jackson's fault.

"I need some air." Celia was right. Sometimes you needed a fresh breeze to restart your brain.

Jackson stood right behind me with his hand on the door. Heat radiated off him as his body brushed against mine. It would be so easy to lean back. To give in and pretend Harlan didn't exist.

"Dad's agenda is not my agenda."

"He's very strong-willed." My code for *a jackass*.

Jackson exhaled, sounding like he had a bit of frustration left in reserve. "Give me some credit. That conversation wasn't about fatherly concern. He's a bullshitter. He's trying to sway me like he would do with a client."

I turned to face Jackson. Big mistake. He stood so close. So huggable. Kissable. Touchable. I cleared my throat twice before I spit out a discernible word. "He's also not totally wrong. Hanging out with me isn't a great political move for you."

"Even if I cared about politics that's not true."

Oh, Jackson. "I have an imprisoned killer for a father and a murdered mother."

"That's not your fault, and I'm not running for office."

Okay, but . . . "I'm a law school dropout. A serial job loser."

Listing my failures like that, being honest, twisted and knotted my insides to the point of breaking. My family history sucked. My ability to build a career and an adult life was nonexistent.

"You aren't any more responsible for your father and what he did to your mother than I am for my dad and how he treated Mom." Jackson managed a half smile, clearly trying to inject a bit of lightness into a dark moment. "About law school. You hated it. Mags's heart issue made you leave quicker than you otherwise might have, but you were right to get out. It wasn't for you."

He understood that I couldn't stay in school while Gram was in the hospital. I never admitted that to anyone and adamantly denied it when Gram insisted I go back, but Jackson knew.

"Don't act like your dad's view doesn't matter." It had to. How Gram and Celia thought about things mattered to me.

"I love him because he's my dad, but I don't like him very much." Jackson looked around the room, clearly trying to find an anchor or a lifeline and failing. "Age hasn't softened him. He is his own biggest fan. He doesn't apologize for pushing or his condescending advice. He's the same jackass who made my mom's final days a misery. Actually, most of her life but especially her final days."

I remembered Jackson's mom. She'd struck me as frail. A beautiful woman, almost doll-like, whose shoulders stooped a bit more each year. Now I knew the weight of Harlan's disregard shoved her down and kept her there. "She deserved better."

"So did you." Jackson trailed his fingers down my cheek. "Please don't leave like this."

It would have been so easy to give in. So simple to ignore the last fifteen minutes and go back to that couch, but I couldn't. Thoughts and feelings crashed inside me. I didn't know what my hazy confusion meant and needed a minute to pull the images apart and figure them out.

I didn't want to hurt Jackson. I didn't know if I had that kind of power where he was concerned, but he had that hold over me. I didn't want to be hurt.

"Maybe we need a little space." I hated saying that, but I needed to.

He rolled his eyes. "We live almost four hundred miles apart. Honestly, I'm sick of all the space."

His face, that pleading expression, wore me down, which was why I needed to back up and take a break. "We'll talk tomorrow."

I should have walked away without . . . no. I cupped his face in my hands and kissed him. It was sweet and too short but enough to keep a connection pulsing between us despite his father's wishes.

"Tomorrow. I promise." I whispered the word against his lips and meant it. I had a lot to think about before we talked again but we would talk soon.

I tended to run from difficult and confusing emotions. Not this time.

CHAPTER THIRTY-ONE

I did the same thing for the last eighteen hours that I did whenever I ran up against an uncomfortable moment: pivoted and focused on something completely unrelated. Immature and unproductive, I know. I'd perfected the art of avoidance in response to taunting.

You don't get to celebrate Mother's Day because you don't have a mom. Yeah, but I wrote this story about a possum.

Your dad is a killer. Let me tell you this joke.

You can't hold a job. Have you ever tried a cinnamon muffin?

See a roadblock and go around it. Find another street. Take a bus. That's how I operated. I jumped over the minutiae. Kept my focus blurry and engaged in selective hearing.

Years ago, when a ten-year-old classmate figured out why I lived with my grandmother and not my parents, she announced that I was an orphan and blared it all over school. My life turned upside down. My embarrassment-free world disappeared. I learned how to maneuver through a school hallway without getting surrounded by girls pelting me with nasty names.

Survival skills. I called on them now.

The only way I knew to block the sound of Harlan's voice in my head, to blunt his words, was to immerse myself in another project. Last night I stared at the television, not seeing or taking in a word while Gram and Celia explained their favorite show to me in painful detail. This morning I jumped on a new task. One that circled back to Abigail Burns and her dead husband.

Gram and Celia had given me the green light to create the impromptu tickler system for the business. That approval provided the necessary excuse to sit in the baking annex office and go through the business's client and delivery information. No more sneaking around, though I had to admit I missed the adrenaline rush of playing covert operative.

I sat twenty feet from Gram and Celia, watching them through the wall of glass that separated the office from the rest of the room. Gram scurried around, gathering ingredients as she prepared to make muffins and finished off a pie. Celia stood at a table rummaging through labels. She'd decided Mags' Desserts needed a better logo. She'd been eating lunch at a run while playing with samples and fonts since I arrived in North Carolina.

With them preoccupied, I went to work looking through business docs for dead husband intel while trying to invent a better business notification system. It was a multitasking extravaganza and the perfect way to take my mind off any male with the last name Quaid.

After a few hours of intense focus I needed a cupcake and a neck brace. My back ached from hunching over the desk. The star references appeared to be gone forever. I scanned every file looking for a hint of the deleted information and nothing. Then I tried making a list of female client names and searched online, using my phone, to see if there were any deaths, suspicious or otherwise, linked to each name. A tedious project.

Sometimes I found dessert orders in connection with funeral services but that didn't help. I needed a delivery close in time to a death. I'd check a name, make some notes, then delete the internet search history because Gram would check. I'd be disappointed if she didn't.

Trying to build a case and convince Jackson of a possibility based on two names hadn't been totally successful. I couldn't blame him. Even I still didn't know for sure and wasn't fully convinced Gram and Celia assisted in killing bad men, but the suspicion had grown every time a piece of evidence disappeared or their ties to the now-widows had become clearer. I totally thought the women had offed their spouses. It was only Gram and Celia's role that remained fuzzy.

I needed more information before I could confront Gram and Celia and point-blank ask them. And, if my suspicions were correct, I needed to act fast. Neither of the ladies would fare well in prison, though their fellow inmates would learn more than they ever wanted to know about pie.

At closer look, every gift order went out with something extra. A tea towel or a homemade card. Candles for birthdays. The customer files included a list of what items were included with each gift to avoid repetitive items going to the same household for different events. I admired the branding and the extra care. Both were reasons for Gram and Celia to keep the business exactly how it was now. Private and curated. Big corporations wouldn't appreciate the attention to detail. It was too expensive to exploit.

Abigail's delivery hadn't been for a special occasion, but the ladies sent along a towel and a recipe. The notation relating to the recipe said *raisin*. Sounded like a pie rather than a cupcake, although I'd never tasted a raisin pie. I couldn't remember Gram and Celia ever making one.

Curious, I did an internet search. I vowed to be quick and get right back on track. I flipped through photos then I saw it. Raisins, sugar, lemons. An old-fashioned raisin pie. Looked tasty but that's not why I froze in the chair.

Funeral pie.

That was the ominous informal name for this dessert. A coincidence, surely. But . . . was it?

Reading more information didn't help to calm my snapping nerves. The recipe originated in the Pennsylvania Dutch community. For years funerals meant big food spreads and special desserts and who had the money for that? The raisin pie, an inexpensive option, became a favorite decades ago. Some people made the pie to signal to the community that a death was imminent; others brought them to memorial get-togethers. Hence the name funeral pie.

A mix of disbelief and dread churned in my stomach. This could mean . . . but, no . . . too obvious, right? Well, obvious but totally not because who in this century would associate a notation about raisins to poisoning bad husbands?

I forced my body to relax. Panic knocked but I refused to let it in.

Breathe in. Breathe out.

Think, think, think.

Another search in the client information and delivery files, looking for other raisin notations. If all the clients during a certain time period got a copy of the same recipe, that would remove the punch from finding something called a funeral pie in the client file of a lady with an unexpectedly dead husband.

If only Abigail got the recipe, maybe it was something she requested and not a big deal.

A few clicks and . . . yeah, neither of those things was true.

Abigail got the raisin recipe. The other woman from the now-deleted star column, Delilah Rhine, also got one. Over a ten-month period, four ladies got the recipe. Another three women got a recipe for "raisin and custard." After a second online search, I knew that some people made funeral pie with custard and some without.

Stop or press on? I could back away and never peek at the business's documents again. Pretend ignorance and hope the ladies covered their tracks. Mind my own business.

Yeah, that last one wasn't really my thing.

The steady buzz of baking continued just outside the office. Gram and Celia laughed about something. I could see mixing bowls and spatulas with yummy bits left on them. I wanted to go in there and take a lick, but I couldn't.

Thanks to the wonders of computers and search engines, I had my answer in twenty minutes. None of the three women who received the raisin and custard recipes had a dead husband or other dead family member mentioned in the press. That seemed like a good sign except there were news stories about two of them. One referenced a domestic violence altercation that resulted in a restraining order against the husband. In another case, the woman's husband was arrested for stealing money from his office. An unnamed informant tipped the company off.

More coincidences.

This is the point where Jackson would caution me against jumping to conclusions. No chance of that. I jumped, leapt, and bounced to a conclusion. Suspicion morphed into something bigger. I didn't have to squint to see Gram and Celia's fingerprints all over this. Were they running some sort of informal charity to assist women with shitty husbands? Knowing them, quite possibly.

The coincidences pile-up continued when I figured out that all four ladies who received the raisin pie recipes—no custard—lost their husbands unexpectedly and within a short period of time of getting the recipe from Gram and Celia. The questionable timing included Delilah and Abigail.

So . . . yeah. Mission accomplished. Sort of. I now had more information. The women who got these "special" recipes, one version or the other, mostly had obviously problematic husbands and a few were now widows. Potentially scary information that may or may not link Gram and Celia to poison and dead men.

I looked up and saw Celia's face through the glass. She smiled at me. Waved. Pointed to a batter-covered spatula, inviting me to take a taste.

Delicious desserts. Desperate women. Recipe cards. Funeral pie.

What the hell had they done?

CHAPTER THIRTY-TWO

I seriously thought about hiding in the office for the rest of my life. Take away the glass walls and maybe. With Gram and Celia both staring at me, pinning me down, my options dwindled. I had to go out there. Had to confront them. Had to talk with Jackson. The only question was the proper order for all of those things.

What a mess.

I pretended to work for another five minutes. There was no reason to rush this. The problem—and what an understatement that was—wouldn't magically resolve itself and go away. Any chance of bolting ended with the funeral pie recipe discovery. Ignoring the situation ceased to be an option, to the extent it ever was.

Almost three o'clock. Hours before I could fill in Jackson and drag him over here. He'd probably leave work and come running if I raised the alarm, but what could he do now that couldn't wait? The dead husbands weren't coming back. We had enough problems without that horror.

My stomach growled. I'd worked through lunch. It was only a few minutes to the informal tea and dessert time I'd been enjoying with Celia and Gram most days. The in-between pseudo-meal meant to calm and soothe. Today everything could go to hell if I wasn't careful.

I opened the door into the main room before my confidence faltered. The strategy of listening more than I talked made sense but Gram could beat most schemes with her bullshit radar. She could tell when someone, namely me, was withholding information. That skill had destroyed many teenage plans before I could launch them.

I was older but so was she. Wiser and more cunning, too. I didn't stand a chance of getting through the next hour without spilling all my theories.

"Are you hungry?" Celia called out the question from the middle of the room.

"Always." Not a lie but not my main concern at the moment. It was difficult to ignore the potentially poisoned elephant in the room.

Act cool. Do not panic. My brain sent out those commands. Would have been nice if it included a how-to guide.

Celia pointed to the place settings on the small table off to the side used for breaks. "We have some pastries and tea, but if you want—"

"Yes."

Too quick. The way Celia and Gram looked at me. My response had them mentally switching to high alert.

"Sorry. I blame the missed lunch. The lack of calories makes me grumpy." Again, totally true. I operated more effectively on a full stomach.

Gram didn't say a word in response to my fumbled explanation. She hummed.

That deadly accurate humming.

"What's wrong?" I immediately regretted asking the question.

Neither of them responded. They were too busy doing that spooky communicate-without-talking thing they'd perfected.

Acting normal meant licking spatulas and enjoying an unhealthy dose of batter. I glanced around at the bowls and utensils, making sure I picked the right snack. Nothing said I couldn't enjoy while I stalled. I eyed the delicious, totally unhealthy array of unused icing and batter that begged to be tasted and picked one.

The only bowl in the sink won. I leaned over the counter, balanced on the edge, and swooped in to grab the spoon resting on the side. My feet barely hit the floor again when Celia rushed over.

"No!" She slapped the spatula out of my hand before it reached my mouth.

The spoon made a clinking sound as it landed. Batter splashed in a spray across the floor and the tips of my sneakers. We all stared at the sugary puddle. It looked like a crime scene but stained with yellow instead of blood.

I liked drama as much as the next gal, but an explanation would be nice. I stopped staring at the lost batter and turned my attention to the two ladies who'd better start talking and soon. "Uh, hello?"

Celia winced. "Sorry, I panicked. You can't eat that."

Incorrect. Nothing wrong with eating off the floor. I wouldn't only because I had some self-control. Not much but some. "Well, not now."

Gram dropped a towel on the batter spill. Without a hint of hesitation, she used her foot on the cloth to wipe up the mess. "It's bad for you."

Because of the poison? They didn't say it, but I could fill in the blank. Now I wanted to hear how they verbally danced around the truth.

"I eat batter all the time. Germs be damned. I'm not choosy."

"That is the golden milk cupcake batter," Gram explained.

Celia's wide eyes and pale face didn't bode well. Panic still thrummed off her. "Right. Golden milk."

The description sounded kind of delicious. I'd have to lick it off the floor to find out. Any other day, definitely. "Which means what?"

"It's made with milk mixed with cinnamon and ginger," Gram said.

That didn't sound like a recipe for poison. And the answer didn't clear up my confusion. The good news was that they didn't want me sucking down potentially contaminated batter, which I appreciated.

"It also has turmeric and you've had an issue with turmeric in the past. An intolerance." Celia visibly calmed down. Her jerky movements smoothed out and her eyes returned to their normal size. "Belly discomfort."

"Last time you ate something with turmeric you threw up for a half hour."

Thanks, Gram. As if I didn't know what Celia meant.

Celia continued. "It's too dangerous to take the risk. You can eat something else."

They possessed a lot of turmeric information all of a sudden. But they weren't wrong. The memory of the turmeric chicken and rice dish haunted me. Seven years ago. I came home from college during spring break. One of Gram's friends had brought over a one-pot meal for us to try. It smelled delicious and had this pretty yellow tint.

So much vomiting. At first I blamed the fact I ate three full plates of food in record time, but no. So, it was true. The turmeric wouldn't be great for me.

Neither would poison.

All their talk sounded plausible, but they might be saving me and themselves by making up a story. Proving that struck me as impossible now that Gram had mopped up the evidence. I could sneak the spoon out of the kitchen and have the batter remnants tested. The thought floated through my mind then back out again. As if I knew how to test for poison or who was qualified to do it.

"Tea?" Celia smiled as if the last ten minutes hadn't happened.

I looked at my batter-stained shoes. Looked at Gram. Tried to believe this was how my day had turned out. Then shrugged. "Sure."

Time for a showdown. Right after I ate a non-poisoned muffin.

CHAPTER THIRTY-THREE

Before I could take another step Harlan came in. Harlan. Of course, Harlan. Apparently the man didn't have a job other than to show up wherever I was in Winston-Salem and make me miserable.

He smiled. "Good afternoon."

Friendly. Warm. His expression put me on the defensive. In graph form, Harlan and the concept of genuine charm were two nonoverlapping circles.

"I thought it might be teatime and I could join you." He gestured in the direction of the table Celia and Gram had set up for the break. "May I?"

It was a table set for three, but sure. Celia and Gram wouldn't kick him out. Actually, Gram might. She didn't possess the play-nice gene like Celia did. What likely saved him from a one-way ticket out of the annex was his friendly tone. No pontificating. No self-congratulatory bullshit. His usual punch of ego and fake chivalry mysteriously had gone missing.

Until I knew what game this was and what his sneaky little plans were, I would watch and wait.

Gram looked as skeptical as I felt. "This is new. You stopping by in the late afternoon for no reason."

A major slip-up on his part. Do not come uninvited and

expect to be fed. I hoped Gram's narrowed eyes meant she planned on ushering him out of the building soon.

Through it all, his smile didn't waver. "We're family, after all."

Hell, no.

Gram looked ready to spit. "Actually—"

Celia stopped Gram's incoming lecture with a hand on her arm.

Bummer. I say let Gram loose.

"Come on in and join us." Celia motioned to Harlan then to me. "Kasey?"

Celia had to know how much this sucked for everyone, including Celia. Only Harlan had the power to ruin a dessert and tea break. His presence put me on edge and guaranteed I wouldn't be able to eat much.

The four of us sat down. The baking frenzy in the annex had calmed down about an hour ago when the assistants left for the day. Gram had insisted she could finish up. Of course, she hadn't expected the turmeric incident or for Harlan to descend on her.

With the tea poured and the plates passed around, I fought to come up with a nice, neutral conversation topic.

"This is delicious." He sipped tea, leaving the piece of pie in front of him untouched.

Strike two. First the surprise visit and now the failure to dig in to dessert.

Whatever thought ran around in his little mind was going to come out and really suck. I'd bet the $634 in my checking account on it.

"I should be upset, you know." He delivered the comment in a light, conversational tone.

I knew better than to be fooled. He had an agenda. He'd made that clear when he suggested Jackson rekindle his romance with Anna. The adrenaline pumping through me said Harlan's seemingly innocuous comment about the tea was a windup. He was easing us in, which would make the hit so much harder.

Gram took the bait. "About what?"

"You're keeping such a big piece of news from me." He glanced in my direction then looked at Gram again. "You could have come to me for help. I would have been happy to step in and guide you."

He shot another glance in my direction. This one lasted a bit longer, delivered with a hint of a challenge.

Oh, shit.

Celia frowned. "Guide us where?"

"What are you talking about?" Gram's voice suggested she wasn't in the mood for Harlan's riddles.

That made two of us. Letting him play his game could lead to a dark place. I tried to pivot. "Maybe we should enjoy the tea?"

"Harlan should explain first," Gram said.

Yeah, I figured that derailment wouldn't work.

Harlan set his teacup down nice and slow. Made a big, dramatic scene of it, ensuring he had our collective attention.

Then he lowered the boom. "The sale."

Gram snorted. "Excuse me?"

"What sale?" Celia asked at the same time.

I was in hell.

Harlan picked up that stupid little cup again and sipped the tea like he was at a cotillion. "There are rumors. This type of information finds its way to me because of my position in town and my work with people in power."

It looked like his ego had arrived.

"Are you enjoying your tea?" Harlan asked me.

I waited for the floor to open up and suck me down. Make that *hoped*. I hoped for that to happen.

Now the unwanted visit made sense. This was a message for me. He was coming for me in his usual *look how important I am* way, not caring who he took out with his shot.

"Harlan, what are you talking about?" Celia refilled his cup. "What sale?"

"There's a rumor going around the business community that you two plan to sell Mags' Desserts."

Boom.

"More specifically, that you are looking for a buyer to step in and handle additional expansion." Harlan continued, clearly impressed with his ability to choke the life out of a room. "Someone who would take over the running of the business, make the decisions, pay you a fair amount of money, of course, then become your partner. Senior partner."

Celia stopped moving. Mouth hanging open, cup tilted.

Gram's face turned red as she prepared to explode.

I sat there hating Harlan.

"Naturally, I was skeptical. Clearly, you would have brought something like that to me before taking it to others, especially firms out of state." He stopped to take another sip of tea.

Well, crap. He knew. This jackass had figured out my pitch problem or dug around and made an educated guess. No way did Jackson fill him in. Jackson wouldn't do that. He could be rigid and overly certain he was right on every issue, even a tad unbending, but he wouldn't pretend to work with me while selling me out.

This was all Harlan. He looked too sure. Too proud of his bullshit. And . . . wait. What had Brock said during our last heated meeting? Something about neutralizing Jackson and the legal end of the deal. That couldn't mean . . . but . . . I looked at Harlan's smug face and knew my fear was correct. Brock and Harlan. I'd rather take my chances and eat a shovelful of turmeric than deal with those two together.

Celia shook her head. "We didn't go to you or anyone else because we have no intention of selling."

"Where did you hear this nonsense?" Gram sounded spitting mad. "People should be ashamed of themselves for telling these sorts of lies."

Harlan glanced at me again. "I'm trying to remember exactly who told me."

Get out in front of this. An offensive strike. It was a little late but my one chance. "I think—"

"I got a call." Harlan set his cup down again and waved off Celia when she went to refill it. "See, I'm the man in North Carolina who outsiders go to with proposals like these. I have a reputation for assisting in deals that would benefit the state and, frankly, in persuading outsiders to look elsewhere if the deals are a detriment to the people who shape local interests."

Talk, talk, talk. So many words and all of them aimed at telling us how important he was. His ego needed its own chair at the table.

He kept right on yapping. "It's true this isn't my exact area of expertise, but it's related due to the sale implications. I can connect like-minded successful business professionals and also clear some of the regulatory hurdles and paperwork requirements. I know the players. And, as you would expect, the people who run the state like to keep the money and businesses in the state."

The room spun. The round and round made the kitchen smear into this hazy blur. Dizzy. Nauseated. Pissed off. I managed to be all three at once.

"Take your expertise in whatever you're an expert at and go somewhere else. A sale is not happening." Gram made that sound like an order.

"It's okay." Celia rested a hand on Gram's arm but kept her focus on Harlan. "Again, we're not interested."

Harlan nodded before looking at me. "What do you think, Kasey?"

That he should leave. Get in his fancy car and go back to his fancy house or fancy club.

I went with an answer that didn't involve stuffing his head in a toilet. "Gram and Celia are in charge. If they say they're not selling, you should drop it."

Gram pointed at the table, drumming her fingertip into the wood. "And tell your crusty-suited friends to keep their hands off my business."

"Mags, it's okay." Celia gave Gram's arm a squeeze. "This is a misunderstanding. Harlan can see that."

"Sounds like I received some faulty information." Without warning or touching his pie, he stood up. "I'll look into the rumors and report back. It's important that you know who's trying to undermine you."

Trip him! The tempting message shouted in my head.

Celia gave him a tight smile. The kind that silently said *get out.* "We would appreciate that."

"People have some nerve." Gram talked to the room in general. She didn't aim the words. She didn't have to.

Score one for Harlan. He got exactly the reaction he wanted. He put me on notice without showing his full hand. He let Celia and Mags know something was brewing. If my heartbeat ever returned to normal, I might be able to stop shaking. Anger gripped me and my brain begged to lash out.

"Kasey?" Harlan had the nerve to smile at me again. Like we were dear friends, which we weren't, dear or otherwise. "Why don't you walk me out?"

Gram was too busy grumbling and Celia was too busy trying to calm her down to notice I was being led to the slaughter. "Sure."

We walked across the big room in silence. He opened the door and stepped outside, leaving me standing there staring at him.

"I came today specifically to speak with you. I like you, Kasey."

So smarmy. "Obviously."

"I need you to understand the lengths I'll go to in order to secure Jackson's future and ensure he doesn't overlook the tremendous opportunities in front of him."

A future Harlan didn't want me to be a part of. Got it. "I'm not sure why you're so worried about me. I'm in town to visit my family."

"That's not what my informal poking around suggested.

You'll be happy to know your boss was very receptive to my offer of assistance. He seems to think the deal has stalled. I promised I would step in, use my contacts, and be very persuasive on his behalf." Harlan smiled. "He's a smart man and appreciated how beneficial it would be to have an open line through me to the power brokers in the state."

This jackass was every bad TV politician rolled into one. "All of this effort because you think I'll corrupt Jackson."

"I'm trying to help you. Mags and Celia never need to know you're the one who put their business in the spotlight. Ripe for the picking." His smile faded a bit. "It would be best if you removed yourself from suspicion and went back to DC. If you're not here I can provide cover. Otherwise, my hands will be tied."

There was nothing subtle about that threat.

Harlan glanced at his watch, as if to make sure I knew how little this conversation meant to him. "I took Jackson out of the middle of this. Because I didn't want you to get in trouble with Mags, I took you out. Everything will now go through me."

Was I supposed to thank him? "What do you get out of all this interference?"

"That's not your concern." He winked. "Have a safe trip home."

Blowhard. Annoying. Controlling. I tried to imagine Jackson as a kid, looking for love and validation from this empty suit of a guy. Expecting Harlan to cheer him on at sporting events and when he got into Princeton then learning that Harlan couldn't step away from the mirror long enough to put anyone else first.

"Next time call before you come over. It's rude to show up where you're not wanted." I shut the door in his face before he could offer a snide reply.

His backroom maneuvering wouldn't win this time. No matter what it cost me.

CHAPTER THIRTY-FOUR

The satisfaction of dismissing Harlan didn't last long. Not when I turned around and saw Celia and Gram standing there, waiting for me to rejoin them.

"What was that little side conversation about?" The pissiness hadn't left Gram's voice. Harlan's game playing had set her off. It would be hours before her grumbling and whispered swearing disappeared.

In her volatile mood, I didn't want to challenge her. Not in any mood, actually, but especially now. I turned to my go-to move. Babbling.

"Nothing important. The usual." I shrugged because it fit with my futile attempt to pull off no-big-deal energy. "Not really . . . You know."

Gram's eyes narrowed. "I don't. Explain."

Pivot. Pivot. Pivot.

"To be fair, no one *wants* to talk with Harlan. Doing so makes us all a bit testy," Celia said as she moved around the table, picking up Harlan's used cup and eliminating any evidence he once sat there.

Thank you, Celia.

She dumped the uneaten pie in the sink. "We deal with him, on as limited a basis as we can make it, because he doesn't give us any choice."

I waited, hoping Celia's comments would shift Gram's focus. And . . . they did.

"I should have known when he came by for tea that he had an ulterior motive." Gram sat down and poured herself a fresh cup of Earl Grey. "He doesn't drink tea. He doesn't even recognize a good dessert when it's sitting in front of him. Did you see the pie? He didn't touch it." She snorted. "Outrageous."

Never change, Gram. "Yes, the most annoying thing about Harlan is his lack of pie appreciation."

Celia sighed at both of us before returning to her seat at the table. "Maybe you two can lower the sarcasm level for a few minutes."

"And this sale nonsense? Where did that come from?" Gram went ahead and answered her own question as she sat down. "From Harlan's tiny head. That's where."

Well, actually . . .

"It's a mistake, Mags. Bad information. Nothing more." Celia put her hand over Gram's and held it there for a few seconds before moving on to scone distribution.

"He's tried this before. Remember?" Gram shook her head. "He never learns."

"What?" I sat down and listened because this was news to me. "When?"

"It's no big deal." Celia kept pouring and setting out plates. "We said no, and he stopped lobbying us."

Another snort from Gram. "He's clearly not done trying."

"Hold up." They'd lost me, likely on purpose. "What exactly did he do?"

"He presented us with a proposal about a year ago. Talked about how he'd usher the deal and spouted off his *with me you'll get the best deal* nonsense." Gram mimicked Harlan's voice in a way that would have been funny if the words weren't so familiar. "His idea was to take the company national. Expand the customer base. Become a household name and bring more attention to North Carolina ingenuity."

"And more attention to him. It was clear he wanted to leverage our business to increase his profile and convince those in power that he was irreplaceable," Celia said.

The play sounded familiar. NOI excelled at that type of maneuvering. Brock bragged more than once about finding a business's weakness and leaning on it to "convince" those in charge to sell.

Why the hell did I drag Mags' Desserts into this vicious world?

"Harlan talked about us getting a paycheck with *lots of zeros*. He kept saying we'd never have to worry about money again." Gram blew by a snort and moved right to her famous *pfft*. "I don't worry about money now, not regularly. We're fine."

Celia shot me an intense look. "We are."

They didn't need Harlan and his money. They didn't need NOI or my interference.

A gnawing tension moved in and ticked up in intensity. Once these ladies knew the whole story about the business sale the usual calm of the room would shatter.

"I surely don't need businessmen coming in here telling me how to make a damn pie," Gram started muttering under her breath.

I caught a few words. Some were profane. None of them were nice.

Celia ripped her scone into pieces. "Mags's mood is a reflection of a provision in Harlan's proposal that would have limited our ability to make desserts and sell them even to friends."

"Prohibited it thanks to some noncompete nonsense." Gram's voice grew louder with each word. "He acted so helpful. Even said he'd run the business until sale. Him."

Gram like to refer to Harlan as a toad. She was right. The guy was a toad.

"A betrayal. That's what that was." Gram sounded fighting mad. "What does he know about desserts? Nothing."

True, but I'd be happier if they didn't throw words like "betrayal" around so freely.

"A sale." Gram worked in one more snort. "As if I'd forfeit control and put that man in charge."

"Well then." Celia sent Gram a stern look that said *that's enough* before turning to me. "I'm sorry you were here for his visit."

Gram wasn't ready to stop. "I'm sorry any of us were."

"We don't like to bother you with assorted business details." Celia finally dropped the scone remains. She had crumbs and pieces scattered all over her plate like pastry shrapnel.

Celia didn't engage in nervous fidgeting. She tended to be the calm one. The one who didn't grump and stomp around. Seeing Celia in a restless state started alarm bells ringing in my head.

"It's not your job to worry about us," Celia said, as if she knew the direction of my thoughts.

Nice try at placating, but she was wrong about this. Dead wrong.

"That's not actually how family works." I pointed at both of them. "You two taught me that."

"Harlan's wishes are irrelevant. We had no intention of selling back then and no intention now." Celia managed a partial and completely unnatural smile. "We've expanded fine without his help."

Gram continued to fume, lost in her head and unable or unwilling to move on from Harlan's bombshell. "Why would anyone be targeting our company? And to reach out to him of all people? Ridiculous."

The room spun to a stop. The sudden jerking movement made me sit up straight and hold on. All the talking and mumbling from Gram and deflecting from Celia amounted to wasted energy. I knew the truth. The harsh, unflattering truth that thrashed and screamed, begging to escape.

I shoved my plate and scone to the side. My hand shook from the force of the adrenaline coursing through me. I swallowed. Cleared my throat. Nothing eased the clogging tension. "About that . . ."

The ladies kept talking. To each other. Over each other.

"I doubt anyone had been fishing around. I'm sure Harlan was taking liberties with the truth, as he does." Celia put a napkin over her scone carnage. "Bless his heart."

I'd waited for one of them to use that deadly phrase during this conversation. It took longer than expected.

"Lying. He was lying." Gram ramped up again. "Some company calls him out of nowhere? That's ridiculous gibberish. This time he thought he could weasel his way in during tea."

Celia winced. "The timing was bizarre."

Enough. I could stop this. I needed to stop this. Time to be brave and take the consequences and figure out how to weather the fallout. "Gram."

"He's gone too far this time." Gram's voice crept up to a higher range. The one she used when she got really pissed.

This was partially my fault and I needed to own that. "Gram."

Celia glared at Gram before plastering on the world's fakest smile. This one was even less genuine than her last one. "You don't need to worry about this, honey. We'll take care of Harlan."

"He refers to our business as a *hobby*," Gram added.

Celia waved off the comment. "He says a lot of asinine things."

When she pushed the plate with the scone toward me again I had a choice. Snatch it up and eat every crumb. Keep mentally running and hope this would blow over . . . or be a grown-up.

For the first time in more than a week, I landed on the right decision. Terrifying as it was to disappoint them. "Okay. Look—"

"No." Celia's hand covered mine. "We're not letting him ruin our tea."

It was a little late for that.

Celia eyed the plate in front of me. "The scones are the peach ones you liked."

"There's no reason to skimp. Take a muffin and a piece of pie." Gram's voice sounded better. Not normal but out of the high-octane range. "You need to eat."

I couldn't do this.

"Both of you stop for a second." I shoved all the plates to the side. "It was me. I'm so sorry."

Celia shook her head. "Harlan isn't your responsibility."

"No, you don't understand."

Celia didn't but Gram did. Those intelligent eyes refocused. Thanks to years of practice, she heard my fumbling and reacted.

Gram sat back with her hands folded on her lap. "Explain."

The clipped tone grabbed Celia's attention. She sat in a pose identical to Gram's. "Kasey?"

"I'm the one who proposed the sale of your business." It hurt to shove the words out. Hurt more to watch them as I confessed. "Me. Blame me."

For a few seconds neither of them said a thing. They stared at me with identical, unreadable expressions.

Then Gram looked at Celia. "I told you."

CHAPTER THIRTY-FIVE

The last few minutes had been a blurry mess of silent plead-ing and too many words. But I heard Gram's comment. Her really scary comment. "You told Celia I was the problem?"

Celia sighed. "Not exactly, but yes."

"We've known you a long time, young lady." Gram loved to pull out the *young lady*. "You can't shock us."

"We guessed you being home had something to do with your job. At first, I assumed you lost it because you were be-ing secretive, but your odd behavior suggested it was some-thing else. Something you were afraid to tell us. Then Harlan showed up." Celia made a face that suggested she wanted to be done talking about him.

"He thinks he's so smart but asking you to walk him out?" Gram snorted. "That was the tip-off that you were messed up in something big and he found out about it."

Defeated by age, wisdom, and subterfuge weaponized by two sneaky ladies with CIA-level skills. They should have been undercover operatives. Knowing these two, maybe they were. They sure proved they could keep a secret.

I waited for a smack of emotions. Anger, frustration, relief. All I could muster was a massive case of confusion. A big ball of *what the hell*. All that worrying and guilt . . . well, that was justified. I deserved both, but still. They'd conned me, the brilliant little devils.

"Was that fake outrage over Harlan's comments? Were you two trying to teach me a lesson?" *If so, bravo.* Their teaming up with Harlan made me want to spit, but the rest of their act was pretty impressive.

"Heaven's no." Gram's clipped response didn't bode well.

Oh . . .

"Not at all." Celia's tone and delivery were a bit less abrupt. "The shock over him trying to weasel into our business was very real."

"The toad." Gram continued without further defaming toads. "But there's one thing I don't understand. Why not come to us and ask first?"

Her words were a reminder that I had so much left to disclose. "That would have been wise, yes."

"And why would you enlist Harlan's help for a sale?" Celia asked. "Your company must have other investors, ones not tangentially related to us."

They thought I was working with Harlan? Talk about a communications misfire. "I didn't. No way. His plans are his plans. I didn't know about them until he unloaded over tea."

Celia looked like she kept sorting through the information she'd gathered and couldn't put it together. "What about the call he says he received? Was that from your company or was it a lie?"

"That beady-eyed guy with the California name. That's where it came from." Gram made a *tsk-tsk*ing sound. "Must be. He looked like trouble."

Brock strikes again. He was the answer in my theory, too. But even I had to admit Brock didn't touch off this cascading disaster. The honor of lighting the initial fire went to me. "Yes. Well, no. I caused it. Sort of . . . mostly."

Gram's mouth flatlined. "Explain."

"Now, Mags." Celia put her hand over Gram's. "We're prepared to listen and be fair."

"We'll see." Gram didn't even snort this time. She didn't need to. Her tone said enough.

The green light kick-started my brain. No more stalling or being careful with my words. The truth tumbled out. Every last piece. That ambush at the business meeting. The part about my job being in jeopardy. The pressure from Brock that led to the spontaneous pitch. My panic. My guilt. The regrets that piled on every day I stayed without being honest with them. Coming home and enjoying being here. Ignoring my grown-up responsibilities.

Self-preservation be damned. I verbally vomited all of it. Every last unattractive detail.

Then I waited.

Silence descended. Intense and crushing. Who knew the absence of noise made a pounding sound? It echoed in my ears and vibrated through me. It sucked up all the oxygen in the room and squeezed, touching off a tightening in my chest.

Gram didn't react to the suffocating stillness. Her facial expression stayed the same. An atmosphere of foreboding wrapped around her. Celia rubbed her forehead as if my long-winded, topsy-turvy explanation gave her a headache. I had one, so it could happen.

The quiet stretched on. Every so often I'd think about stepping in and saying something else, but Gram's *don't you dare* glare stopped me.

After what felt like an hour but was likely a few minutes, Gram let out a long exhale. One of those loud ones that signaled a change in mood and not necessarily a good change. She slowly turned to look at Celia. "I told you she didn't get two weeks off."

My unexplained vacation time couldn't have tipped her off. Grandma radar wasn't that sensitive . . . was it?

"You were right. I'd hoped . . ." It was Celia's turn to deliver a dramatic exhale. "It doesn't matter."

The wallop of guilt almost knocked me off my chair. "The love I have for the two of you. Worrying about you. Wanting to be here. All real."

I needed them to know they weren't props to me. The business scenario made it sound like I used them to avoid trouble, and maybe I did, but I never meant to hurt them or disappoint them or threaten their control of their business. I really didn't mean to shine a spotlight on their activities, poison or not.

"How did you think this sham was going to end?" Gram asked. Her voice hadn't returned to normal. Fire still burned beneath the surface.

The question. She sounded like Jackson. Man, I wished he'd show up. Pop in and provide silent support even though it served me right to navigate this alone.

"I didn't think it through. While I've been here I've been doing a combination of ignoring calls from the office and trying to keep Micah and Brock away from you and the business. I don't want you wrapped up with them or their investors."

Gram's blank expression faded. "Micah? Is that the weird one who changed his name?"

Might as well spill it all. "Yes. He was at Graylyn. Part of their surprise visit to the area. Micah and Brock. They insisted I meet them there."

Gram nodded. "That explains some of Charlotte's photos. She should have done a more thorough job."

"Yes, that's clearly the lesson here." I needed to meet this Charlotte person and tell her to stay out of my business. And stop taking photos. "How mad are you?"

The million-dollar question. How much damage had I done?

Celia winced. "'Mad' is the wrong word."

"Oh, no. Please don't say 'disappointed.'" *Not that. Please not that.*

"Well . . ." She hesitated but not for long. "We'll get over it. Probably by dinner."

Gram glared at Celia. "Don't tell her that."

Celia hadn't let go of Gram's hand and didn't do it now. "We know all about panic and bad decision-making. We can cut her a break."

Nice. Good. Lovely, even. Also, way too easy. "But?"

"If you didn't want us to even consider the deal, why poke around in the business and show the sudden interest in helping out?" Celia might think her disappointment in me would soon fade but her tone said otherwise. "I'm guessing designing a new tickler system resulted from whatever you collected while snooping. That invasion of privacy is hard to ignore."

Gram responded before I could. "You didn't share the information with Mr. California, did you?"

"I wouldn't do that." Not with Brock or anyone.

Gram's snort said she wasn't convinced.

"Okay, I deserved that, but it's true." I didn't have the moral high ground here. I had to suck up all the sighs and snorts and whatever else Gram threw my way. While I did that I could clarify a few points. "Brock is a jackass. I don't like him or trust him. The fact he and Harlan found each other and joined forces is not a surprise. They share a lot of the same personality traits."

Celia went in for more reinforcements—more tea. "How would they have met?"

Gram hummed. "Harlan is a toad but a smart toad. He knew Kasey was in town and probably checked up on her."

Okay. That part. Harlan's weird obsession with me. That was new and very annoying.

Gram started to say something but Celia cut her off. "Let's stay on topic. We need more information from you."

I didn't have much more to admit, but fine. "Take a shot."

"Why specifically go through our computer files? Not the new tickler system you're designing. I mean before. Right after you got here."

I was wrong. I had a few admissions left . . . so did they. "You were both acting weird. I thought the business might be in trouble and tried to check. I figured you hadn't said anything because you didn't want me to worry."

Gram didn't look impressed with my attempt to shift the spotlight to them. "And you checked our financial solvency by sneaking around?"

"The point is you could have asked us," Celia suggested.

"We all know you wouldn't have answered." The paralyzing anxiety that had settled in and pressed down the minute we started this conversation loosened. The easing of the grip bolstered my confidence. I wasn't the only one in the room with secrets. Big secrets. "While we're disclosing things, how about you two take a turn."

"I'm not sure why you think we're done talking about you and your choices, young lady."

That tone usually worked. Gram knew when to use it and when to ratchet up tension. Not going to happen this time. If we were opening up and sharing, they needed to open up the vault and take a turn.

"The locked-up cupcake supplies, which are now not locked. The disappearing stars on your spreadsheet. The funeral pie recipes." I didn't go into greater detail because I shouldn't have to.

"I don't know—"

Celia sighed. "Mags, don't even try. She clearly put some of the pieces together."

An ally. A reluctant one, sure, but Celia wasn't hiding or putting me off. I wished that made this conversation easier. "I poked around on your work computer then did a bit of research . . ."

Gram frowned. "What research?"

Nope. Nice attempt at derailing, but nope. "On your clients, the delivery of pies, and dead husbands. I know those things are related. You're involved. Somehow."

I waited for a *don't be ridiculous* or *that's a wild story* or a similar line like *we could never*, but they didn't say anything at all. That was their answer. The truth waited in the quiet, lurking and ready to spring.

Thinking something was true and knowing it were two dif-

ferent things. Did I celebrate my ingenuity or find them a lawyer? Maybe rush them into hiding?

No matter the fallout, one truth couldn't be ignored. "Oh
my God. You really did poison Cash Burns, Abigail's husband."

More silence.

This time Celia broke it. "Not exactly."

CHAPTER THIRTY-SIX

D id you just say *not exactly*?" Jackson's even voice cut through the still room.

I turned, for once hoping not to see him, but there he was. Standing with his hands hanging by his sides and his gaze locked on his aunt.

No, no, no. "You should leave."

He couldn't play the role of attentive nephew right now. He couldn't help or even listen to this. He needed . . . What was the term? It came to me in a shot. "Plausible deniability." Cover from the fallout. Political career or not, his job was to keep his hands clean.

The color left Celia's face. "Shouldn't you be at work?"

Yes. That. He should. I counted on his twenty-hour work-day, but he'd parried when I least expected it. He picked today to take off early. Of course. If I'd known he was on his way over I would have locked the door. Saved him from this con-versation and the ramifications of having my poison theory confirmed.

I glanced at the clock. It was a little after four. "Why are you here?"

"I texted you a couple times and didn't hear back. I wanted to come by and make sure everything was okay after that mess yesterday." He blew out a haggard breath as he walked across the room to join us. "Apparently it's not."

I slipped my cell out of my pocket. There they were. Four texts from Jackson, all smooth until the last one, which read as if his agitation had spiked.

Okay, that was on me. I couldn't fix that mistake, but I could avoid another one.

I stood up and grabbed his arm. Tried to tug and drag him away from the table and the overflow of confessions. "Really, though, you need to go while you still can pretend you didn't hear anything."

Moving him didn't work. He stared at me like I'd lost it but didn't shift an inch.

"Celia is my aunt. I love Mags and Celia. What happens with them matters to me. If they're in trouble I'm going to help."

The sweet words made my heart do a little jump.

Well, he needed to rein it in. So did I. The dark energy swirling around the room reflected just how serious this moment was. He had to feel the kick of that dark energy.

"That's lovely but not relevant." Yes, I'd made him my investigative wingman. I regretted that.

"We didn't want either of you involved in this." Celia's voice sounded stronger now. Like that of a high school teacher who had seen enough and was putting an end to the chaos.

"What is the 'this' you're referencing?" Jackson looked at Celia over the top of my head as he asked.

Loving him was going to kill me. There. I admitted it. My feelings for him weren't random or fleeting. They also covered things like not putting him in danger. I never intended to do that but did. "Do not ask more questions."

I didn't realize until right then that I held Jackson's arm in a death grip. My fingers wrapped around his impressive biceps. We stood just inches apart. I could feel his breath near my ear. Smell him.

"Sit down. Both of you." Gram gave the order.

My balance faltered. "I don't think—"

"Kasey Adelaide Nottingham. Do not argue with me." Gram's message was clear. She was done playing.

I balanced my forehead on Jackson's shoulder for one blissful second then went back into the fire. I let go and fell in my chair, defeated. "Right. Caution be damned."

Without a word, Jackson sat down at the table. The strain of the moment caught up with me. I wanted to curl up and slouch against him and will this discussion away. The rolling admissions needed to happen but coming clean about my role in the business pitch had stolen most of my strength.

Celia rested both hands on the table. She stared into her cup of tea. "I'm not sure where to begin."

"With men problems." Gram dropped that like she'd said a full sentence. "They're the cause of all of this heartache."

"Jackson, you might not understand this, but there are some men who can't be reformed." Celia sounded hesitant, like she was trying to wade in and be careful with her words.

He already looked confused. "Why wouldn't I understand that?"

Celia touched her crime scene of a plate then moved it away from her. "Mags and I came from difficult household situations. Different types but both required an escape."

"Don't sugarcoat it." Gram rushed in as if she needed to get the words out fast so she could go back to forgetting them again. "Some men are positively rancid. Edmund Dennison being the most obvious. He's the kind of evil that should be wiped from the earth."

My biological father. The most hated figure in Gram's long life. She was right about him.

"The women in our family have a habit of picking bad men." Gram stared at me for a few seconds before moving on. "My husband, Kasey's grandfather, was not nice. He wanted the drapes closed at all times so the neighbors couldn't see. He kept the walls, the furniture—everything—in a monochrome brown and black. Darkness inside and out."

Gram's love of color and wild prints now made sense.

"He didn't believe in compromise or partnership. He led with his fists, and anything could set him off. When he was angry or tired or hungry. When he had a tough day. Because his boss hated him. Because it was Tuesday. He always had an excuse and a reason why his anger was my fault."

My stomach roiled. A mix of fury and sympathy caught in my throat. I knew the broad strokes about Gram's married life but not the details. Hearing her talk in that flat tone about being hit, imagining her trying to duck but not being able to outrun her husband's wrath, would play in my head for a long time. How did she dodge the terrifying memories for all these years?

Another round of silent communication passed between Gram and Celia. This time I could hear it. Maybe I just guessed the words, saw the comfort. Celia sat there, listening, and taking in every harsh fact with her hand resting on Gram's arm. Celia was Gram's tether. Her lifeline.

"I tried to stay out of his way, be perfect, not cause trouble or wake him, and it was never enough. I never offered the right response at the right time. And if I tried to get away or fight back . . ." Gram's words faded. "Life got worse."

"Gram." She'd experienced more heartache than anyone deserved. She was strong. A survivor. I didn't want to say or do anything that suggested I viewed her any other way.

"The worst part was the impact on your mother. I have so much guilt. So much . . ." Gram's voice broke.

Celia didn't try to hide her pain at seeing Gram's despair. "Mags, you can take a breath."

"I need to say it. Get it all out." Gram lovingly covered Celia's hand with hers. "Even though I tried to pretend, to protect her, Nora knew what your grandfather was. He never used his fists on her, but she saw and heard what he did to me, and the damage was done."

"Sonofabitch." Jackson mumbled the word but his anger rang through loud and clear.

"I'm convinced she married Edmund Dennison because she craved a home and stability. She wanted to secure her future then help me escape my situation, and she thought he was her ticket."

Gram had never hinted at this before. I'd read a lot about spousal abuse and spousal violence over the years, trying to understand how things could go so wrong. I'd assumed Mom's choices fit a pattern. She'd married a man like her father because that's what she knew, and the cycle continued.

"Edmund Dennison seemed fine at first. A bit too smooth-talking for my taste, but attentive to your mother. Something sinister lurked under the surface. Something he hid until he exploded. He convinced people he was one thing when he was really a monster. A narcissist who valued how the public viewed him above all else."

Jackson took my hand under the table in an unspoken gesture of support. I grabbed on.

"His controlling behavior escalated at home. Nora saw the signs. She knew what a dysfunctional household looked like because she'd grown up in one, but he couldn't allow her to leave and . . . you know the rest." Gram's words abruptly stopped, the pause echoing through the house. "It keeps me up at night to think she didn't come to me because she thought I would tell her to stay with her husband like I did."

The haunting words sat there. Hearing them, seeing Gram's stark expression as she opened the vault to her most secret memories made every sentence sound so much worse.

"You and Mom deserved better. I'm so sorry you lived like that." Gram had made sure I didn't. I'd thanked her many times over the years. How she raised me was a gift I never wanted to take for granted.

The stress around Gram's mouth eased. "I know, honey. It's been years. While I can't pretend the trauma didn't leave a mark, and I am nowhere near ready to forgive the unforgivable, I have moved on. I married your grandfather to escape my father and all his drunken screaming and then walked into a much worse situation. Nora repeated the pattern. That's my fault. My failure."

"You're not to blame for how either man acted." Celia's soft tone didn't match her message.

"It's okay." Gram nodded. "I was blessed with Nora and Kasey. I got a second chance with you. I found love and a much better life."

Jackson nodded. "I don't know how but you thrived. Despite the odds, you trusted Celia and then the two of you built a life with Kasey. That's the kind of personal strength people claim to possess but don't. You actually do."

Hearing him say the words confirmed what I already knew. He wasn't anything like his father. Jackson might resemble Harlan on the outside. On the inside, Jackson surpassed Harlan in every way.

"Your aunt's situation was different from mine. Her husband was a loser. Insecure. Incompetent. Far beneath her and threatened by how much smarter she was." Gram squeezed Celia's hand. "He took everything. Lied. Ran up debt in her name. Squandered every cent. She had multiple jobs while he wasted it all."

I couldn't hold one job and Celia had juggled multiple jobs. The women who raised me impressed me more every day.

"The medical supply business. A department store sales job. For a time, some bookkeeping work. I also cleaned offices at night. Anything to keep food on the table. My car that I had before marriage and thought was paid off got repossessed. That's when I found out my husband had leveraged it and forged my name to do so. The house foreclosure notices. All those calls from the credit card people for cards I didn't know he had."

Jackson's pained expression showed his sympathy. "I'm so sorry."

"We know." Celia treated Jackson to a small smile. "After all we'd been through and all we'd lost, we tried to teach Kasey she deserved better. That she deserved an equal who loves and respects her."

"Not every woman knows her worth or believes she has value outside of her marriage. Add in children and money strains and other daily issues and walking away becomes an unscalable mountain," Gram said.

"We felt sick and angry and helpless whenever a new rumor popped up and traveled around town about a woman in an abusive household," Celia said. "We vowed to help them."

I dreaded asking this, but the topic was how we landed here. "Is now the right time to ask about the poison?"

"Poison is only part of it."

Thanks, Celia. Not exactly the answer I was hoping for.

Gram was more direct. "It would be too obvious if we drugged every abusive man in the area. They'd be dropping all over town." Gram glanced at Celia and waited for her nod before finishing. "So, we came up with a compromise."

I bit back a groan. "I was afraid you were going to say that."

Gram treated me to a satisfied nod. "This will teach you to snoop around."

CHAPTER THIRTY-SEVEN

Vigilante justice. People debated the appropriateness of terrible individuals who did terrible things to their supposed loved ones facing retribution outside a formal system. What was fair? What did justice require? No one ever asked the victims those questions. The burden to survive rested on them while the attacker could depend on the prejudices and faults within the system and the fickle demands of society to escape culpability.

Despite that, we had choices. We were sitting in a house, not operating in a courtroom with all its rules and limitations. This was real life, where the answers weren't so clear. If you felt alone and no one stepped up to help then that bright line between right and wrong could blur.

Maybe that's why I would have made a terrible lawyer. From my vantage point, the law malfunctioned many times when needed and delivered harsh blows often when unnecessary.

Celia traced her finger over the handle of her mug. "I deleted the star references in our business documents after I realized you'd been in the computer system."

That explained that. "So much for thinking I'd been stealthy."

"When Mags turned on her computer she saw that the spreadsheet was open to the column with the stars. She hadn't been looking under that tab when she stopped working," Celia said. "Next time make sure you return everything to its rightful place after you're done poking around."

Gram cleared her throat. "There won't be a next time."

When I realized Gram was staring at me, I answered the unasked question. "Yes, ma'am."

"We didn't know if you figured out what you saw or realized it had significance." Celia shrugged. "Erasing the potentially damning evidence seemed wise. You were also in and out of the kitchen, so we locked some items in a cabinet in the pantry until we could dispose of them properly."

I didn't want to ask . . . but I really did. "What was in the cabinet?"

Celia seemed to think about how to answer before spitting out an explanation. "It doesn't matter. It's gone."

Gram focused on Jackson. "How did she convince you to get involved in all of this?"

"I was a willing participant."

That wasn't quite true, but I loved him for saying it. "Jackson begged me to be cautious and not jump to conclusions."

Gram sighed. "The conclusion being that we were killing men around town with our pies."

"Didn't I get that right? Wait . . ." I focused on Jackson. "Last chance for you to leave. You can bolt before they answer."

"I'm in this now."

"You can go look. We don't have poison in the pantry." Gram acted like her comment closed the subject.

She'd been mighty specific with her words. "That seems smart, but did you and do you keep it anywhere else now?"

Gram didn't answer me.

Celia skipped right over the poison question as well. "We are part of a network of like-minded women who are concerned about this issue."

No, that didn't sound ominous at all. Who knew coming home for a few days of pastries could be so stressful?

"Women around town who have dealt with abuse in their own homes or by watching someone they love struggle." Celia kept playing with her mug. Touching it. Turning it. Running her finger down the side of it. "We started with a few women in key places—in the Junior League, at country clubs, tennis clubs and golf clubs, through advocacy groups, and even in government and leadership positions throughout the county."

Jackson whistled. "That's a lot of women."

He wasn't wrong. It sounded like Gram and Celia didn't half-ass this. They'd built a community based on the most desperate kind of need.

"It started small but has grown as we reach out to more women. We help a woman and then, if she's able, she looks out for other women and reports back when she hears anything of concern," Celia said.

The strain around Jackson's eyes grew more pronounced as the weight of each sentence pressed down on him. "How do you keep it a secret?"

"Our network and what we offer are not secrets to the women who need help," Gram said.

"This issue touches every economic group, education level, ethnic background, race, and religious affiliation." Experience had taught me that. Those books I read confirmed it.

Jackson wore a pained expression. "I don't know how you trust any of us."

"It can be hard." Gram responded by patting his arm. "The men in my family tree are regrettable creatures but I do realize not all men are terrible."

"Some are lovely. Some pretend to be lovely. The latter is when problems arise," Celia said.

"If a woman is in trouble but early in the process, like she doesn't know where to go or how to leave, the woman who reached out to her delivers one of our pies along with a recipe, specific information aimed at her circumstances, and a burner phone for confidential communication."

Gram knew about burner phones? She couldn't work the remote control for the smart TV, but she engaged in complex clandestine operations. Society tended to dismiss and ignore older women. Big mistake. Never underestimate a woman due to her age.

Every word made me love and respect Gram more. She could have sat back and celebrated her escape. Stayed quiet and healed in private. No one would have blamed her, but she took a different path. She looked at the suffering passed in silence from generation to generation and said *enough*.

"If a woman is at a different stage, ready to leave or in extreme danger, they get a slightly different pie recipe in their gift basket that leads to advice and information specific to their circumstances," Celia explained. "Both cards include password-protected links to files we've put together over time."

Now I got it. The notations. The gift baskets. "A recipe for the funeral pie with custard versus a recipe for the funeral pie without. You use one or the other, depending on an individual woman's situation. The recipes are a notification system. A way to distribute information."

Celia nodded. "Yes. We thought it was safe to use the two pie recipes since we don't actually offer funeral pie as an option. And the nickname for the pie drives home how imperative the help is."

Jackson looked lost again. "Wait. Is funeral pie the real name for this dessert?"

"Yes. I'll give you the history later." Then I'd remove the phrase "funeral pie" from my internal dictionary, just in case. "So, you don't actually include poison or that specific pie in this care package? And please feel free to give me a definitive no."

"We do not deliver poison or funeral pie directly to a woman's door during an initial contact." Celia sounded pretty sure about that.

Gram rushed to clarify. "But we do give ideas on what a woman can do if she can't escape."

"So, poison." The way they danced around the poison question, taking it off the table then adding it back in again, switched my senses to high alert.

Gram shrugged. "Some men deserve a horrible end."

"It certainly sounds that way," Jackson mumbled under his breath.

I wanted to shout with pride about their ingenuity. I couldn't, of course, this would have to be a family secret.

"You're evil geniuses. But are you also in danger?" I feared both law enforcement involvement and a stray angry husband who might come looking for revenge before he met his fate.

Celia did the most Celia thing possible. She started serving tea. Probably from nerves and the need to keep her hands busy, but she didn't stop explaining. "We take a lot of precautions.

The passwords are on a one-time-use setup. After that we establish a direct link between the woman who needs help and a mentor of sorts who walks her through the process. There are layers of people who perform different tasks—identifying women at risk, meeting with them, delivering the pies, and for us, making the pies—and we never specifically advocate for killing a bad husband."

Specifically? "Good?"

Celia remained calm through the entire explanation. "That's a last resort option."

"Can this last resort option be traced back to you or the business through these packages and recipes?" Jackson asked like the good lawyer he was.

Gram shook her head. "There's no poison in the actual pie that's delivered."

"It's the way you say those words that worries me." The fact there was, at least for a time, a locked cabinet in the pantry that they had to get rid of suggested there was poison somewhere on the property until very recently.

Gram waved off the concern. "The goal is to let these women know they have support and provide options, even if they're not ready to reach out for help. Even if they are in fear for their children's safety. Even if they don't have access to money. Even if they think they have nowhere to go."

"There's also a lockbox they can access when they're ready," Celia explained. "The mentors personally set that up."

"But, and let me be very clear, poison would be included with every pie delivery if I had my way. Celia insists we be more subtle."

Good Lord. "Thank you, Celia."

Jackson focused on the positive. "You save lives."

They did. They made a difference through their food and their top-secret advocacy.

"No one tried to rescue us. We want better for other women." Celia reached out and took Gram's hand. "Even women we don't know."

"Which is why this business takeover push, or outside financing, or whatever the proposal is, needs to stop. We can't have Harlan—"

Jackson made a weird noise. "Dad?"

"He's acting as Brock's surrogate." I hated to drop that truth but there it was.

"How in the . . ." Jackson let out another strangled sound. "Never mind."

"We can't have anyone poking around in the business or asking questions. It's too risky," Gram said.

Right. Exactly. Turning this around fell on me. "Then I'll kill any talk of a deal."

Celia shook her head. "You'll lose your job."

No question. "So? I'm an expert at that."

"We could refuse any further discussion on a buyout and lie low. Let Harlan and that Mr. California find another hobby."

Too risky and Gram had to know that. The ladies shouldered enough of a burden without adding more. Then there was the other problem. "I'm not really great at waiting around and seeing how things go."

Gram snorted.

"No kidding," Jackson said with equal drama.

Celia went with a sigh. "We know, honey."

Not exactly the cheer of support I expected but probably the response I deserved.

"My point is I made the mess. I'll fix it." This one time I wouldn't screw up.

CHAPTER THIRTY-EIGHT

Two hours later I sat on Jackson's couch with my feet balanced on his coffee table. On the drive over here, Jackson and I debated if the poison was still somewhere on Gram and Celia's property. No matter how many times we'd asked we never got a clear response. Celia and Gram were determined to keep some secrets to themselves.

Jackson leaned back into the cushions. "This has been a hell of a day."

We sat side by side, sprawled out, thighs touching, and more than a little unnerved by the information we'd just heard. "I know you're tempted to blame my presence in town as the reason for the slightly chaotic way your week is going."

He lifted his head and looked at me. "Slightly?"

Yep. Ignoring that. "But, today, that conversation was not my fault."

He frowned but couldn't hold the mood. Amusement lingered just under the surface and peeked out in subtle ways. In his voice. In the way he fought a smile. "I'm surprised you didn't throw your back out jumping to that conclusion."

"Look at you being all funny despite the lawyer thing." He really had lightened up since that Anna chick left.

To be fair, she was probably very nice, because Jackson wouldn't date a mean girl, but their personalities didn't match . . .

or maybe they matched too well. Not sure what the problem was but I'm not sad she'd moved on.

"I have many skills," he said.

I never would have guessed making me feel at home, welcome, would have been one of them but here we were. We each had a glass of wine, but they sat untouched on the table, as if moving required too much energy. We were content to snuggle into the cushions with not a breath of air between us.

"It's weird I'm not more upset about women offing their bad husbands." Chalk it up to my father or my grandfather, but the idea of violent men being removed from society permanently barely caused a minute of uncertainty. Women's safety trumped all other concerns.

"It's hard to root for an abuser."

I'd been prepared to argue and defend the ladies' position but he didn't express reservations. Sometime in the future we'd likely circle back and walk through the fairness issue but not today.

"Hearing Gram talk about . . ." No. I didn't want to relive the description or hear the sound of her voice in my head though I knew I would. I'd never known my grandfather and couldn't remember my father. One more gift Gram gave me.

"I know." Jackson reached over and took my hand.

A sense of calm settled over me like a warm bath. The harsh facts didn't disappear, but they faded into the background. Touching him, being this close, sharing this intimacy, the reassuring comfort of it all, restored my balance.

"I mean, I knew, but knowing and *really knowing* are two different things." That was enough babbling. "I'm just grateful Gram found Celia. They're good together."

"They are."

Okay, but did he understand the nuances of their relationship? I always wondered because we never talked about how much Gram and Celia meant to each other and in what way. Their love for me and each other was a constant that grounded me and a reality I never questioned. I wasn't clear where he fell on this topic. His answer would impact how I viewed him.

"You know what I'm saying, right?"

His thumb rubbed the back of my hand. "About what?"

"They're not just friends. Gram and Celia, I mean." I shifted until I faced him, never letting go of his hand. "Yeah, they keep separate bedrooms but that's just for their clothes. They've always slept in the same room."

"Okay." His expression didn't change. His thumb kept drawing that lazy and very sexy pattern over my skin.

Everyone avoided clarity today. I tried to break that pattern. "Jackson, they're a couple."

His hand went still. "Do you really think I don't know that?"

"You should see your face." He looked miffed that I'd suggested he lagged that far behind. I almost laughed, not because I thought the topic was funny or didn't take his reaction to what he clearly thought was an insult seriously, but from the relief shooting through me. It rushed to my head and made me feel . . . silly happy. For once in my life the description fit.

"I'm not clueless." Now he sounded indignant.

I couldn't blame him. I'd tiptoed into what shouldn't be a difficult or uncomfortable topic but was for many people. Not him. "I wasn't sure if you were ignoring the truth or if you, maybe, had problems with the state of their relationship."

"Who other people love doesn't affect me. I say the more happiness the better."

Okay, yeah. I loved him. Not a crush. Not a teen love that never matured. Love. Like, I grumbled about not seeing him and claimed we had "unresolved issues" but, really, I just wanted to be with him. Which was going to make leaving and going back to DC really suck.

"For a very long time Aunt Celia has been the most important woman in my life. She supports me. Loves me. Even though she doesn't think I know, she also advocates for me with Dad."

Him. Harlan. The one thing—a six-foot-two annoying thing—that could be a problem. "Does he understand the nature of Gram and Celia's relationship?"

"In public, he insists they are two *very good friends* who combined their money because it's hard for single women out there." Jackson lifted our joined hands and rested them against his chest. "That's not a direct quote but close."

"Wow." At least Harlan was consistent. Consistently not great.

Jackson smiled. "You can't possibly be surprised."

Harlan thought he deserved a wife who waited on him and girlfriends who satisfied him, so no. "I'm trying to imagine someone at the club making an offhand remark and him giving a lecture about how very close older women can be friends without anything more."

"I've heard it. It's astounding in its lack of awareness."

I looked at the way my hand fit in Jackson's . . . who knew hand-holding could be so romantic?

"So long as he doesn't bad-mouth them or act disrespectful,

I let it go. Mostly because Celia told me, for her peace of mind, to ignore Dad's views on this topic."

That sounded like Celia. Gram would have taken a different approach, one a bit more hostile. Both worked.

All this talk about his dad made me anxious, a sensation I did not love. "Not to sound unappreciative, because I am grateful you suggested we give Gram and Celia a minute of privacy and come here, but is your dad going to pop up again? I don't really have the energy for another run-in with him today."

"We have a Dad reprieve."

This time Jackson lifted our hands and kissed the back of mine, sending my ability to concentrate into a nosedive. "Is he out of town? . . . she asked hopefully."

"He dropped off some paperwork earlier then left me a text, talking about an informal business meeting with a client from out of town that he couldn't reschedule and saying we'd talk tomorrow."

Don't be here tomorrow. *Check.* "Lucky you."

"I need to add the business issue and your boss, Brock, to my list of discussion topics with Dad. You can join us if you want."

Nope. "I'd rather go running."

"Whatever he dropped off is on the dining room table. I haven't looked at it because I wasn't home until now. I'm also not in the mood to have another battle with him over who gets to decide my future." Jackson gave my fingers a squeeze. "The answer is me, if that wasn't clear."

That was very . . . wait. "Hold up. Are you saying your dad has a key to your condo?"

Jackson winced. "In hindsight, not my smartest move."

Sweet hell. "I thought you were supposed to be a genius."

"It's for practical purposes. I have one to his house. He has one to here. Just in case."

I couldn't think of anything nice to say and didn't want to kill the relaxing mood winding around us, so I went with the most benign sentence I could think of. "The man does enjoy playing games."

"He's an expert at that sort of thing." Jackson let out a long exhale. "That and getting married."

"Three former wives and who knows what he has planned for the future." Why any woman would say yes to him was the mystery.

"I think he doesn't want to be alone, which is interesting since he doesn't like most people. And don't think I haven't figured out that Dad is one of the bad men in Mags's eyes."

In Gram's. In mine. In Celia's. In the eyes of every woman who strayed across his path. "I know he's your dad but he's . . . a lot."

"I wish I could say he meant well and wanted what was best for me, but—"

I borrowed one of Gram's snorts. "You don't like to lie."

"Something like that." Jackson shifted until his head rested against mine. "At one time he was more attentive. We'd golf and he'd come to my high school games but his interest in parenting would fade in and out. We didn't have a huge amount of family time when I was growing up."

"That sounds like a wild understatement."

"He couldn't handle Mom's illness and how the cancer kept

coming back. He acted as if she got the disease to spite him. She could barely move near the end, and he would rage about missing this event or this meeting to take care of her." There was a *no big deal* vibe in Jackson's tone that sounded practiced but very fake. "I think a part of him blamed me for her being sick. He'd talk about how she was healthy until I was born."

It was a miracle Jackson had come out of that household intact. "That's demented."

"Despite all that, I was luckier than many. I've had a lot of advantages. I had what I needed."

Except unconditional love. I didn't say it out loud but we both knew.

"Loving Dad because he's my dad and liking him as a person are two different things, which is why the last few years I've tried to set boundaries."

That was a news flash. "How's that going?"

"I'm not sure he even noticed."

Jackson understood his dad. He didn't praise him or hold him up as perfect or misunderstood and I was grateful for that honesty. "Let's agree not to talk about Harlan, the pie business, or dead husbands any more tonight."

"Done." Jackson's fingertips trailed up my arm. "There are much more interesting things we can do, right?"

That sounded like a promise as much as a question. The answer was yes.

CHAPTER THIRTY-NINE

I didn't try to slow Jackson down or talk reason. I dove in.
This, us, was going to happen. So many of my fantasies started this way. Me lying on top of him. Him hovering over me. I didn't care about the position. I just wanted to rip his clothes off, drop every inhibition, and get there.

"We could talk about the kiss we shared. The grown-up one," Jackson said. "That wasn't on your list of barred topics."

"An oversight." I'd barely been able to keep up my end of the conversation for the last five minutes as the memories of kissing bombarded my brain. Remembering the last time. Wanting a *this* time.

He turned to face me. "Was that a once only thing?"

His breath blew across my cheek and his scent wrapped around me. The heat pulsed between us. How did we manage to carry on a conversation at all? "You really need to call all those fancy colleges you went to and hand your degrees back because you aren't talking like a smart person right now."

"I was hoping you'd say that. Well, not all of that, but you—"

Enough talking. I reached out and brought his head even closer to mine. He didn't fight me. I didn't pretend I wanted to go slow. Our lips met and the same blinding heat roared through me as last time. This felt good. Right. A little naughty, but in the best way.

As the kiss raged on, my defenses fell. The flimsy shields I threw up to fight off my attraction to him collapsed with a resounding thud. Him, me, cuddling on this couch, the exploring and touching. I craved all of it.

"This is a bad idea." A comment I felt obliged to make. I lifted my head long enough to get the words out then dove right back into the kissing.

"Terrible," he mumbled against my lips.

We shifted and rolled until our legs tangled together and my hands traveled over his chest. I was on top of him now. Balancing my hands on his shoulders and straddling those impressive hips with my thighs.

"Once you see me naked things will change."

Why was I still talking?

His mouth went to my neck. He licked and nipped, crashing through the last of my control and setting my nerve endings on fire. "I've seen you naked."

Whoa . . . I sat up, straight up, kissing on hold while I stared at him. "Uh, hello? What are you talking about?"

His fingers continued to move, working their way under the edge of my shirt to find the bare skin of my stomach. "Four years ago. You were in the shower and passed out."

Thinking about that day made me queasy. I'd gone for a hike, which was always the wrong answer. It was one of those times when I started listening to that nasty, demeaning voice in my head that said I wasn't good enough. Hence the outside exercise kick. That ended when I became dizzy. My blood pressure took a nosedive and dragged my hiking enthusiasm down with it.

All true. Him being there wasn't. "You weren't in the house."

"I took Celia out to lunch that day, but Mags called in a

panic before we got to the end of the street. She said you'd come home groggy and weren't making sense and then she found you. We turned around and rushed into the house to help." He had the nerve to smile as he finished his explanation. "And there you were. Naked, wet, and unconscious."

I was an adult and all, but the idea that he'd seen me without clothing and not said anything . . . my mind refused to accept it. "Gram pulled me out."

He made a humming sound. "Not exactly."

"Oh my God!" A nightmare. A full-fledged nightmare.

His fingertips continued to dance over me. The brush of skin against skin threatened to shut down my brain.

"Celia thought it would embarrass you if you knew about my role in the rescue, so we said Mags lifted you out and never spoke about it again."

"You've all lied to me for years?" They never even dropped a hint. "I think I should be outraged."

His hands stopped moving. "You didn't think it was a little weird that a seventy-something woman lifted you out of the tub and onto the bed?"

"With the right motivation Gram could lift a house."

"Fair point."

"The only fact saving me from complete mortification and an accompanying mental breakdown is you saw me naked for medical purposes, which is not the same thing as real naked." Saying it and convincing my brain were two different things.

His hands returned to my hips and tugged me closer. "Okay . . ."

"You weren't *looking* looking." *Sure, that made sense.*

"Would you feel better if I agreed with you?"

Not even a little. But I had a better idea. My hands slid to the cushions behind his head, trapping him there with my chest resting against his. "Seems to me if you've seen me naked then I should get to see you naked."

He nodded. "It's only fair."

"I thought you'd agree." Smart man.

His fingers slipped under the edge of my bra. "In this scenario, are we both naked?"

If he kept touching me like that we'd be naked before I answered his question. "What do you think, lawyer boy?"

He kissed me again. This one started out slow and soft. Tender. Learning and exploring until my heartbeat thundered in my chest. The tension built and anticipation swirled around us. His hands cupped my breasts. My thighs pressed against the sides of his legs.

I never needed anything as much as I needed this.

"Be sure." He said the words against my mouth.

Consent. He had the brightest green light ever. "I'm absolutely sure."

Then his mouth crushed mine and the talking stopped.

CHAPTER FORTY

The fantasies I'd always had about us faded out before we got to the morning-after part of sex. As expected, the guy with the big brain knew exactly what to do with his hands and my body. Jackson's sexy voice. The way he used that tongue. Hours of touching, and exploring, and pleasure. It was amazing my heart didn't explode.

Regrets? None so far.

Awkwardness? Unclear because he was still asleep. I took his exhaustion as a compliment to me . . . or him, or both of us.

No, it was me. Definitely me. I did that to him. I had him breathless and whispering my name last night. I was taking credit for his inability to wake up and get moving.

This one time in my life I appreciated running. Him running, not me. His stamina. Those muscles. That flat stomach. Damn.

Wrapped up in his robe, I wandered through the house with my mind on a muffin. I couldn't exactly call Gram and ask her to bring a few over. She hadn't texted to check on me. She knew where I was. I could imagine Gram and Celia chatting about this turn of events all morning. I had no idea if they approved, but that was an issue for the afternoon. Food was the immediate concern.

Jackson's fancy kitchen called out to me. There had to be

food here somewhere. Before that, caffeine. I stared at his silver coffee machine willing it to magically make me a cup. This thing had a grinder and an attachable container for milk. So many buttons with little pictures of cups on them. You'd think they'd give me a hint about where to start but I couldn't even identify some of the named drinks. What was a doppio? That sounded totally made-up.

I bet if I looked up the price of this contraption online it would cost more than my car. Breaking it would not leave a good post-sex impression, so I went with water. Jackson would wake up eventually. Sooner rather than later would be nice.

Crawling back into bed sounded so tempting but I needed to take a breath. The collision of my fantasy world and reality scrambled my brain. My common sense took an unexpected vacation when it came to Jackson. Every promise I'd ever made to myself about not getting too close—gone. Last night was unplanned and amazing.

Now what?

I bit back a caffeine-depleted groan as I sat down and dropped my head on the dining room table. Yeah, I needed that coffee. Time to experiment with the fancy machine.

Being as dramatic as possible, I swept my hand across the table as I sat up. The stack of papers teetering on the edge made a whooshing sound as they fell to the floor.

"Crap." I hated when things went sideways in the morning.

My groan escaped this time. I dropped to my knees and gathered up the papers. I picked up the file lying upside down and . . . my face stared back at me.

"Uh, hello?"

A quick look to verify and, yep, this was some sort of report with Harlan's name on it and the name of an agency of some sort. It had been prepared for Harlan. I knew because that's what the attached note on the front said. *Per your request.*

What had Harlan done now?

The document noted my name and date of birth. A bunch of basic info about the addresses where I'd lived. There was a line for "investigation type" and it said "domestic services."

What the hell did that mean?

On the next page . . . holy crap. Information on the men I'd dated. No, that wasn't invasive at all. The list of "partners" wasn't long but that really wasn't the point, was it?

I kept flipping through the pages, scanning the paragraphs about my education and job history. This thing included a list of my closest friends and living relatives. The latter being a very short paragraph. Details about my parents. The stark and official outline, not the more emotional version Gram gave yesterday.

There was a separate section on my father's criminal case. It had dragged on far too long and included so many of his excuses and false statements. *My wife had a mental illness. She came from a violent family and could be volatile. I needed to protect myself so I could be there for my daughter.* Nonsense justifications as he blamed her for her own death. His arguments failed and he ended up with a life sentence. Good riddance.

Seeing my history broken down into a few bleak lines of black ink separated by cold topic headings made my stomach heave. The report went on for ten pages but said nothing. It spelled out my boring life and the trauma that shaped it. The

"recommendations" section at the end was the most enlighten-
ing part. It actually said *inappropriate mate for subject with political
aspirations*. It said a lot of shitty stuff, but that line stood out.

Harlan had been a busy boy since I got to town. To say I was
irritated didn't come close to covering my rage. This jackass
commissioned a report about me for the sole purpose of con-
firming I was wrong for Jackson.

Under the demeaning and infuriating file was a second
folder. This one was thicker and a bit imposing. I opened the
cover, thinking it contained more information about my life,
and . . . *shit*.

He couldn't. He didn't.

But he did and I needed to warn Gram and Celia right now.

CHAPTER FORTY-ONE

I drove straight to Gram's house. Bolted in the door then slammed to a halt. Gram and Celia sat at the kitchen table. They'd been smiling and talking when I burst in. Now they stared at me in charged silence.

I wasn't sure how to start but Celia saved me the trouble. "Are you wearing a robe?"

"Am I . . ." I looked down. *Oh, shit.*

"Why in the world are you running about town half dressed?" Gram, always one to get right to the point, threw that out.

The last fifteen minutes played in my head. I'd read the report then found the second one and left Jackson in bed. Alone. Without an explanation for my absence and grabbed the robe. That's all I wore. Really, that was it. Nothing underneath. No underwear or shoes.

No, this wasn't embarrassing at all.

Push through. That was the answer. "What I'm wearing doesn't matter."

"I think it does." Gram nodded in the direction of the empty chair across from her. "You can't just flit around like that. You'll get sick."

She was worried about my catching a cold. Interesting. If they'd put together my near-naked state this morning and my leaving with Jackson last night, and what that meant, they hadn't spit it out yet.

I needed to take control of the conversation and direct it away from the robe question. "We have an emergency."

Gram snorted. "Clearly."

Do not take the bait. Do not take the bait.

"Would you like a scone?" Celia didn't wait for an answer. She got up and brought back another plate.

"I'm not . . ." When she put the scone in front of me my hunger surged. "Well, yes, but that's not why I hustled over here."

I didn't run but I came close to a jog, which was way faster than my usual speed. I sure sprinted from the driveway to the porch. Also "borrowed" Jackson's car, which might not go over well. That's how serious this mess was.

"Please tell me you didn't jump around on the streets wearing that." Gram shifted in her seat, looking under the table. "Where are your shoes?"

Excellent question. Why didn't I slip them on?

That stupid report. Actually, reports. I saw the words. Panic swamped me when I realized how grave the situation could get. The need to protect overwhelmed my need for clothes.

Celia guided me to an open chair. Even stopped to pull the lapels of Jackson's robe closer together and halt the unintended peep show. "Let's get you some coffee. That will help."

She said the magic word—coffee.

"Why does she need help?" Gram looked toward the door. "And where is Jackson?"

"He's in bed." Too much information. "I mean, I assume he is. He's a grown-up. He can do what he wants in the morning."

Why couldn't I stop talking?

Gram frowned. "Are you okay?"

No. I wasn't sure if I'd ever be okay again. It probably wasn't possible to die of embarrassment. At least I hoped not.

"We know you were with him last night, honey." Celia returned to the table. "That's his robe."

Admit it? Don't admit it? I wasn't a kid, but I still didn't know how to maneuver through this situation. "I don't—"

"I bought it for his birthday." Celia dropped that bit of information then grabbed a scone for herself.

"Ah." Of course she did.

"Did Jackson do something to you?" Gram asked.

Wow. How did I answer that?

Celia let out a little gasp. "He would never."

Depends on what we were talking about because Jackson absolutely did, and it was great. I felt pretty lucky today as a result.

"Maybe that's how she looks after . . ." Celia waved her hand in the air. "Sexual relations."

Oh my God. "Please, stop."

"Kasey!"

I jumped at the sound of Jackson's stern voice. He sounded angry but looked adorable. His hair went every which way. He'd thrown on a T-shirt and pants but looked like he'd just rolled out of bed after a night of hot sex to find his car missing.

He stormed his way across the room and stood by the table. Frustration thrummed off him.

"Oh, dear," Celia mumbled under her breath.

All of his attention was on me, and his tone wasn't sexy or sweet. "What the hell is going on? Why did you leave?"

Gram snorted. "At least he put clothes on."

"The way young people court these days is confusing." Celia shook her head. "What exactly happened last night?"

Jackson's expression was priceless. "I'm not giving you a play-by-play."

"You need this." Celia put a scone in front of Jackson even though he hadn't bothered to sit down yet. "And I wasn't referring to the sex. I can guess about that part."

Maybe I could walk back to DC. "I'd like this conversation to be over."

Gram didn't make one of her usual warning sounds but she did smile. "I'm sure you would."

"Kasey, I'm serious." Jackson sounded like his patience had finally run out. "I thought you were making coffee then I couldn't find you. Then I couldn't find my keys. I had to call a rideshare to come over here."

That was a lot of information and none of it made me look good. "Your coffeemaker is confusing."

His mouth dropped open.

"So, you drove over here to use this one? Wearing only that?" Celia asked.

I gave in and split open the scone. This conversation didn't show any signs of winding down and I still hadn't eaten. "No, of course not. That would be ridiculous, as opposed to this discussion, which is totally normal."

"I didn't know about the report." Jackson blurted that out.

He stared at me, like he was willing me to believe him. What a waste of energy. I already knew.

"What report?" Gram asked.

Celia started to get up. "Maybe we should give them some privacy."

I wasn't falling for that. "Oh, please. You don't mean it."

"It looks like Dad had a private investigator throw together a report on Kasey." The words rushed out of Jackson as if he needed to make his argument before he lost the floor again. "She clearly read it and panicked without talking to me."

"Harlan caused all of this?" Gram sounded less than impressed. "That man is a—"

"That's not quite what happened." I put an end to whatever she was going to say because it wasn't going to be good, and Jackson still had to be related to the guy.

Jackson kept talking, refusing to get sucked into the hurricane of weirdness swirling around him. "You left the report open to the recommendations page. I know you read it."

"Kasey." Celia sighed. "We've talked about this. You need to leave a space exactly how you found it or people will know you were snooping."

Yes, that was the important lesson here.

"I was skeptical before but it's good advice," Gram added.

Time to end this so I could eat the scone instead of just holding it. "I wasn't . . . okay, everyone listen to me for a second. I wasn't snooping. I knocked over the papers and then, yes, read them but only because I saw my picture on the first page."

Gram made a noise that sounded like *huh*. "How do you define 'snooping'?"

A fair question. "I didn't actively go looking for inflammatory documents. I wanted coffee, as we've already established."

Celia looked ready to respond but Jackson beat her to it.

"I don't care that you read the report. I care that you think I asked Dad to hire a private investigator."

Now I felt bad. Poor Jackson rushed over here thinking I suspected the worst. I'd pushed him over this edge.

The scone would have to wait. "Then we don't have a problem. I don't think you had anything to do with the report."

"But you . . ." He stood there for a second without talking. "Okay, good."

"You two should work on your communication."

True but not helpful. "Gram."

Another snort. "I'm not wrong."

Jackson sat down next to me. I almost held his hand. Only the presence of our nosy and overly involved audience stopped me. "The report looked like a Harlan-created invasion of privacy. He ordered it, or whatever you do when you hire an investigator, to prove that I'm ruining your life and your political aspirations."

Jackson frowned. "I don't have political aspirations."

"Ruining his life?" Gram sounded offended. "He'd be lucky to be with you."

The tension eased from Jackson's face and body. He almost smiled. "I agree."

Did he just say . . . "Back up for a second."

"If you know the report was my dad's doing and nothing I care about, why run?"

Yeah, that. A new mess I created. "The second report."

"Two reports?" Gram made a sound I couldn't even identify. "Harlan has been a busy little toad."

Jackson put his hand on my knee and pulled my attention

right back to him. "Are you serious? I only saw the one then bolted over here."

"Your dad is very enterprising. A second report was on the stack he left for you. He had one done on Gram and Celia and the business." I took the rolled-up summary I'd ripped out of the report and put in my robe pocket. "Here."

"Have you been holding that since you came in?" Celia asked.

"His nonsense is out of control," Gram said at the same time.

Jackson took the pages and started reading.

I broke the contents down for Gram and Celia, which was the point of my partially clothed, completely spontaneous visit in the first place. "There are sections about sales and deliveries. A list of the items you offer. There's also a reference to the 'special' gift boxes and pie recipe cards."

Jackson read the beginning of that section out loud. "*An undetermined amount of money is spent on packages that are off the menu, including information on a raisin pie that is not for sale otherwise.*"

"Does it talk about poison?" Gram asked.

Oh. My. God. "Should it?"

Jackson finished reading. "This doesn't connect the pies to the customers with dead husbands. The line I read is under the financial section, which makes me think the point is about spending habits and nothing else."

"How we spend our money isn't Harlan's business." Gram's grumbling echoed throughout the room.

Jackson lowered the offensive report summary and set it on the table. "You left my condo to warn Gram and Celia? Not for any other reason."

"Like what?" Celia asked.

"Don't interrupt when it's getting good." Gram thumped her finger on the table. "Answer the man, Kasey."

The mood flipped. Chaos gave way to a tingling that felt like excitement. I blocked out Celia and Gram and gave all my attention to Jackson. "I didn't intend to leave you. I didn't want to go."

He smiled this time. "I was hoping you'd say that."

"Okay, now we really should give them some privacy." The chair skidded across the floor as Celia got up. She motioned for Gran to join her.

Gram answered with a snort. "It's our kitchen."

"We have to get ready to go anyway," Celia pointed out.

Gram continued to grumble and snort and aim all kinds of grumpy noises in my direction. "You're lucky we have church, or I'd stay in that chair all morning."

Yeah, I felt lucky. "Enjoy the service."

It took another few minutes for Gram to stand and move some dishes around. Her stalling was not subtle. Finally, Celia guided Gram out of the room, leaving me with Jackson and a heap of energy pinging between us.

"This is a uniquely embarrassing situation."

He shrugged. "I'm not embarrassed."

"Of course not. You've got clothes on." He looked great without them. Just saying. "Who would have guessed you owned lounge pants."

He took my hand and leaned in closer. His voice dropped to a whisper. "I thought you woke up and regretted what happened between us last night."

Every woman's magazine I'd ever paged through suggested

to go slow and play coy in this situation. Don't be the first one to make commitment-like noises and risk scaring him away.

I ignored every syllable of the lame advice. "I don't. You?"

He played with my fingers. Lacing his through mine. "I regret we didn't continue this morning."

He got more adorable each day. "Sweet talker."

"You look cute in my robe." He touched the space where the lapels met.

His fingertip brushed against my skin, making my breath hiccup in my chest. "Let's keep this G-rated. I'd bet the house Celia and Mags are spying on us right now."

He raised an eyebrow, looking all sexy and playful. "You could come over tonight and return the robe."

"Should I be wearing it?"

He winked. "Definitely."

"Gram was wrong. We're communicating just fine."

CHAPTER FORTY-TWO

A few hours later the house settled down. I'd returned Jackson's car keys—but not his robe because I might never give that back—so he could scamper, probably off to work. A hot shower and two cups of coffee helped to get the day back on track.

First stop, the kitchen. A pre-lunch scone waited for me. So did Gram and Celia. They'd clearly attended the shortest church service ever or skipped out on the after-service gossip, which they never did.

"You're back." I tried to make that sound like a good thing.

Celia smiled. "We are."

An ambush. *Great.*

They'd retaken their seats at the table. Gram had made an early switch today from a hot beverage to her beloved sweet tea, which meant she planned to linger as long as it took for her to get the information she wanted.

Apparently no one in Winston-Salem needed fresh pastries anytime soon.

I made it the whole way to the table and my plate before Gram spoke up. "You certainly know how to liven up a Sunday morning."

Celia nursed a cup of coffee, holding it close to her mouth but not drinking it. "Leave the poor thing alone."

"She's the one who came crashing in on our breakfast."

Celia nodded. "We've all been there."

Wait a minute. What were these two doing while I was in DC? "You've been caught wandering around town in a man's robe?"

Gram snorted. "You'd be surprised."

We'd hit on an interesting topic filled with messiness and mistakes that weren't mine. Finally. "Let's talk about that for a few minutes."

"No." Gram's tone didn't leave a lot of room for disagreement. "So, what does all of this mean?"

"You and Jackson. Together."

I figured out the context without Celia's help. "Yeah, I know what Gram is referring to."

Gram poured herself another glass of tea and hunkered down, ready to interrogate. "I'm still not hearing an answer."

That was on purpose because there was a limit to the amount of sex talk I could have with my grandmother. Celia was Jackson's aunt. This situation had *ick* written all over it. "I thought I could finish my scone first."

Gram pushed a plate full of scones in my general direction. "You can do more than one thing at a time."

Gram was not backing down. She wouldn't be happy until I presented a PowerPoint presentation on yesterday evening's activities. "You understand this is embarrassing, right?"

Celia crossed the room and picked up the jam and clotted cream. If she intended to force me to talk by stuffing me with scones . . . yeah, that would likely work.

"It shouldn't be. We've all had sex with men before." She launched that bomb as she sat down again. "Admittedly, for me, not great sex. He had no idea what he was doing."

"Men always think they're so good at it." Gram delivered a well-placed snort. "All that fumbling and grunting."

Celia made a face that showed how distasteful she thought that was. "At least it was over quickly. That was the one benefit of the lack of skill."

Gram nodded. "Falling asleep right after as if only his pleasure mattered."

The images that ran through my head would take years to forget. "I'm begging you to stop the conversation there. No details."

"What did we always tell you?" Gram brought out her angry nun tone.

We weren't Catholic but I'd watched television and assumed this was how they sounded. The *your time is up* edge to Gram's tone left little room for me to maneuver.

I gave in because they weren't going to move from those chairs until I did. They'd spent hours giving me the sex talk all those years ago. This was not how I intended to use the information, but it was shaping up to be that kind of day. "You said if I wasn't mature enough to talk about sex I shouldn't be having it."

Gram nodded. "And?"

There was a lot more, but this was the main point. "Always have safe sex. Don't depend on the man and his promises. It's your body."

"Exactly."

"Kasey." Celia's approach was calmer and less confrontational. "We know this is private and none of our business."

If true, they were hiding it well. "Do you?"

"We've noticed on this trip home that you might . . ." Celia added to the drama by drawing this out. "Have feelings for Jackson."

Gram snorted. "Wearing his robe after spending the night together confirmed that."

Honestly . . .

"We love Jackson," Celia said.

Here it comes. I braced. "But?"

"That's it." Celia spread a thick layer of jam on the nearest scone. "We love both of you. If you have feelings for each other, we're happy for you."

"Really?" Could it be that simple? No concerns about how different we were or how we fought and snipped at each other growing up . . . and sometimes now. How he was a big-time lawyer and I was whatever the opposite of that was.

"Really," Gram said. "Although living so far away is a problem."

There it was. Gram's practical side had popped out. I appreciated the way she set out the problem. I knew better than anyone how confusing and potentially messy a relationship with Jackson could be. Unfortunately, we had more than one barrier to clear. "That's only the beginning. I'm not sure I'm his type. Our lives are very interconnected, so what happens if this goes sideways? And Harlan. Enough said on that last one."

Gram shook her head the second I said his name. "Only the last one is a problem. A big toad of a problem."

She wasn't wrong. The comment made me think about Savannah, Jackson's mom. She'd married Harlan and stayed with him for years. I remembered her hugs. She wore this ever-present smile. It wasn't until I got older that I realized her sunny disposition was a mask she wore to survive each day.

Pain and depression from a life spent dealing with repeated

bouts of cancer and devastating test results. I blamed Harlan for the rest. His coldness. His dismissal. His inability to keep his pants on. His lack of empathy. "Was he always like this? Like, Savannah met him and was all *he's the one for me*? That's so hard to imagine."

Celia hesitated for long enough that it looked like she might not answer. "We grew up in a religiously strict and insular household. We never had friends over. We weren't allowed to participate in activities or on teams. No dating. No television. Our lives consisted of home and church and little else."

Celia hadn't grown up in a cult. Not exactly but close. I researched the church when Celia mentioned it years ago. The rules left no room for imagination or questions.

"My parents ran a hardware store. Harlan came in and announced he now owned the property and was their landlord. He was charming and handsome. He said the right things." Celia sounded sadder as her explanation went on. "I think Savannah saw a way out of a life she hated."

Gram's hand disappeared under the table, and I knew it was on Celia's knee. Gram, so outspoken and fierce, had few weaknesses but Celia was one of them.

"It's not an unusual story. It mirrors mine. I married because I wanted a child. Mags married to get away from her father. Sometimes escaping leads to a new kind of hell." Celia looked lost in her vivid memories. "We didn't think we had a lot of options, which is part of the reason we made sure you did."

"We're hoping you break the cycle of the women who came before you. To do that you need to find your way," Gram said.

Celia nodded. "We're here for you."

I agreed but thinking about all of this right now felt like too much, so I tried to lighten the mood. "You still haven't told me what you think I should be when I grow up."

"Easy," Celia said. "You should write."

Gram nodded. "Get paid for those wild stories you create in your head."

They spelled out my dream. Make up stories. Write all those fantastical ideas that I shoved aside as soon as I entered the workforce. But I had to be realistic. "How do I afford to eat in this scenario?"

Celia leaned over and squeezed my hand. "You will always have a soft landing here."

Always. I knew it, felt it. Saw it every day in how they treated each other and supported me. I messed up repeatedly and their only requirement was that I get back up and try again.

Jackson told me he was lucky about how he grew up. Actually, I was the lucky one. Not during the first six years but in every year after.

"I know it's probably terrible to say but I'm happy both of your husbands died earlier than expected and you two found each other." I could admit that here, in private, at this table. Anywhere else would be a big no-no. Wishing people dead wasn't the polite Southern thing to do.

Gram snorted. "It took them long enough to go."

"Mags."

"What? I'm not wrong." Gram took a sip of her tea. "It took so long in my house that I had to help the process along."

Every thought I had screeched to a halt in my brain. I could hear the crash and pileup. "What did you just say?"

Celia gasped. "She doesn't need to be burdened with this part."

"She can handle it."

That comment touched off a back-and-forth between Celia and Mags. One that didn't include me. They continued with each throwing out an argument and the other one ignoring it or talking around it. I caught only pieces because they talked in code. Phrases rather than full sentences. At one point, Gram even used an acronym I couldn't decipher.

All the bickering led to one conclusion. A fact that was both shocking and not. Their secret. It was all but set out in lights in front of me.

"You both poisoned your husbands." Yep. I said it. That was the answer we'd avoided until now.

"Not quite." Celia put up her hand as if to stop the runaway conversation. "Mine really did die in a car accident. That's when I discovered he'd squandered all the money and used my name and social security number to acquire more debt."

Gram pulled out a snort here. "He got lucky because he deserved a harsher way out."

Okay. Wait a second. "Worse than dying in a fiery crash?"

Gram shrugged but Celia pushed on. "We don't kill other women's terrible husbands. The women decide what they need to do."

Gram saved her biggest snort for right now. "We would if we could get away with it."

Celia didn't flinch. "Sometimes removing the threat is the only way out. Not always, not even most times, so we present all other options first."

"If all else fails, we provide a how-to guide and the necessary supplies," Gram added.

Supplies . . . yep.

How in the world was I going to explain all of this to Jackson? Or keep these ladies from getting arrested? Those were two of the questions banging around in my head at the moment.

I needed this one answered first. "I don't want the two of you to get in trouble. So, where are these *necessary supplies* now that they're no longer in the locked cabinet?"

I was wrong. Gram had one snort left. "What did you think we kept in that locked shed in the backyard?"

CHAPTER FORTY-THREE

The shed. Not the pantry. Not the baking annex. The shed. After a wildly eventful morning and a delicious lunch of leftover pot roast, I stood outside, looking at said shed. I'd spent my whole life assuming the most interesting thing in there was the lawn mower. In hindsight, who would lock down a lawn mower? Then there was the fact Gram had a gardener who took care of the grass, and he brought his own equipment.

The lock stopped me from getting in there and . . . what? My next move was a bit fuzzy. Find the poison first then assess. Removing it from the property or destroying it would be the next problem to tackle. No poison, no jailtime. It worked that way, right?

I could ask for the key, but Gram was already ticked off about the business pitch thing. I knew because she reminded me about it at lunch and how Harlan, Micah, Brock, or some combination of them could drop by for a visit at any time, and she couldn't be held responsible for her actions.

Brock and Micah and their annoying texts would need to wait.

The shed wasn't huge, but poison probably didn't take up much space. No windows. Made of wood and freshly painted, which was interesting. I hadn't noticed before because shed maintenance wasn't on my radar.

I walked around the structure just in case there was some sort of trapdoor I didn't know about. A woman could hope.

"What are you doing?"

At the sound of that voice, I lost my balance and reached for the nearest thing to grab on to. Unfortunately, that was a rosebush with no flowers but lots of thorns, which then led to a lot of swearing.

Only Harlan could cause this much trouble.

"When did you get here?" I really wanted to ask *Why in the world do you keep showing up wherever I am?* but refrained out of respect for Jackson.

"My assistant ordered a dessert tray for my business partner's birthday tomorrow. She usually handles these things, but I was in the neighborhood and figured I'd save her a trip in the morning." He nodded, clearly pleased with his pathetic excuse for informally stalking me. "I pulled into the driveway and saw you. Thought I'd say hello."

Believable? Not really. Seemed to me a dessert tray for tomorrow would be packed up fresh for pick-up *tomorrow*. I glanced at the side of the house and couldn't see anything but the side of the house. We were tucked in behind the building. I didn't hear traffic. Only the gentle sway of the tree branches in the wind.

It sucked to foist him off on Celia and Gram, but I did anyway. "The ladies are in the kitchen. They said something about testing mini cupcakes."

Gram actually said the whole concept of mini cupcakes was

ridiculous because why not just eat a normal-sized one. Gram thought a lot of things were ridiculous. She was right about mini cupcakes. Making them smaller only meant I had to eat five of them, which meant they'd have to make a lot of cupcakes.

"I wanted to speak with you anyway, so this is convenient," he said.

For him, maybe.

He studied me for a few seconds. Probably his attempt at intimidation. Only Gram had that power, but he could try.

"I'd like for us to come to an understanding that would serve both of our interests."

This morning's embarrassment looked like it might be the best part of my day. I couldn't even hope for a rain delay. There wasn't a cloud in the deep blue sky. "About what exactly?"

Harlan glanced at the shed. It held his attention for longer than it should have. Long enough to make me jumpy. He couldn't possibly know why the shed mattered. Unless he planted a listening device in the house . . . and now I had something new to worry about.

"Look, I know you're in trouble at work." He smiled. "Let me help."

He sounded so virtuous, like he was doing whatever he was doing for my benefit. Now I understood why Gram snorted all the time. Sometimes it felt right. Like now. "You've been hanging out with Brock."

Harlan crossed his arms in front of him. His body language telegraphed his willingness to listen to reason. None. He had none. "Your boss and I have business interests in common. We've been discussing how we might help each other."

Worst. Sentence. Ever.

"I've lobbied for you, of course. Explained that you're young and inexperienced and needed time to settle into a new job," Harlan continued.

I could see it now. Harlan's condescending manner would fit in well at NOI. "Exactly how much time have you spent with Brock?"

"Enough to know you're treading water." Harlan closed the gap between us. A show of intimidation even as he used his smarmy fake charm to win me over. "I don't like to say this, but the truth is you're out of your league on this deal. We both know negotiations aren't your strength."

This guy needed a class in *how not to be a jackass.*

"Brock and I have worked on a draft proposal. One that calls upon my connections in state government and one that will greatly benefit your grandmother and Celia," Harlan said.

Gram warned me about men who wouldn't take no for an answer. She said to avoid them and if that didn't work to kick them where it would hurt the most. Harlan was getting mighty close to a kick in the balls.

"They aren't interested. They really aren't interested if I'm not involved." The former cut off any chance of the latter, but I wanted to make the point.

"Let's be realistic. They're not getting younger. They've taken this enterprise as far as they can. While their drive is commendable, they can't sustain it." Harlan nodded as if we'd entered into some sort of conspiracy. "We both know that."

No wonder Gram hated this guy. "You should tell them all that. I'd love to be in the room when you do."

"Then there's the harsh reality they can't ignore." He hesitated, as if the moment weren't tense enough. "A business like theirs depends on referrals and recommendations. On the support of others."

That smell? The stench of an incoming threat.

He must have enjoyed the sound of his own voice because he kept yapping. "I send a great deal of work their way. I'm happy to do it, of course. But I wonder if I'm doing them a disservice. Would it be better to refrain so they could see the rough road ahead and exit now with a great deal of money in their pockets rather than face an inevitable downturn?"

I'd been shifting my weight, crunching the grass under my sneaker. Now everything inside me froze. He'd hit on the one threat that would work. I'd do anything to prevent an attack on Celia and Gram, even one that supposedly was for their own good.

"Celia is your sister-in-law."

"Yes, exactly, that's why I originally stepped up. I've given time and resources. Used my contacts. It was the right thing to do when they were getting started, but is it now?" He took a long look around the yard. "This place can't be cheap to run and would be impossible to hold on to without an ongoing income stream. I'd hate to see them lose it."

No way did adorable, brainy, very skilled with his hands Jackson come from this empty shell of a guy.

"Gram and Celia have never been anything but welcoming to you." It was a guess based on Celia's personality. Gram would have booted him out of her life long ago if she'd had the choice.

"And I enjoy their company."

Sure, he did.

"If you stepped aside. Went back home. I'd take over. The buyout would be quick and painless. I'd even give you the credit for the initial referral as a way of helping you maintain your job." He oozed confidence. Stood there as if he didn't doubt his ability to win this round. "I would do that for you. For them. If I was the only one here and in charge. You understand."

I'd seen the threat coming but it still landed with a hard thud and vibrated through me. "You want me out of Winston-Salem? The place where I grew up."

"That's overly dramatic. I'm trying to ease the way for you to return home. To Washington, DC. That's where you live now. Not here." His smile had a sinister edge to it. "You have responsibilities there. Bills to pay. I'm willing to help you do that."

"Was money trouble listed in your little investigative report?"

His smile fell. His mood flipped that fast. "Jackson showed you?"

Sure, let's use that word. "I've read it, including the recommendations."

Harlan let out a long, I'm-ticked-off exhale. "That's routine in political matters. The financial backers need assurances about the nonpublic aspects of Jackson's life."

Blah, blah, blah. I didn't need a law degree to understand this. He was vetting possible future Mrs. Jackson Quaid candidates as if Jackson was a client and not his son. Under all the fake *I'm doing this for you* crap, Harlan wanted me to know I'd been considered and eliminated as a potential partner. He also planned to use my love for Gram and Celia to remove me from the area entirely.

Harlan held up a hand as if to swat away any arguments. "I love my son."

Clearly. "What an interesting way to show it."

"Do not doubt my feelings or how far I will go to secure Jackson's future. We don't always agree but he's very intelligent. Driven. Practical. He understands his obligations and what a failure it would be to waste his potential. He'll come around to the right answer."

Was Harlan trying to convince me or him? I couldn't tell.

"We want the same things, Kasey."

"I really doubt that."

"Success for you and success for Jackson. Not together. I'm sure you see that. But I do want to help you. I just need to make sure we have an understanding about your role." He reached into his pocket and pulled out his car fob. As far as dismissals went, this one was pretty clear. "Can you imagine how awful it would be if Magnolia and Celia had to sell the business and the house at a very reduced price?"

"You're an—"

"Harlan. I didn't see you drive up." Gram shouted her welcome as she walked across the pristine yard. "Usually people call before they visit. That's the appropriate way to do these things."

"You're correct and I apologize for the intrusion. I needed to pick up an order and—"

Gram snorted. "You? Today?"

"I saw Kasey in the yard. I wanted to say hello. My understanding is she'll be leaving town soon."

Gram took a quick look toward the driveway. It looked like she doubted his I-can-see-through-buildings explanation, too. "Who told you such a thing?"

"I have a meeting, so I need to leave." The car fob and a few keys on his chain dangled from his fingers. "I'll talk to you soon."

With that, he broke away from us and headed toward the driveway. The driveway you couldn't see from this angle.

"Harlan?" Gram called out, stopping his overconfident steps. "Have you ever had raisin pie?"

Oh, shit.

He frowned. "I don't believe so."

"Maybe I'll make you one."

Harlan nodded and left. I waited until he disappeared around the corner to confront Gram. "You can't kill him."

"We'll see." Gram shrugged. "Why are you out here?"

"Getting some fresh air." I said a silent thank-you to Celia for that lifetime excuse. Not that it was true. I'd asked about seeing inside the shed earlier and Gram had handed me a cupcake. The trick worked to delay my snooping, not erase it, which was why I stood right here.

"Stop worrying about the shed. I have it handled." She stared in the empty space where Harlan had just stood. "What did he say to you?"

This required a delicate dance. The last thing I wanted was for Celia and Gram to worry about Harlan's pontificating. *"You should be in DC. Jackson has a future here without you.* You know, the usual."

"That nonsense about Jackson? Ignore it." Gram added a *pfft* in there to drive home her point. "He's a grown man. He knows what he wants."

My thoughts about Jackson, our relationship, and his feelings about it jumbled together. The moving pieces refused to stop shifting long enough for me to put the puzzle together. "Maybe, but you still can't feed Harlan poison pie."

Gram didn't respond for a few seconds. When she finally did, she hummed. "You'd be surprised what I can justify."

CHAPTER FORTY-FOUR

This morning started with finding the report, continued with an unwanted visit, complete with a side of not-so-subtle threats from Harlan, and ended now. In Gram's backyard. It was pretty sad this moment was the high point of my day.

I held the bolt cutter I bought this afternoon. The guy at the home improvement store looked concerned when I said I needed whatever tool would help me break a lock and that I needed the most powerful one he had. Because what did I know about heavy-duty versus regular when it came to bolt cutters? Better to go big and be safe.

I hadn't had this much excitement since my DC neighbor carved *I suck at sex* into the side of her husband's—soon to be ex-husband's—car when she found out he was having an affair. I was there for the "after" when the husband came home and saw it. He didn't appreciate the decoration and called the police. The wife stumped the officers when she explained that her name was also on the title, so she could do whatever she wanted to the car. All in all, a very interesting three hours.

"When you said we should go out tonight, I thought you meant on a date." Jackson leaned against the shed. "Not that sneaking around Mags and Celia's backyard isn't fun, but we haven't had dinner yet and you lured me here with the promise of a predinner muffin. Where's the muffin?"

He looked more adorable than usual. He'd refused to wear all black because, and I quote, *we're not robbing the place*. He really needed to work on his killjoy tendencies. After I promised to model the tie to his robe—without the robe—when we got back to the condo, he conceded to putting on jeans and a black sweater. Close enough.

"Admit it. You enjoy the drama."

"I can see why you'd think so." He looked at the bolt cutter. "Are you ready to explain why you're holding that?"

I'd tucked the tool away on the far side of the shed, near the old greenhouse, after I bought it. I'd waited until we got in the yard to pull it out. Jackson took the reveal surprisingly well. He didn't initially ask what we were doing, but Jackson being Jackson, now he had questions.

I stuck to a simple answer. "To break the lock."

It was just after eight. The sun had gone down about fifteen minutes ago. The porch light clicked on via timer just as Gram and Celia settled in to watch some sort of FBI show.

"There." I pointed behind him.

He stood up straight. Scanned the area. Frowned. "The shed?"

"It's weird it has a lock, right?"

"No."

That answer wasn't helpful at all. Of course, I hadn't exactly told him why we were here or given him a complete rundown of my conversation with his dad, then Gram. All Jackson knew was that I wanted to stop by to check on something, then we could have dinner.

"Gram said she keeps the poison in here. Or did. Honestly, I was too stunned by her admission to ask follow-up questions, so the timing isn't clear."

"When did she tell you this?"

"Earlier today."

"Was the timing unclear because she plied you with a dessert?"

The amusement in his voice threatened to sidetrack me, but I stayed focused on the shed door. "Don't just stand around looking adorable. Help me."

He didn't move. "One question. How are we going to find the poison?"

"With our eyes." Seemed obvious to me. "The shed is, what, six-by-eight? There won't be many places to hide it."

"Uh-huh."

That tone. He doubted my plan and now he had me doing it, too. "Come on. How hard can this be? We'll know it when we see it."

"Do you think it will be in a jar that says 'poison'?"

Kind of?

He sighed at me. It sounded like he'd been holding it in for a while. "There are different kinds of poison. Some—"

"Nope." He'd fully downshifted into lawyer mode. We didn't have time for that. "As much as I'd love to hear you talk on this subject, let's get moving. Those ladies are nosy. They could come out here at any time."

"Second question." He held up two fingers.

I didn't need the hand gestures. I also couldn't afford this delay. "You said you had one."

"Consider it the second part of my initial question." He talked fast enough to block any interruptions. "Why do we want to take the poison out of the locked shed, to the extent it's even in there and we can identify it? Theoretically, isn't it safest in there?"

We needed to bury it. Destroy it. Hide it away from the property. But mostly to keep it from Harlan. "Could we talk about this later?"

"We could until I saw your expression just now." Jackson folded his arms in front of him and sent out a strong *we're not doing anything until you talk* vibe. "What happened?"

"Nothing."

"Kasey."

I debated engaging in the time-honored skill of ignoring a direct question, but Jackson would be all over that sort of subterfuge. "Fine. Harlan. He said some things."

"When the hell was this?"

"He reiterated the same stuff that was in the report. I'm not girlfriend material and so on."

"Are you serious?"

"Look, none of this is important." I tried to wave off the concerns but from the strained look on Jackson's face I'd failed. "Your dad is on a mission that's somehow spilled over into my work mess. If he comes over here, or convinces the ladies to listen to a pitch, he'll be walking around, maybe with Micah and Brock, and we can't risk them stumbling over the poison."

"Are you saying or, more accurately, trying not to say Dad threatened you?"

Jackson seemed to be stuck on the point I'd tried to dance around. "Harlan talked about the business and how Gram and Celia depended on his goodwill for clients. He chose his words carefully, but you know how he is."

Jackson took the bolt cutter out of my hand and set it on the ground. "Tell me exactly what he said."

"The point is Gram and Celia won't cave to your dad's relentless lobbying unless they have no choice. He could make things miserable for them and force them into a position they can't escape."

Jackson swore under his breath. "That must have been a hell of a conversation."

I'd killed off Jackson's good mood. The flirty, cute side of him vanished in favor of the ticked-off side. I knew his frustration wasn't aimed at me but that didn't make being the person delivering the news any easier.

"It will all be fine." I'm not sure I believed that, but . . .

I refused to dwell on what this all meant for what was happening between me and Jackson and how it would play out. Right now, I was taking life one minute at a time, avoiding any talk of the future. To act in any other way would let my mind wander into dangerous territory and paralyze me. Lock me in a state of confusion and sadness that might be impossible to escape.

"You're giving Dad too much credit. He's not that powerful."

Someone should tell Harlan that.

"And he's way out of line. I've placated Dad on this political thing and clearly that was the wrong call."

"It's understandable. You wanted a relationship with your dad. That's probably a healthy thing." Sweet, actually, but I didn't have any experience on this particular topic. "I know you don't want to lose contact."

"That will be up to him."

I didn't like the sound of that. "What are you saying?"

Jackson brushed his fingertips over my arm. He took my hands and put them on his hips. Held me close. "What if I asked you to trust me?"

"I do trust you." Totally. That had never been a question.

"Then trust me to handle Dad."

This time his fingers skimmed my cheek. The temptation to lean into his touch swept threw me. My body swayed and my self-control bobbled. "What if he—"

He leaned in and kissed me. Soft and quick. Sweet and inviting.

"Trust me." He whispered the plea against my lips.

"The poison—"

His hands slipped up my back and his fingers plunged into my hair. "Isn't going anywhere tonight."

My concentration blinked in and out. I struggled to hold on to my original plan because Harlan clearly didn't intend to back down. "What if we can't beat him?"

"You continue to underestimate my skills."

No, I feared the potential blowback on Mags' Desserts from the mess I'd created. "If I get even a hint of this going sideways, I'm breaking into the shed, stealing the poison, and hiding it."

"I can and will beat him." He finally smiled. "But now is the time to concentrate on a more enjoyable topic."

Really. So cute. "Eating muffins?"

He pretended to think about it. "I guess we can do that naked, too."

CHAPTER FORTY-FIVE

After a second night with Jackson, in his bed, snuggling with him in his condo, talking about nonsense things and important things, I walked around in a daze. Every kiss dragged me further under his spell. Problems that used to stick out, like how different we were, started to fade in importance.

The hopeful, in-love side of me battled with the *this could go really bad* side. I didn't know which side would win, but I feared I knew which one should.

Jackson headed for work later than usual and dropped me off at Gram's. The scene had a homey feel to it. The only thing that could make the morning better was a scone. Warm with jam. I dreamed about the taste during the car ride over here.

One step into the kitchen and my scone fantasy vanished. Gram and Celia sat there, talking with Abigail Burns. *The* Abigail Burns. For the second time. The ladies had to know Abigail's visiting should not become a habit. Not while she still was a murder suspect.

I inhaled, preparing for whatever storm was gathering strength on the horizon. "Good morning."

Gram sipped her tea. "Kasey, you remember Abigail."

All too well. "How are you, Mrs. Burns?"

"Abigail, please."

We shook hands. Mine swallowed hers. She was so petite. So pretty and polite. It was the other *p* words that caused the problem—"poison" and "prison."

She looked like a lot of the women in town. Blond, and almost doll-like with how perfectly she sat and talked and walked. The type of woman that always wore the right clothes and knew the right people. She likely performed huge amounts of unpaid work for local charities and had once done the same in parent groups at Austin's schools.

Abigail probably enjoyed a full life before marriage and certainly deserved one now. From all the whispers around town, Cash had viewed her as the perfect trophy wife for someone with his pedigree and credentials. A trophy he could put on the shelf and ignore. A trophy he could break.

Gram gestured for me to join them at the table. "Abigail was just telling us about the initial findings in her husband's death investigation."

No buildup. Gram dove right in.

I was afraid to move. Afraid I might say the wrong thing. "Good."

Not my smoothest moment but how exactly did one handle a situation like this? We all knew the truth, or pieces of it, but were pretending we didn't. I loved to make up stories but I'm not sure I could have created one like this.

Celia frowned at my word choice. "The police believe Cash was poisoned."

Not new information. The fact the ladies tiptoed into this topic meant something. With my luck, something very bad.

"The police have narrowed down the contamination to his water bottle. It had traces of arsenic in it," Gram said.

Abigail twisted a napkin between her fingers. "He had this thing about staying hydrated. He used the bottle at work. No one else could touch it. It was a rule of his."

Convenient and helpful for Abigail's plan. There must have been two bottles and some big switch I couldn't figure out, but I could imagine Gram coming up with this scenario.

"Apparently arsenic is odorless and can't be detected by taste, so it's easy to administer." Gram took another sip of tea. Then one more. "It often isn't detected in the bloodstream after death because no one thinks to test for it."

Look at Gram knowing all the arsenic facts.

"The dose must have been high enough to kill him. He called me that day and complained about stomach pain. He'd started vomiting." Abigail cleared her throat and her fingers kept clenching that napkin. "Naturally, I thought it was the flu or maybe food poison . . . poisoning."

Sure, she did.

"The police were skeptical about the death being from natural causes from the start. Something about the way he was clutching the water bottle when his assistant found him tipped them off," Abigail continued. "That's why they tested everything in his office, including the watercooler. And ran the appropriate tests on him."

All three of them acted like they were sharing some shocking reveal, but their body language didn't match their words. They held their bodies stiff to the point of snapping.

I tried to think of a question to ask. The kind of question

someone who didn't know anything would ask. "How would the arsenic get in the bottle?"

I really wanted to ask where one would get arsenic. You couldn't just pick it up at the store or order it over the internet . . . unless you could. I was the only one at the table who was not an expert on arsenic. But since the answer to that hypothetical question would likely be *Gram* I skipped it.

"No one knows. The poison wasn't found anywhere else in the office or in the water supply. There were security cameras in the lobby and outside the building, but there wasn't anything unusual or unexpected on the video. The police checked at home, too, of course, and found nothing."

Gram nodded. "The whole thing is so unfortunate."

Oh, Gram.

After a bit of stammering, Abigail continued. "The water bottle was out in the open. On his desk. It only has Cash's fingerprints on it. The police have no clue what happened or how."

For a second, so short, the pain cleared from Abigail's face. She looked relieved.

"Scary." And by that I meant it was scary how good these ladies were at this.

The three of them had the discussion down. They'd delivered the information without flinching and with only a few minor bobbles. Maybe they'd performed this same show many times, with other women. It's also possible they'd rehearsed what to say and when to say it, to be safe. Except for the tension pulsing through the room, they'd completely sold this version of the story.

"So, now what?" I asked, because the possibility of having to bail Gram and Celia out of jail still lingered.

"The police are waiting for more forensic findings, but they don't have a suspect or a motive," Abigail said.

There was that flash of relief again. Abigail really needed to work on that.

"Well, thanks for listening and for the coffee. I wanted to deliver the news in person since you both have been so kind." Abigail smiled at Gram and Celia as she stood up. "As you suggested, I'm going to stay with my sister in Nashville for a while. There's nothing much for me here, except good friends."

Celia took the cup Abigail had been using and placed it in the sink. "When do you leave?"

"Due to the circumstances, we're having a private memorial service for Cash. I need to help Austin figure out his next steps. He's talked about returning to college, starting in the summer."

I was going to need to know which college so I could stay away from it.

"The police said as long as I kept them informed of my location and was accessible, I didn't have to stay in town. I'll probably leave in a couple of weeks."

Celia hugged Abigail. "We'll talk before then."

"Definitely." Abigail treated Gram and Celia to one final, small smile before turning to me. "It was nice seeing you again."

I waited until Abigail left, even watched her slip out and get in her car, before saying anything. "Did I walk into the middle of some sort of session to make sure you all have your alibis straight?"

"We don't deal in arsenic."

It was the way Gram said things these days that put me on edge. "You're telling me you didn't give her the poison or show her how to use it?"

Gram nodded. "Correct."

"We provide advice and an ear. We listen. What a woman does from there is her choice," Celia said.

A lovely speech. "So, if I break into the shed I won't find arsenic?"

Gram frowned. "I told you to stay out of the shed. There's nothing in there you need to worry about. Not now."

"Let's stop talking about the shed. It's not relevant to Abigail's situation." Celia picked up a plate piled with freshly baked scones. "Want one?"

I didn't know what to do with all the questions floating through my head. I went with the most obvious and troublesome one. "There's no way the arsenic can be traced back to you two, right? All I care about right now, which is a terrible thing to say because a man is dead, is if the arsenic connects to you in any way."

"It won't." Celia didn't evade this time. "We don't know anything about arsenic. I promise you Abigail did not get that from us."

A scary but clear answer. My stomach started to unclench. For a few minutes, all the bad news and conflicting information bouncing around the kitchen made the muscles in my neck seize. I rubbed the sore spot.

"Abigail went rogue. We wouldn't have told her to use arsenic." Gram drank the rest of her drink. "Not when there are much easier solutions out there."

The tension crawled right back up my spine. "Meaning?"

Gram sighed. "Don't ask questions when you don't want to know the answers."

CHAPTER FORTY-SIX

The next day in the afternoon, for the first time in, well, ever, I called Micah. I wanted to end the charade, explain that the ladies had decided not to sell, and slam the door shut once and for all on a partnership between NOI and Mags' Desserts. Handling that mess would leave the Harlan problem sitting out there like a blaring alarm, but I wasn't ready to tackle him or his ego yet.

Micah's assistant said he was out of the office today and tomorrow on something business-related. His trip provided a small reprieve and time for planning my next move. When he got back, I hoped to talk him into letting me work from here for another week. That would give me a few more days and nights with Jackson.

I'd tell Micah I needed the extra time to ferret out what other food deals might be possible in the area. Winston-Salem already gave the world yummy doughnuts. There were many other decidedly Southern food delicacies around here I could pitch as a possible investment.

Jackson was at work. Gram and Celia were engaged in baking prep. We'd talked and thought about poison enough for the past few days—for a lifetime, really—so I could concentrate on something much more important. Cupcakes. The delivery schedule had referenced a bridal shower and a children's charity event. Both required cupcakes, which meant there would be unused batter waiting for me in the baking annex.

I walked in expecting to find the room humming with activity. The ladies baking. Maybe an assistant or two flitting around. None of that was happening. Gram and Celia sat at the table drinking tea. Celia was willingly sharing Gram's pitcher of sweet tea, which meant Celia was either trying to calm Gram down or trying to convince Gram of something.

Either way? Not great.

"What's going on? I was looking for a tub of unused batter and a spoon."

Neither of them answered me. Celia pointed to a bowl on the counter and the spatula balancing on its edge that had something that looked delicious on it.

Tempting, but the sugar fix would need to wait until I waded through whatever this was.

I sat down, dreading the incoming conversation. "What happened and how bad is it?"

Gram poured herself another glass of tea. "Harlan is on his way over."

"Oh, come on." He did not give up. Some people might praise his tenacity. Not me. "Good grief, why? What now?"

His not-so-gentle suggestion that I leave or the business could lose clients repeated nonstop in my head. He hadn't directly issued an ultimatum but came damn close. I hadn't filled in Gram and Celia. With all the conversations and information bouncing around, I'd left them out of this one. Harlan clearly planned to drag them in.

"He's bringing a man he wants us to meet." Celia's voice sounded rougher than usual, as if she'd been arguing with Gram for quite a while before I walked in. "A man who has a business proposition for us."

Oh, no . . .

Gram snorted. "It's the beady-eyed rat."

The perfect description of Brock. "Okay, I still have the same question. Why, as in why agree to a visit? You are not selling. End of story."

"True, but Harlan wasn't going to stop pushing, so we offered to hear him out," Celia said.

She sounded so calm. So unemotional. That shook me more than the idea of Harlan strutting in here, throwing his weight around, and unleashing hell.

"We'll listen for as long as we can tolerate this nonsense, then we can say no and throw Harlan and his sidekick out." Gram made her famous *pfft* sound. "At least this time Harlan remembered his manners and asked first before dropping in."

Good job, Harlan. He finally got something right.

"A showdown of sorts was inevitable." Celia took a sip of tea then put the glass to the side. She'd probably had enough sugar in that one mouthful to last a week. "Harlan is relentless. Always looking for new angles. He thinks he can pummel us into submission with his charm."

Gram made a grumbling noise that was tough to describe. "He'd have to go find some charm first."

"He'll lose this round, then eventually come crawling back again, with a different proposal and new players, and try again," Celia said.

"So, why bother to entertain him now?" I knew the answer. They'd agreed for me and for Jackson. Gram and Celia spent their lives trying to make things better for us, trying to protect Jackson from Harlan's pressure and interference.

We were all so busy helping each other and being secretive about it that Harlan had slinked in when our defensive shields were down. When this was over, and it had to end soon or my thumping headache might become permanent, I needed to sit down with Gram and Celia and explain that it was time they put themselves first. They'd given enough.

"We'll keep doing this until Harlan tires himself out or he finds a more lucrative business opportunity," Celia said.

They knew him but did they know he viewed himself as their pastry savior and wanted to take over? "That's a lot of attention from a guy who thinks your business is a hobby."

"If he says anything like that today I'm going to make him a funeral pie. Neither one of you can talk me out of it." Gram sounded serious.

"Let's stay positive."

Celia had to be kidding. She also had to know giving Harlan any opening was a mistake. I might not be a lawyer, but I knew that. "I think we shouldn't—"

One sharp knock then the annex door opened. Harlan and Brock stepped inside. They both wore dark suits and sunglasses. They held folders no one sitting at the table wanted to see. They shared a smarmy vibe. They marched in sync.

Matching jackasses.

"Thank you for agreeing to see us here today." Harlan watched Gram during his greeting.

Her noncommittal response wasn't a surprise. "Hmmm."

"Brock Deavers, this is Magnolia Nottingham and Celia

Windsor." The wattage of Harlan's smile didn't flicker when he looked in my direction. "You know Kasey."

I was about to see Harlan in his finest lobbying form.

"Of course. She's been doing advance work for me on this proposal." Brock's *do not blow this* expression dared me to disagree. "Assistant work."

Calling him a jackass had been too nice.

"Magnolia, it's a pleasure." Brock extended his hand to Gram.

She took it but delivered a shot as well. "Call me Ms. Nottingham."

Score one for Gram.

"Please sit." Celia gestured toward the other side of the table. Doing so meant she avoided a formal greeting from Brock. Good choice.

They all sat down. I pulled over a chair and joined them.

"Kasey, I can handle the details and overview. You don't need to wade through the finer points with us." Brock opened a binder and pulled out what looked like a report. Apparently he'd been busy in between his rounds of golf. "Why don't you—"

"My granddaughter stays."

Second point to Gram.

Brock wore a tight smile. "Of course."

"We're happy to have Kasey here," Harlan said but couldn't possibly mean. "We're talking about a proposal that benefits the entire family."

"Uh-huh." Gram wasn't giving an inch.

"Right. Well, you know why we asked to see you today." Harlan relaxed into his chair, coming off very much at home in the annex, where he wasn't actually welcome.

Gram looked Harlan up and down, letting him know she was not impressed. "Not really since we've made it clear the business is not for sale."

Gram reached for her glass of tea. She didn't offer anyone else a drink. That had to be killing her. Southern hospitality and a certain level of graciousness were ingrained in her DNA. She'd been the perfect hostess for most of her life. Not greeting her guests with a smile, not putting out a spread of fresh pastries and suitable drinks, went against everything she believed in. They might not know it, but her actions telegraphed how little she thought of her unwanted guests.

"I know you've said your position is firm, Mags." Harlan passed glossy-covered folders around the table. "I think once you've heard the offer you might change your mind."

"Doubt it."

Honestly, Gram didn't need me for this. She could hold her own with almost anyone. People mistook her cute, tiny grandmother persona for weakness. The dumbasses. She had a backbone of steel and a deep dislike of Harlan, so this could devolve quickly.

"Kasey knows this is a good deal. One you should consider." Brock stared at me. Put his whole you're-about-to-be-fired *hmpf* behind it. "Correct?"

Since I expected to lose my job within the next few days, possibly minutes, what did I have to lose by going against him? Hell, I was shocked I still had the job, so whatever punishment he thought he could levy didn't really pack a punch.

My real concern and the reason I refused to move from my chair was Harlan and his whims. I didn't trust him as far as I could drop-kick him . . . and I really wanted to drop-kick him.

What was stopping him from running me out of town and out of Jackson's life and still waging a campaign of destruction against Mags' Desserts? In Harlan's mind, absolutely nothing. He wanted the business and was willing to destroy his relationships with everyone around him to get it.

"Are we interrupting?"

I spun around at the sound of Jackson's voice. He walked in with . . . Micah.

I did not see that shocker coming but now I knew exactly why Jackson asked me to trust him. The man had a plan.

Let the fireworks fly.

CHAPTER FORTY-SEVEN

Harlan's posture was the exact opposite of relaxed now. He sat up straight, looking ready to spring. "Your office said you were in a meeting all afternoon."

"Right. This one." Jackson skipped right over Brock to smile at Gram and Celia. "This is Micah Bainbridge, the owner of NOI and Kasey's boss."

"He's Brock's boss, too." I didn't need to add that bit but seeing Brock sitting there bubbling with anger and unable to release it made the moment worthwhile.

"We seem to have a misunderstanding about who is handling what issue. We should clear that up now." Jackson stood there, fully in charge and unimpressed with the hurricane of frustration building in the men at the table.

That thing where I used to think of him as stiff and unbending? A tad dull? Dead wrong. There was nothing boring about this man. His voice, that stance, the way he stormed in here at just the right moment, all said sexy.

He had an air of confidence that never tipped into jackass territory. Intelligent. Competent. So unbelievably adorable. The sexy combination made me feel sorry for his ex, Anna, for losing him. Not sorry enough to say it out loud or find her phone number and tell her, but that woman did miss out.

Harlan stood up. "Jackson, I need to speak with you outside for a moment."

"Of course."

Harlan started to move. "We can—"

"After we straighten out this confusion. I know you want to resolve this as much as I do."

Harlan's jaw clenched so tight I could hear the snapping sound. "Correct."

Oh, damn. Harlan would blame me for this. He would never accept that Jackson was a grown man with beliefs and dreams separate from the family name. That he had a strong enough ego to fight when necessary and to back off when appropriate.

Where Harlan didn't have an off switch when it came to things he wanted, and plowed ahead and pressured, his son had boundaries. And Jackson came out swinging here.

"I called Micah yesterday afternoon about a business opportunity." Jackson didn't offer more even though there was definitely more to say.

Celia frowned. "You did?"

"Interesting." The bulk of the fury drained out of Harlan. His unreadable expression said he didn't know if he'd won this round or not. "We do have a misunderstanding or a scheduling issue because if I had known we could have combined our talents."

Jackson had made a promise to me when we stood at that shed two days ago. I counted on him to follow through. That's who he was. Harlan might be cautiously optimistic and growing in confidence but if my instincts were correct, we were about to see a fiery crash.

Good thing I was sitting down because the fallout from this wreckage could get wild.

"I went directly to the person responsible for making the major decisions at NOI." Jackson nodded in Micah's direction. "The man in charge."

Harlan glanced at Brock. "I may have gotten the wrong impression. I thought Brock was handling this acquisition."

Micah watched as the conversation unraveled around him. "Handling?"

For once the repeating thing didn't bug me. Not when Micah aimed it at Brock and wiped the smirk right off his face.

"Neither the sequence of events nor the employee directory of NOI matter right now. The point is, I contacted Micah about a client of mine."

This time Gram flinched. "Jackson, should we—"

"Let me explain this first, Mags. See, I represent a company that, for years, has been invested in agriculture and forestry in the state. With the age of new environmental awareness, the company wants to expand into the area of carbon offsetting." Jackson let that tidbit sit out there for a second or two. "Kasey suggested I contact Micah because this is a topic of great interest to him."

Micah nodded. "Great interest."

There it was. The assist I didn't know I needed when I landed in North Carolina two weeks ago.

Jackson's comments could go anywhere next but the jumpy, unsettled sensation that overwhelmed me when Harlan walked through the door subsided. The tension that had been trapped and flailing without restraint ran out of me. The room still pulsed with dark energy, most of it coming from Brock's side of the table.

I trusted Jackson. Whatever road he was about to walk us all down had been planned out and perfected. All done in record time because I'd only dropped the information about some of this, particularly his dad's excitement at screwing over Gram and Celia, two days ago.

Buckle in.

Gram must have felt the strain loosening as well. She took a deep breath, acting more like herself and less ticked off the longer Jackson spoke. Celia smiled. Harlan looked ready to drag Jackson out of the room.

And Brock? It was hard to describe his look. Shock. Panic. The same look a little kid got when he accidentally wet himself in public.

Couldn't happen to a nicer guy.

"Micah is an environmentalist and the type of leader who gets out in front of emerging technologies and creates opportunities to integrate them into his business plan."

Jackson should write Micah's bio because *yikes*. So much bullshit and Jackson somehow made the words sound true.

He wasn't the only one who could throw the bullshit around. My turn. "Micah's great appreciation for the environment and need to make different decisions going forward is one of the reasons I wanted to work there."

"Great appreciation." Micah sounded pleased with the praise.

The color drained from Brock's face, but he stayed quiet.

I could play this game all day.

"I met with Brock a few days ago around lunchtime," Jackson said.

"We didn't exactly—"

Jackson raised a hand to stop Brock from continuing. "I informed him that, as the attorney for Mags' Desserts, all discussions and proposals needed to run through me. That I would deal directly with Kasey because she'd been integral in convincing the ladies to even consider the possibility of outside investment."

Micah nodded as he'd been doing almost nonstop since walking in the door. "Informed him. Yes."

Brock made a strangled sound. Like, he saw the boiling pit of crap waiting in front of him and desperately wanted to steer around it.

"That's exactly what Jackson told Brock." Jackson didn't need my help, but why not. This was the first time I'd enjoyed any part of my job.

"Unfortunately, Brock's pushing and his attempts to work around me and, more importantly, Kasey convinced the ladies that any sort of joint venture with NOI was impossible," Jackson said.

"Exactly." Gram must have been loving the show because she was not the type to sit back and let someone talk for her. She ceded the floor to Jackson again without so much as a twitch.

"But Kasey had spoken so highly of you, Micah, that I made that call yesterday. I'm happy I did," Jackson said.

"Agreed. I think NOI and your client, with your guidance, can do significant and important work together." Then Micah turned to Brock. "We'll discuss all of this on the way back to the office."

"You don't understand."

"A long discussion." Micah acted like Brock hadn't said anything. Almost like Brock didn't exist.

Sounded good to me.

"Kasey, you've worked hard over the last two weeks and while this deal did not come to fruition in the way we anticipated, your efforts directed me to other leads. That's the sort of teamwork NOI is built on." Micah smiled, clearly pleased with whatever he was saying. "Take a few days and we'll see you in the office next week."

The comment made me worry about Micah's ability to analyze a situation, but I wasn't about to correct him. "Thanks."

"Brock? We should go." Micah turned to Gram and Celia. "I apologize for the inconvenience but I'm grateful for your granddaughter and proud to have her as part of the NOI team. Her work ethic is a reflection on you."

I knew he thought that was a compliment, but . . .

"Thank you for understanding, Micah. Some people can't take a hint." Gram glared at Brock. "I appreciate that you can."

With that, the unwanted and highly entertaining meeting ended. Everyone said their goodbyes. Except for Brock, who stayed quiet and acted sheepish. Two things he never did.

Jackson walked the NOI team to the door then returned.

Harlan hadn't moved. He stood by the table, not saying a word. Not giving anyone eye contact. Not even looking angry. His expression read more as blank.

I wanted to congratulate Jackson, maybe shoo Harlan away and give Jackson a kiss, but I honored the silence and waited for Harlan to explode.

He finally lifted his head. His gaze bounced from me to Jackson. "That was a huge mistake."

"I'm not sure why you got involved in this, Dad. You know Mags and Celia don't want to sell. We consider them family. I needed to step in before this went too far. Hell, I should have stepped in days ago, but I never imagined you'd turn your lobbying efforts against the people you care about."

Jackson managed to defang Harlan and play the family card in one breath. Impressive. There was no other word for it.

"Thank you, honey." Celia's smile carried more than a note of relief.

Harlan shook his head. "I'm trying to understand why my motives are so hard for you all to understand. Jackson has a bright political future. Mags, you and Celia have an impressive business. I can help all three of you get what you want."

"I want to be a lawyer and I want you to stop pushing." Jackson drew the line and stood on it. "I'm not your client and I don't want to be. It's that easy."

"This is a seismic change. A few weeks ago we were in agreement." Harlan shook his head as if he couldn't believe how the afternoon had unfolded. "Then she came to town and . . . is all of this trouble really for her?"

"Watch yourself, Harlan." Gram was not having this. Her tone made that clear. "Do not drag Kasey into your nonsense."

"I agree." Jackson hadn't moved but he somehow looked bigger, more imposing. "If you want to fight, do it with me. Not her."

The whole conversation made me shaky and breathless and not in a good way.

"You've lost focus. Instead of concentrating on our candidate plan, or even your legal work, you're running around town—" Harlan's abrupt stop likely meant he knew he needed to change direction, and fast.

Jackson didn't let him do it. "What, Dad? Say it."

I wasn't as eager as Jackson to hear what came next. Harlan looked and sounded like a man about to plunge over the edge into full jackassery. If Gram didn't stuff a funeral pie down his throat, I might.

Harlan looked around the room before his gaze landed on Jackson. "I understand the two of you grew up together and are close—"

This guy made my head pound. "You can say my name, Harlan. We all get it. You think I've done something to Jackson. That I can sway him against your political agenda."

"You have an unhealthy hold over him."

"Dad, stop."

"Harlan, be careful," Celia warned.

Harlan kept his focus on Jackson. "I know why Anna left. What she saw at Christmas."

Jackson shook his head. "Not relevant."

Okay, wait. I'd missed something.

"I get it." Harlan waved a hand in my direction. "She's different from your usual type, which can be very exciting, but it's not sustainable because she's not built for the long-term."

"Do not make me come over there and whoop you." Gram sounded ready to do it, too.

"I don't have a choice but to speak up. It's my job as a parent. I'm telling Jackson what he already knows." Harlan stopped. His stern expression looked as if he was gathering his arguments and about to let the worst fly. "I know it's hard to hear, son, but your love for her makes you sloppy. Less driven. Frankly, far less marketable and less appealing to the people who can further your career."

I heard a gasp. I saw a sea of angry faces. Only one thing went through my mind. *His what?*

CHAPTER FORTY-EIGHT

The tension in the room ratcheted up to suffocation levels. Gram got up and took a step in Harlan's direction. Celia pulled her back. I was too lost in the *love* comment to function.

About that . . . "Did you say—"

"I know everyone is upset with me." Harlan's gaze traveled around the room. "But I'm not wrong."

"You clearly don't think much of me or my decisions, fine. We'll battle that out later." Jackson hadn't moved or blinked since Harlan dropped his bombshell. "But leave Kasey out of this."

"How can I?" Harlan turned to me. "You understand my position. If you care about him, and I think you do, you'll back off."

"I'm not the problem here." I really wanted to go back to the *love* part, but the conversation had rolled on and showed no signs of slowing.

Harlan didn't listen. He kept right on talking. "I'm not saying anything we all don't know already. Kasey is what some might call flighty and unpredictable. Not me, but others. And, yes, that can be endearing but someone who can't hold a job for more than a few months isn't the right partner for someone trying to carve out a political future."

Listing out my failures in such vivid detail shook me out of the *love* comment confusion. His facts weren't wrong, but how was my life his business? He was out of line.

Gram tried to slip out of Celia's hold. "I'm going to hit him this time."

"I might let you." Celia let go of Gram's arm while she said it.

While I'd love to see Gram take Harlan down, and she would, this ugly mess needed to end without Gram-induced bloodshed. "Everyone stay where they are for a second."

Harlan being Harlan, he kept pushing. "You told me you knew what the report said about you. That isn't my fault. I didn't write it. I didn't conduct the investigation. I'd hoped for a more positive conclusion, then none of this would be necessary."

"Necessary?" Jackson looked like he'd started a silent countdown in his head to keep from blowing up. "Dad, we're leaving."

I appreciated Jackson's attempt at a ceasefire, but no. "Not yet. I'm done with Harlan taking me aside to pressure me in secret. We're all here now. Let's get this out."

The next ten minutes could get nasty.

Harlan held up a hand as if to ward off the rage directed at him by the rest of the room. "I gave you a hypothetical. Nothing more."

No. He wasn't getting away with that bullshit. Not this time. "You insinuated you could ruin Gram and Celia's business."

"That's it." Gram looked ready to throw a punch.

Jackson took a step and put his body between me and Harlan. Between all of us and Harlan. Jackson looked more like a man on a mission than a lawyer doing a job. "What else did you say about the business?"

"And why are you issuing warnings to my granddaughter?" Gram asked a second later.

I appreciated the assists, but I had this. Harlan counted on being able to sway the crowd because he was *the* Harlan Quaid. That didn't fly in this room. It was time for him to learn that, and I intended to help. "When we talked you made it sound like Gram and Celia owed their clientele to you and that you could turn off that spigot any time you wanted."

He said a lot of other shitty things, including insinuating they could lose the house. I stuck with the highlight because that was crappy enough.

"He said what?" Celia's voice sounded soft. Furious. The same tone she used when she'd reached her limit. It didn't happen often, but when she let go, her temper was a thing to behold.

I tried to keep everyone from rushing in and going after Harlan, although I'm not sure why I bothered. "Gram and Celia wouldn't let you destroy their business. I won't let you. Jackson coming here with Micah today shows he won't let you. I'm also not leaving town just because that's what you want and because it would be easier for you to pressure Jackson without me around. Though, honestly, you're underestimating your son because he absolutely can hold his ground with you."

"Starting right now," Jackson said. "Dad isn't going to do anything to you, Kasey, or to the business. Mags and Celia are safe from any threat. I promise you. Right, Dad?"

Harlan didn't answer.

He was determined to make this day suck.

Gram took over before anyone else could yell or point fingers. "You are no longer welcome here. Get out."

Oh, shit. Gram's voice stayed even but I could hear the crackle of the fire burning underneath. I wanted to sit back and enjoy Harlan being told off, but an exploding fireball of anger wouldn't resolve any of this. Diffusing an incendiary situation was not one of my skills. I tried anyway.

I moved over and with a gentle hand on Gram's back pulled her closer to me. Selling this next part would be harder than when I pretended to do work at NOI. "Harlan understands your anger. You're being protective. He loves Jackson. He cares about Celia. He tolerates the two of us. Despite whatever he's saying now or told me in private, we're the people in his life. The ones he could go to if he needed something. He's smart enough not to blow that apart."

"Within certain parameters," Harlan said. "If Jackson would be willing to consider—"

Gram rolled her eyes. "You never learn."

I wanted to shake Harlan until his survival instincts kicked into life. "You are not going to bribe Jackson into living your dream."

Harlan did a pretty good impression of someone being shocked. "I would never."

"You run for office. You want this so badly. Go for it." An obvious solution. He craved the spotlight. Give it to him.

"That's not how this game is played. Jackson is the one with the opportunity here. He's young. He has a future." Harlan shrugged. "There are some issues in my background that could be problematic."

Talk about an understatement. But he didn't say no. He wanted this and was settling for living vicariously through Jackson. The women. The whole jackass thing. Yep. Harlan likely commissioned a report on himself and saw the red flags.

Harlan was born for political life, so I kept lobbying. Let's see how he liked being on the receiving end of the pressure.

"You have the connections. You have the drive and the ideas. You want it, so take it."

"Kasey is right," Celia said. "You have the right skill set."

Gram snorted. "Politicians act shitty all the time. You'll fit right in. The voters will forgive your pontificating and blow-hard nonsense if you have a strong family behind you. That last part is up to you to fix."

"You're the only Quaid with a political future," Jackson said. "I'm not entertaining any additional meetings or discussions on this. The topic is closed forever."

"When are you leaving town?" The heat cooled in Harlan's voice, but he clearly was not ready to stop viewing me as the enemy.

"As soon as I know everyone I love is okay." That didn't include him but for Jackson's sake I'd try.

"You've all made your point." That fast Harlan's voice returned to normal. He sounded unruffled and sure like he usually did.

The switch in his mood should have been a good sign but it creeped me out. Who changed their position and body language that quickly?

Harlan nodded as he looked at Jackson. "That maneuvering you did to win over Micah? Impressive."

Jackson shrugged. "You didn't give me much choice."

Harlan hesitated before heading for the door. "We'll talk tomorrow."

Gram waited until Harlan stepped outside to hug Jackson. "I've always said the business needed a lawyer. You're hired."

Nice. Maybe too nice. All wrapped up except for one thing. Sure, I should wait until we were alone. Think it through and come up with a game plan. Sharpen my skills in being tactful. But I'd held the question in as long as possible.

"What was that part Harlan said about love?"

Celia winced and Gram rolled her eyes. I got it. My delivery needed work, but they had to admit I'd showed great restraint in not asking before now.

Jackson wasn't answering, so I tried again. "Jackson?"

"Simple. I've been in love with you for years and you're the only person who hasn't noticed."

CHAPTER FORTY-NINE

The ringing in my ears drowned out everything else. I struggled to focus, stay standing, and hear. Basically, my whole body shut down at Jackson's comment.

Before I could ask a question or even think of what to ask, Jackson continued. "I've worked impossible hours, exercised, dated other women, and nothing. I still thought about you. I still missed you."

"So, you're saying . . ." Nope. The words refused to come together in my head. If he said what I thought he'd said? Couldn't be. "What are you telling me right now?"

I wasn't toying with him or trying to make him prove anything. His huge declaration sounded like it matched the decade-long fantasy running through my head. All those dreams I had about him and about us. The one-sided attraction that kicked my butt.

Unrequited love sucked. That's why his professing big feelings now made zero sense

Jackson looked as confused as he sounded. "Did you really not know how I felt about you?"

Gram snorted. "She didn't. She's clueless about these things."

"Okay." Celia took Gram's hand and tried to steer her toward the door. "We should leave them alone."

Gram gasped this time. She did love to unleash a dramatic gasp. "We've waited for two years for this day. For these two to figure themselves out. I'm staying."

What was happening? "Two years?"

"There's a reason Dad talked about Anna. She broke up with me at Christmas because she watched us together. She said it was obvious I was in love with you. I didn't mean to hurt her or lie to her. I really was trying to get over you and I liked her, so dating made sense, but she was right about my feelings."

I sat down hard in the chair. "You barely spoke to me when I was home in December."

"Survival instinct. Self-protection." He stood there with his fingers wrapped around the top of the chair across from me. "I've spent a lot of time trying to ignore you and my feelings for you."

He spoke as if Celia and Gram weren't in the room. As if he wasn't embarrassed about what he felt or the words he said. Could that be right? Admittedly, I wasn't great about picking up on cues, but this?

"But why?" Really, why? I wasn't his type at all. "Your dad is annoying, and his methods aren't elegant, but he got some things about me right. I'm unsettled and chronically unemployed. I have no idea what I want to do with my life. I'm bumping along while I try to figure it out."

"All true."

He didn't need to agree so quickly but fine. "I can be a bit impulsive."

He smiled. "A bit?"

No one was rushing to defend me. I knew my limitations.

I'd been bogged down by them for a long time but a little support from the people who were supposed to love me most in the world would have been nice.

"At times I've been reckless, and one could say overly curious. Those two traits together lead to trouble now and then." When Gram started to say something, I cut her off. "No. Do not mention my snooping or the business pitch that landed us in this mess. I know what I did, and I've tried for days to undo it."

Gram's snort was answer enough.

Jackson knew about my faults. He'd spelled them out for me often enough. Yes, we'd kissed and had sex. All of that meant everything to me. Incredible moments I would pack away and hold on to during the frustrating days ahead.

I figured the flirting, sleeping together, was just guy stuff. Not real and not lasting. An *enjoy the moment and move on* sort of thing.

"Since when are you attracted to me? Not the sex. I mean the bigger attraction. Love." I stumbled a bit at the end because hearing Jackson talk about love still sounded like a mean joke.

"Forever." He threw up both hands. "Well, it feels like forever but for a few years. After you graduated from college and spent the summer here."

Okay, no. I remembered how he acted. Ignoring me. The dismissal.

"When I set fire to the kitchen? You thought, *Yeah, she's the one for me*?" In my defense, the instructions for making caramel were right there on the counter. Gram and Celia had stepped out to run some errand. Of course I tried the recipe. Not successfully but I tried because who didn't like caramel?

"I miss those curtains," Gram said. "The pattern was out of stock, so we couldn't replace them."

Celia sighed. "It was an accident."

"Ladies, please." I loved them but they were not helping at all by playing amateur commentators.

"You were here. We spent time together. You didn't notice how many times I came over for dinner?" He didn't wait for an answer. "I tried to stay away. I warned myself not to get attached. You had turned into this beautiful, funny, charming, sometimes unhinged woman."

I couldn't even be offended because he started the description with the word "beautiful." "Was it the unhinged part that did it for you?"

"You were this burst of energy. This light. You see the world in a different way. You rush in when I would be careful. Too careful. You make me laugh. You make me want to take risks." He shook his head. "My work is serious. I tend to be serious."

Come on. "Tend?"

"You make me want to leave the office and have a life. A full life outside of work."

Oh, wow . . .

"Look, I know I'm not your ideal man. I also know your life isn't here. It sucks but it's true." He drew in what sounded like a shaky breath. "We'll get through this embarrassing moment and go back to normal. Not sure how, but we will. In the meantime, what I can promise you is that I won't let Dad mess with Mags' Desserts."

"Oh, he won't be touching the business." Gram sounded grouchy and resolute about that. "He'll be lucky if we let him in the door."

Jackson kept going. "I'll watch over these two and make sure they avoid more adventures with deadly recipes and suspect pies."

Gram frowned. "We don't need a babysitter, young man."

"Usually," Celia said.

"I'll take care of the things and people you love because I love them, too." He shrugged. "It's that simple."

Simple? Nothing about this whirl of new information was simple. He loved me, a fact that still didn't fit in my head. I loved him and had forever. So, why was he talking about letting me go?

"I made it clear to Micah that you did everything right and Brock was the one who messed up the potential deal, despite our warnings. Your job is safe. Micah said he viewed you as a valued employee." Jackson smiled. "Helping to keep you employed is my small way of saying thank you for sticking up to my dad and giving me the support to do it."

Was he winding up or winding down? I couldn't tell. The only thing I heard was the hint of goodbye in his words. "Okay, wait . . ."

"I need to check in with Dad. Make sure he wasn't telling us what we wanted to hear in the moment while moving in the wrong direction."

Jackson kissed me on the cheek. Quick and light like how he might kiss a distant relative. Certainly not the I'm-hot-for-you kiss I'd experienced the last few days.

"Talk to you soon." He walked away.

What? I watched him head for the door, not sure if I should throw a muffin at him or run after him. He was gone before I could decide.

I turned to face Gram and Celia. "What the hell was that?"

CHAPTER FIFTY

Celia cleared her throat. "Oh, dear."

Gram shook her head. "A dramatic exit. Who knew that boy had it in him?"

"He's always been very sweet. My sister lit up when he was born."

Oh, no. They were not going to cute their way out of this. These two and their CIA-level secret-keeping skills. "You two knew. You knew how he felt and stayed quiet."

Gram managed to groan and *pfft* at the same time. "It was obvious."

I just . . . but they . . . The words piled up in my brain. I needed to shake them loose and concentrate but everything kept spinning. "Not to me."

"He smiles when you walk into a room. He talks about you all the time," Gram said.

"He rushes over here when he knows you're in town. He checked up on you and your job from afar. He lets himself get pulled around on your . . . adventures." Celia gathered plates and a tray of muffins while she talked. She placed the booty in the middle of the table then sat down. "He paid more attention to you at Christmas than he ever had to Anna."

"He also acted annoyed with me most of the time." Where did that fit into their analysis?

"And the sex." Gram reached for a muffin. "I'm assuming it was good. You want it to be good. Don't pretend it doesn't matter."

Gram needed to find a different topic.

Celia passed out napkins as if the conversation hadn't tipped into *OMG* territory. "You both acted like you enjoyed yourselves. I mean, it happened more than once. The sex. It did, didn't it?"

They were killing me. "Can we focus on the love part?"

"Yes." Gram put her muffin down and pushed the plate away. "Do you love him?"

The crescendo of noise in my head clicked off. All the activity and chaos in the room stopped, leaving that one question hanging in the air.

"We know the answer but do you?" Celia asked.

There wasn't any reason to deny it. These two knew everything anyway. "Yes. I had a crush on him as a teen. I've always thought he was kind of adorable even if he was a bit of a fuddy-duddy."

Gram rolled her eyes. "What are your feelings for him now? As a grown woman."

"I've been in love with him for years." The words rushed out because there was no need to hold them back. "It's like this steady hum in the back of my head. He was dating other people here while I was in DC. I hated his social calendar, so I pretended I didn't love him, or convinced myself I didn't."

Celia looked at Gram. "You were right."

These two. "Stop doing that."

"Honey, you love him, which is amazing." Celia reached out and took my hand. "He's good for you. You're good for him.

Your differences complement each other. You lighten him. He grounds you. And the spark when you're together is undeniable."

It was? "Funny how no one bothered to tell me."

Gram sat back in her chair. She looked like the queen ruling over her kingdom. "You have a decision to make."

More adulting. I'd proven I was so good at adulting.

"I don't live here." I threw the excuse out, heard it, and realized how lame it was. "But if I did and, let's say, worked here—not baking, though—"

Celia was the one who snorted this time. "Heavens, no."

"Absolutely not," Gram said.

Rude. "Okay, you made your point. Baking is not my strength. I'm much better at eating." But the idea of coming home, being here, trying to build a life the way I wanted and with the person I wanted, suddenly didn't sound so scary. "Let's be realistic about one thing. If the relationship doesn't work out—"

"What if it does? What if it's better than you dreamed? Do you want to throw away your chance?" Gram asked.

Celia squeezed my hand. "You deserve to be happy. You deserve to have time to find your way and figure out what you want. If you really do love Jackson, why wouldn't you want to learn those things with him?"

I couldn't imagine doing them with anyone else. Now that we'd kissed and touched and lay in bed talking, the thought of dating some DC guy repulsed me.

"You two are pretty wise."

"We're brilliant and we love you." Gram picked up her muffin again. "Now go fix this."

CHAPTER FIFTY-ONE

It took exactly two days to completely turn my life upside down. I changed the focus and the direction. As of this afternoon, I also changed my employment status. Instead of being fired, I quit.

Micah turned out to be very charming. He was nice enough over the phone. He praised me and bargained to keep me. Even said I wouldn't need to report to Brock, which would make Brock melt into a pile of goo, so it was tempting.

I appreciated the ego boost, but I hated that job and really didn't love living in DC. The choice was obvious—quit and move back to Winston-Salem. The plan was to live with Gram and Celia. For the short-term only.

Celia said I could stay as long as I wanted.

Gram said there were nice apartments near Wake Forest University that I might like.

Yeah, I got the point.

Sitting in the kitchen eating muffins all day was not a job. Unfortunately. Gram wanted me to thrive. She didn't use that word, but I sensed it. That meant instead of bouncing from bad idea to bad idea, I needed to settle in and figure out what my *thing* was.

The first step was easy. Writing. I didn't know if I had the talent for books, short stories, or articles. The stories racing

around my head—the characters and plots with shady dealings—
needed somewhere to go. All I could do was try and see if I had
the stamina and drive needed to finish.

The rest of the time I'd be doing non-baking work for Mags'
Desserts. Scheduling, streamlining, and marketing. The mix
appealed to me more than whatever I'd been paid much more
to do at NOI.

No one knew more about and loved muffins, scones, and
pies than I did. No one. I could convince people they needed
all three for breakfast without any trouble. I'd be searching for
more business clients and managing the bulk orders. The only
potential problem was the sample sampling. I planned to eat a
lot. Running was out of the question, but I could burn calories
other ways.

The main way should be here any minute. I glanced at the
wall clock in the baking annex. It was just before four. I hadn't
seen Jackson since he completed his swan dive of martyrdom
out of the room two days ago. I texted and called. He left a few
messages about being swamped at work.

Nice try, Mr. Adorable. As if I wasn't intimately familiar
with that sort of lame excuse. Come up with a better tactic . . .
or don't. Just answer the phone.

Since I couldn't get him here the easy way, I went for the
devious way. He thought he was coming to the annex for my
going away party. Celia told him he had to show up.

There was no party. No people. Just me and an offer I hoped
he'd jump at.

At exactly four o'clock the door opened. Jackson took two
steps inside and stopped. Seeing me sitting on the counter next
to a plate of freshly made scones was, I hoped, his fantasy.

"What's going on?" He held his keys and they jingled when he moved.

His frown wasn't very comforting, but I did trick him into coming, so I couldn't really be grumbly about his confusion.

He started walking again. Came the whole way to the kitchen area and stood about five feet away from me.

Progress.

"We're having a party." Man, if he turned me down this was going to suck. I might stuff him in the freezer. Even Celia would understand the reaction.

"When? Do I have the wrong day?" He glanced at his watch then back at me.

How did he look even more adorable when bewildered?

I continued to sit on the counter. If Gram saw me she'd yell. She was opposed to anyone sitting on a kitchen counter for any reason. She promised to give me privacy with Jackson, so this was my one shot at counter sitting.

"Technically, you're here to celebrate my work news."

"Okay." He looked anything but okay. Disoriented. Tired. Those fit. "Did Micah give you a promotion?"

Jackson, Jackson, Jackson. He really wasn't getting this.

"I left NOI." I looked around the room. "I work here now."

"What?"

"It's true."

"Baking?" He sounded horrified.

"That reaction is so rude."

"Have you ever cooked anything without burning it?"

"You start one fire and right away people think you can't cook." I jumped down. He didn't move back, so the landing put me right in front of him. Just as I'd planned. "Hi."

"Hi." His voice sounded scratchy. Very sexy.

He was always so in control. So confident and practical. He looked a little jumpy right now. I hoped that was a good sign.

I crossed my arms in front of me to keep from wrapping them around his waist and pulling him in tight. Baby steps. "You've been ignoring me."

"I wonder why."

He was not going to make this easy. Lucky for him I liked a challenge. "Me too."

He started to say something then stopped. It took another deep exhale before he said a word. "You get it, right? I admitted I loved you, which I never intended to do. It's embarrassing that I barked it out like I did. The logical solution was to give you some breathing room."

So logical. "You mean hide."

"I'm going with 'breathing room.'" He finally dropped his keys in his jacket pocket. "I know all of this was a lot. The pressure from my dad. The poison. Your work situation. Worrying about hurting Mags and Celia."

"What does any of that have to do with loving me?"

He rubbed his forehead and shifted around. The poor guy looked like he felt uncomfortable in his skin.

Fine. I'd keep going. "You could have answered any of the million texts and calls—"

"Seven. And I did message you about my schedule."

It was cute he kept count. "Terse one-liners. If you would have given me a real response instead of avoiding me, we could have resolved this and spent the last two days kissing . . . and other stuff."

His arm dropped to his side. "What?"

For a smart guy he was having trouble with simple words. "Let's try this. I've loved you forever. When I was a kid it was, yeah, not possible, and weird and all that. But that teen crush gave way to love. Full-fledged, compare-every-date-to-you, excited-when-I-see-you, hate-when-I-don't love."

His mouth dropped open. *"What?"*

I broke him. Not sure how but I did.

Time for a big gesture. I slid in closer. Slipped my hands up his stomach to his chest. "I love you. If you had stayed in this room two days ago instead of bolting, you would already know that."

He didn't say a word.

"What did you think the kissing and the sex were about?"

He shrugged. "I thought you were bored or curious."

"That's not cool." I stepped back but he caught me and dragged my hands to his neck. Wrapped my arms around him and pulled me tight against his chest.

"Sounds like I was wrong." He smiled. "You love me."

"Up until two minutes ago." When he hugged me I gave in. "Fine. Yes."

"You don't sound happy about it."

"You understand what this means, right?" He should but I jumped on the point just in case. "You said you love me, so now you're in this. Us. A couple. Dating. Sleepovers at your condo, not here because *gah*."

His arms tightened around me, but he didn't move.

I tried again. "What, too fast?"

"I've loved you for years, so no." His cute smile made another appearance. "Just surprised. You've called me boring in the past."

Yeah, that did happen. More than once. "I reevaluated."

"You . . ."

"I was wrong." If he needed to hear the words then fine. "You're smart and caring. Charming and decent. Adorable as hell."

That smile of his grew even bigger. "I really like that last part."

"Me too." If his hands kept traveling over my back like that, all soothing and sexy, we were going to do a different kind of cooking in this kitchen. "I know it's scary because our lives are so tied together. The idea of a breakup—"

"Not happening. I intend to make this work."

Well, listen to him. Right answer. "Okay, but you know how this will go. I'm going to be bossy about you taking time off and coming home so we can have dinner and all that."

"Done." He grimaced. "What about my dad?"

Talk about an excitement killer. "Yeah, he needs to be better or at least behave. He's also going to need to learn about boundaries because we will have some."

"I'm looking forward to hearing you tell him all that."

Oh, I would. Harlan and I would come to an understanding. I wasn't going anywhere, so he needed to tone down the jackassery. "I'd rather talk about us than him."

"You know, I left work thinking I was going to a party. A party I dreaded."

He backed us up until my butt hit the counter. It looked like we were finally on the same page. "And?"

He kissed my neck. "I'm off for the rest of the day."

"Oh."

"We could get started on that dating thing." Those impressive hands of his started moving again.

I kissed him because who wouldn't? I put all my energy behind it to show him how committed I was to making this work.

"I like your problem-solving," I whispered in between soft kisses. "I'll bring the muffins."

CHAPTER FIFTY-TWO

Three weeks later . . .

I'd been back in Winston-Salem full-time for three weeks and no one tried to fire me. That might have been a new career record. Gram was good about stuff like employee retention. She had a few simple rules, the biggest being that I stay out of her kitchen except to eat. No cooking or baking allowed.

Today was a special day. Mags' Desserts had gotten a huge order boost. Harlan didn't take credit but the people placing the orders for their business meetings and get-togethers over the last week were his golfing buddies. His fingerprints were all over the rush of new business. Jackson said it was his dad's way of apologizing and as close as we'd ever get to hearing the words.

Baby steps.

Harlan still viewed me with skepticism. That was fine. I wasn't his biggest fan either. We had an unspoken agreement to get along for Jackson's sake. Jackson and I had a similar agreement to hold firm on our boundaries when Harlan tried to shift the line. Since he was "exploring the possibility" of running for office, he was busy elsewhere and I was grateful.

Tonight, Gram was making a special dinner to celebrate

getting all the orders out the door on time. She didn't divulge the menu, but I loved her cooking so knowing the entrée ahead of time wasn't necessary.

Jackson wouldn't be here for another hour. Even I could admit making him leave the office right at five might be too much. He loved his job . . . and whatever.

Now I just needed to find the cooks. Gram and Celia had been in the kitchen a few minutes ago. The delicious smell of roasting onion and garlic wafting through the room gave them away. I'd also heard them moving around and decided to visit in case there was a stray scone left over from this morning that needed to be eaten. I considered that sort of thing part of my job.

I looked out the window over the sink in time to see Gram and Celia walk around the side of the shed and disappear. The only thing back there was a mini greenhouse. Gram used the space for repotting and to experiment with a few plants she feared would take over the garden. She separated them to keep them from "cluttering up" the lawn while she assessed.

Why have them if they could be trouble? I had no idea because I knew even less about gardening than I did about baking. I let Gram handle this and stuck to admiring the flowers she planted and moved to the yard.

Playing with plants and flowers now, so close to a meal, was a bit strange. I slipped outside to check if they needed help. I was perfectly capable of moving pots and bags of soil.

Celia's voice stuck out. She said something about needing to be careful.

Her tone. The edge to it. The bit of panic.

Oh, shit.

The greenhouse door stood open. I took that as an invitation and walked inside. Purple and pink trumpet-shaped blooms in pots lined the floor. We had flowers like this in the yard but not exactly these. "Pretty."

Gram and Celia jumped at the sound of my voice. They both wore gloves and masks over their faces. Gram also wore what looked like a pink velour sweat suit with purple flowers on it and a matching floppy hat.

Where would someone buy something like that?

"Oh, no," Celia said.

"No." Gram backed me out of the greenhouse and into the fresh air. "You should stay out of there."

Celia joined us and closed the greenhouse door behind her. She stood in front of it, blocking my entry. She blushed while she talked. "We had some trouble with poison ivy. We have to be careful while we clean it out."

Their faces. The spewing of unimportant information. The hazmat outfits. Gram had that sweet, could-never-harm-a-fly vibe. She looked all cuddly in her long-sleeved outfit. Never mind that it was eighty degrees outside. Not exactly weather that required being covered from head to toe.

They were lying their cute little faces off. "Try again."

Celia started to say something about dinner, but Gram cut her off. "Can we really avoid this? She's always snooping."

Somehow me finding them sneaking around was my fault. Interesting. "Now would be a good time to explain."

Gram lowered her mask. "Foxglove."

Okay . . . Still confused. "That means what?"

"It's poisonous." Celia rolled her eyes when Gram made a noise. "What? That's why we're doing this. Removing it so Kasey doesn't live near it and stumble over it."

Gram still grumbled. "She does have a habit of doing that sort of thing."

They acted like their bickering answered all my questions. Not even close.

So many thoughts fought in my brain, begging for attention. I went with the scariest one. "How poisonous?"

"What kind of question is that?" Gram had a habit of falling back on grouchiness if she didn't want to give a real answer. Like now.

Nice try, Gram. "The kind I'd love for you to answer."

Celia sighed but started talking. "Foxglove is dangerous to touch. It can cause skin irritation."

Not fun but not scary . . . yet. The adrenaline coursing through me signaled trouble ahead.

"Headaches, vomiting, heart rate issues," Gram said. "And death."

And there it was.

Oh my God. "Ladies."

"We told you we never used arsenic and that wasn't a lie." Gram smiled. "Never had to. We had foxglove . . . and other things."

Celia peeled off her protective gloves. "This is nothing for you to worry about. We're clearing it out now because Abigail called to say she's leaving town tomorrow as planned and, well, we thought it would be a good thing for all of us to get a fresh start without foxglove nearby."

There was no way they'd kept these flowers out here for years and, what, picked a flower every time they needed to kill some bad dude. Right? I looked at the greenhouse door. For the first time I noticed the lock matched the one on the shed.

"You've had a greenhouse full of deadly foxglove tucked away in the backyard just in case." Not a sentence I expected to say today.

Gram nodded at Celia. "I told you she'd understand."

Oh, no. "I didn't say that."

"The important thing is that we're removing all of it. You won't need to worry about touching the foxglove by accident."

Yeah, Gram. That was my issue with the poisonous flowers.

"Have you used this foxglove stuff recently?" What was I saying? Of course they did. "Forget I asked."

"We should have waited to start this chore. We'll take care of the rest of the plants after we eat." Celia acted like it made sense to stop playing with poison so they could go work on dinner.

What did I even say to that?

"No more foxglove. We promise." Celia put up her hand as if she was making a pledge.

"Okay. Good." Not poisoning men seemed like a smart plan.

"We can always plant something else if we need it." Gram dropped that then started toward the house.

"Gram."

"If men behave they have nothing to worry about." She gestured for me to follow her. "Come on. You know I like to eat at six."

I watched Gram and Celia walk away from this perfectly

normal conversation. Heard them arguing about the superiority of green beans over broccoli as a side dish. Smelled the lemony punch of magnolias in the yard. Thought about having a predinner doughnut.

Poison or not, it was good to be home.

ACKNOWLEDGMENTS

Everything I write is fiction but sometimes bits and pieces of real life pop up in my books, including this one. The no clapping rule? An ode to my dad. I clapped in the car exactly one time as a kid. The thing where someone (Mom) tells random stories about people I don't know and have never met? Mom, come on. You know that's you. The horrified reaction to seeing someone sit on a kitchen counter or having someone visit the house unannounced? Those come from my husband. Definitely call or text first.

Living in Winston-Salem and Washington, DC? Those are me. Loving two amazing older women, one sassy and one more home and hearth? Me again. My grandmothers. The lawyer thing? Also me, but I actually stuck it out and graduated from law school. Go Demon Deacons!

The poison? That part is pure fiction . . . though I've been tempted.

This book was a joy to write. The mix of humor, lightness, loss, sisterhood, trauma, family messiness, romance, and jobs-gone-wrong required a balancing act. I hope I hit the *life is full of laughter and tears* tone just right. If I didn't, that's all on me, because my editor, May Chen, is a gem. She makes everything I write better. My gratitude is heartfelt and abundant.

Thank you to May and to everyone at HarperCollins for shepherding my work from draft to finished project. You're amazing and I literally (correct use of that word) could not do this without you all.

Thank you to the two amazing agents who promote my work and make magic happen—Laura Bradford at Bradford Literary Agency and Katrina Escudero at Sugar23. I'm so happy to have you both on my team.

I also want to thank my readers. I can only enjoy a writing career (and not go back to being a lawyer) because of you. If I could come to your houses and hug each one of you (in a non-stalkerish way) I would.

To all the bookstagrammers, librarians, reviewers, and book lovers who promote my books, buy my books, talk up my books, post about my books, and show off my book covers—thank you! I am so grateful.

A special shout-out to Tonya Cornish and everyone involved with Thriller Book Lovers: The Pulse. It was a huge honor to see *The Usual Family Mayhem* featured as the launch book for your new all-genre division, The Buzz. I am your biggest fan.

As always, thank you to my husband, James, who is one of the good ones. I got very lucky there. No poison needed. And I promise never to sit on our kitchen counter (again).

ABOUT THE AUTHOR

HELENKAY DIMON is a former divorce lawyer with a dual writing personality. Her work has been optioned for television and featured in numerous venues, including the *New York Times*, the *New York Post*, *Cosmopolitan*, the *Washington Post*, the *Toronto Star*, PopSugar, Goodreads, theSkimm, and HuffPost. In addition to writing thrillers as Darby Kane, she is now writing stories centered on family hijinks with a bit of suspense and humor, and she hopes you'll go on this new writing journey with her. For more information go to helenkaydimon.com.